PIECES OF YOU

JESSICA GOMEZ

This is a work of fiction. Unless otherwise indicated, all the names, characters, businesses, places, events and incidents in this book are either the product of the author's imagination or used in a fictitious manner. Any resemblance to actual persons, living or dead, or actual events is purely coincidental.

Copyright © 2024 by Jessica Gomez

All rights reserved. This book or any portion thereof may not be reproduced or used in any manner whatsoever without the express written permission of the publisher except for the use of brief quotations in a book review.

Published in the United States by Chandler House Publishing in Northville, Michigan
For purchase information please visit WriterJessicaGomez.com

FIRST PAPERBACK EDITION
Paperback ISBN: 979-8-9899348-0-5
Hardcover ISBN: 979-8-9899348-2-9
eBook ISBN: 979-8-9899348-1-2

Printed in the United States of America

TEXT DESIGN BY BROOKE GILBERT

For Ronan -

The only one who could teach me what it means to be a mother.

ONE

Nora stole a glance in her rearview mirror, but all that she found was darkness. She hunched her delicate shoulders over her steering wheel, powering through a translucent fog that lingered just above the pavement. She tried to unclench, but it was a pointless exercise. Her nerves were frayed. She hadn't anticipated leaving Jimmy's Bar later than ten. Certainly not alone.

Thick towers of trees lined the winding road, surrounding her as if to say *You're not welcome here.* Her headlights only allowed for a few feet of visibility, making it impossible to see what lay ahead. In the absence of streetlights and a sliver of moon as her only guide, silhouettes crossed the road and danced past the trees. She quickly tapped her brakes before realizing there was nothing in the street - just her eyes attempting, and failing, to adjust to utter darkness. She slowed her pace and held her eyes open as wide as they'd allow, pressing her fingers harder into the wheel.

She had no choice but to replay the events of the evening in her mind. She'd arrived early at the bar and perched herself in the back booth, excited but flustered to be out of her decidedly small comfort zone. According to Ryan, a sweet, slightly nerdy outdoorsman she'd met online, Jimmy's Bar in Woodbridge was a halfway meeting point between them. She faced the door so she could see when he came in, smoothing her hair and wringing her hands to stop them from shaking. She'd had a long ride in from Philadelphia and had practiced what she'd say when they finally met in person, making a mental list of conversation points in the case of an awkward moment.

She checked her phone often for a message from him, but a tiny X where bars should be taunted her. She hoped that at least the food would be good since the decor was drab and the tired-looking waitress was rude, but it wasn't. She eyed each patron sitting at the bartop as she picked at her soggy fries, how they all looked different but somehow exactly the same, forty to fifty-somethings in their tattered t-shirts, downing bottles of beer in near silence. None of them resembled Ryan. She flicked through her screenshots until she got to the sole photo he'd sent her and studied it, comparing it to the men sitting at the bartop. Their eyes were sunken where his were kind. One of the men caught her staring and she quickly averted her eyes, and fished her e-reader out of her purse.

She engrossed herself in a heartbreaking novel as if she had always intended to eat alone, that she hadn't been stood up, that she had planned to come to a dimly lit bar in the middle of nowhere to catch up on her reading. Her heart lifted each time the door swung open. And then the crushing shame arrived when she finally understood, definitively, that he wasn't coming.

Though she'd known no one in the room, a self-conscious haze consumed her. She didn't know why she cared that these strangers might see that she had been stood up, but she did. So she kept reading, and before she knew it, nearly three hours had passed. She finally departed with slumped shoulders, sucking in fresh air as she crossed the threshold, and hurried to her SUV. Woodbridge was isolated from its surrounding cities, and the locals didn't exactly roll out the welcome mat. They had all done a double-take at her when she entered, making her feel foolish in her favorite low-cut black V-neck, the one that gave her thin frame extra curves and illuminated her bronze hair, her skin-tight olive green pants that matched her eyes, and her stilettos that she could never steadily walk in, no matter how many times she tried.

Her mind began to wander as she drove through the trees, taking in her surroundings. Between the silence and the overwhelm of the night, her thoughts became harder to tame, and she began to indulge them. She'd felt a nagging discomfort at the bar and assumed it was nerves, but maybe it was something more. Had someone been watching her as she read? She instinctively checked for headlights behind her, but the blackness in her wake reaffirmed that no one followed. She shook her head roughly, as if she could shake the bad thoughts out. *Focus on the road. Just keep going.*

The gentle hum of crickets and a soft whir of wind seeped through her open window. Despite the humidity, the leather from her seat was cold against the backs of her arms, generating tiny, rough goosebumps across her skin. Her hands gripped the wheel tightly at the ten and two position, her eyes flitting back and forth to keep herself apprised of any wildlife that may attempt to dart out in front of her.

Inhale: One, two, three. Exhale: one, two, three she chanted in her head, holding her breath and slowly exhaling, an exercise she'd learned in therapy to keep her anxiety at bay - one that didn't seem to be doing much for her on this trek. Her stomach tensed as the car hugged the edges of the serpentine street, winding left, then right, then left again as she followed along with the curvature displayed on her GPS, willing the highway to suddenly appear.

She wished she wasn't alone. She wished she never would have agreed to come out here in the first place. Maybe if she wasn't so desperate, she would have done as her best friend Erica had advised, and made Ryan come to her. She didn't want to rock the boat, and it was only fair, meeting halfway. But why would he pick such a strange place to meet? How did he even know a place like that, so far off the beaten path? Now she was hours from home, in a town that, for a reason she couldn't quite pinpoint, made the hair on the back of her arms stand on end.

A sudden, pale movement, almost an apparition, caused her to gasp aloud as she slammed the brake to the floor and jerked the wheel to the right. Bursting from the trees, draped in a nightgown streaked with blood, a barefoot and frail woman frantically threw herself in front of Nora's car, as if she meant to be hit. It happened within seconds, but time somehow slowed. Nora veered off the road in panic, a harsh squeal of tires against a silent backdrop, straight toward the woods. She swerved, and for just half a moment locked in with wild, pleading eyes. The figure's mouth was twisted in a look of haunting desperation. And then came the impact.

Gasping. Crunching. Horn. Then nothing.

Only quiet, and darkness.

TWO

Nora lifted her head, heavy and throbbing, from its resting place on an airbag that had deployed only after her forehead bounced off the top of the wheel. She let out a long groan as she reached for her phone, using her fingers to feel for it through the darkness, but only receipts and nameless gunk were in the console where she normally kept it. It must have been thrown somewhere in the car when she slammed on her brakes, but she couldn't see where. Her body felt worn, as if she had just been on the losing end of a boxing match. She hoisted her arm above her head with another groan and clicked the emergency button on her OnStar. After a few seconds, Ronaldo from OnStar's voice flooded her speakers, his deep, soothing voice promising help was on the way. Within minutes, a bustle of paramedics and police officers were barking instructions at her: "Don't move!" "Can you move?" "Can you walk?" "Sit down!"

As she sat in the back of the ambulance after the EMTs arrived, red and blue lights painting the black sky, a young paramedic shone a flashlight from left to right as he asked her the date and who the President was. She opened her mouth to answer but stopped as a pair of uniformed officers sauntered up. She stiffened at the sight of them. They seemed unassuming enough - both of them thin and not much older than she was, but she could feel herself clamming up just as she did with any authority figure. She swallowed roughly, her throat dry, as the smaller of the two officers removed a lined notepad from the front pocket of his shirt next to a badge that read Crenshaw.

"Name?" he asked, and Nora jumped at the harshness of his tone.

"Nora. Nora Aberdeen."

"You been drinkin', Miss Aberdeen?"

Nora's eyes widened.

"No. No, sir," she stammered. She was telling the truth, but somehow found her hands sweating as she stretched the cotton on her V-neck to cover the breadth of her chest.

"How'd this happen, then?" He gestured to her SUV, the front bumper crumpled against a large oak tree. She winced and closed her eyes, trying not to think of her mom.

"Someone...a girl. A woman, I think. She ran in front of me."

Crenshaw looked quickly at the second officer, whose name tag read Mable. Mable met his gaze with narrowed eyes for half a second before turning his attention back to Nora. She could begin to feel her heart thundering in her chest.

"Ma'am, we have a lot of wildlife out here. You probably saw yourself a deer and got spooked," Mable said dismissively, gesturing toward the woods. Crenshaw lifted the pen from his pad.

Nora had never felt so small as she desperately shook her head.

"No. It was a woman. She looked like she was in trouble."

"Yeah? How do you know that?" Mable asked, one eyebrow raised speculatively.

"She looked...scared. She was wearing a nightgown. It looked like it could have been... bloody. Maybe she was hurt. She looked like she needed help."

The officers exchanged another silent glance, so quick it was almost indecipherable, but she noticed. Then they carried on.

the fact that she looked like she might be injured, or why the hell she had been in desolate woods, alone, in the middle of the night. Crenshaw had written a short, indecipherable scribble on his pad. What had they written down? Did they even believe her? She'd tried to protest without sounding pushy. The girl couldn't have made it very far on foot, but Nora doubted that they intended to look for her.

There was no television in her room, not a radio or even amateur art to distract her. Just the dated machine dispensing IV fluids through her left arm, the thin, cold sheets of her uncomfortable bed, and an empty whiteboard that Nora could tell had been erased hundreds of times from the residue left behind. So she put her energy into remembering the details.

Female. Caucasian. Early twenties, if that. Dark hair. White nightgown. How tall was she? The moment she saw her was over so quickly that it had been impossible to tell. And those eyes. The bright green, desperate eyes. The whole thing had felt like an out-of-body experience. Nora ran the details over and over in her mind, nervously biting her lips and cracking her fingers as she sat rigidly against the hospital bed, a dull ache in her back making itself known. She wanted to remember everything she had seen. She'd binged enough true crime documentaries with Erica to understand that eyewitness accounts can be very helpful or very hurtful, depending on the reliability of the witness. She didn't want to be one of those people who she and Erica would laughingly toss popcorn at on the screen as they groaned over their accounts of what happened, as they swore what they testified to seeing was true, only to be proven wrong later.

She shook her head and rolled her eyes. She was getting ahead of herself. The cops actually had to show up, to *care*, before she needed to worry about her reliability.

Had the officers assumed she was drunk and trying to give an excuse for the accident? She may have been disoriented when she came to, and her head still felt a bit foggy, but she knew what she

"I don't know what you think you saw, but there's nobody out here, miss. I think you oughta get that head checked out. Let these folks do their job." A nod and a condescending smile from Mable, and Crenshaw flicked his notepad shut.

"Is that it? Don't you need more information?" Nora asked, panicky.

"We'll meet you at the hospital, once you're...feeling better. You take care, now."

Nora's mouth fell agape as they turned and walked back to their cruiser, their boots crunched over the gravel, a hushed conversation she couldn't make out coming from their direction. She found herself caught in the flurry of people surrounding her, and before she knew it, she was being delivered to a tiny hospital.

As Nora lay in a hospital bed, shivering from cold and adrenaline, she could not shake what she'd seen that had caused her to crash. Though the figure appeared seemingly out of nowhere and she was dressed all in white, it was no ghost. She'd only seen her for a second, so she worked hard at keeping the image alive in her mind. A young woman, so thin she was bony, running directly into the road, almost like she was unaware that she was so close to being struck. Her hair was dark and untamed, and tiny leaves were tangled in the strands. She wore a dirty, sleeveless nightgown, something suited for a person much older than what she looked like. And then there was the blood.

She looked through a murky window at the old plastic clock in the hallway above the empty room that sat across from hers. 1:45 A.M. When were the police going to show up? She arrived at the hospital over an hour ago and hadn't spotted anyone from law enforcement since, and she'd been taking care to check often. All she'd noted was the occasional nurse in faded scrubs hurriedly walking past, as if they were afraid Nora might call to them for aid, their soft white tennis shoes padding quietly over the rundown yellow linoleum until they disappeared down the corridor.

The officers, curiously, did not seem interested in the girl, or saw. The way the officers had looked at each other stuck in her mind, and she started to get angry. Nora hadn't drunk any alcohol at the bar so as to keep her wits about her on her date, so the blood alcohol test she was sure she was given when they drew her blood when she arrived at the hospital would prove that she was sober. But what about the girl? *Who knows where she is by now.* She felt a pang of guilt that she hadn't pushed them more to look for her, but the police had always made her uncomfortable, like she was going to get into trouble even though she never broke any rules. She was always careful to respect authority, but maybe this situation had called for a little push-back. If she'd just been a little more assertive, sounded a little different, maybe they would have believed her.

Maybe she sounded like she was making it up. She was shy and intimidated by the police presence, and felt guilty that she'd caused so many people to come to check on her. It hadn't seemed necessary for that many people to show up just for a one-person accident. The attention had made her uncomfortable, and the combination of paramedics barking orders and the police asking her questions so rapidly had made her lightheaded and flustered; she was sure it made her sound uncertain of her answers. If she could have made herself sound more believable, more self-assured...maybe they would have searched. Would have done *something.*

The more Nora thought about the girl running in the road, the more it made her blood run cold. What was she *doing* out there, all alone in her nightgown? She didn't remember seeing any houses for miles. *Didn't she see my headlights? And why was there blood on her gown?*

Was it blood? She started to second guess herself. It could have been...dirt? *Oh God*, she thought, annoyed with herself. *Get your shit together.*

Another nurse walked by her room, and she called out to her.

"Excuse me? Nurse? Do you know if the police are here yet?" Her soft voice cracked.

The nurse, ruddy faced and stocky, stopped in her doorway and narrowed her eyes as she rested a hand on her hip.

"Police?" She sounded confused and irritated, disheveled though Nora was certain she was one of the only patients in the hospital.

"They told me they would meet me here to get my statement from the accident."

"Oh. Never heard that one. I'll check in the front." The nurse once again disappeared into the corridor. As she watched her go, Nora had the distinct feeling that the nurse wasn't going to be checking anything, and that she wouldn't be seeing her again.

Of course she had never "heard that one." She lived in a Podunk town where probably nothing ever happened. Maybe when someone accidentally shot a hunter, or got run over by a tractor, then she'd actually have to do something at work. She had a slight chuckle to herself, but instantly felt remorseful for thinking like that.

She felt her eyes grow heavy as she fought the longing to start bawling. She wanted her mom; the one person she couldn't have. She imagined her reaction. Angry at the police for not listening to Nora. Angry at Nora for trying to meet up with someone she'd never met in person. Baffled and worried, asking Nora way more questions about the girl she'd nearly struck than the police had. But she'd be scared, more than anything, for Nora. She'd hug her, she'd cup her head in her tiny hands, she'd grip Nora's hand and not let go until Nora told her to and assured her she was fine. Tears welled in her eyes, but she wiped them away as quickly as they came. She couldn't go down that road right now. As badly as she needed her mother, she'd learned long ago to push through. But she knew she didn't want to be alone anymore.

She instinctively went to grab her phone from the bedside table, then realized that she had never retrieved it from wherever it had flown in her car. *Shit.* She was sure they were towing her car at that very moment, and then who knows if she would ever get her phone back? She reached for the hospital landline, and dialed a number she knew by heart.

"Eli? It's me. Sorry to wake you," she said, even more meekly than she'd intended to sound.

"You didn't wake me," Eli said. She searched his voice for signs of heavy sleep, for a stifled yawn, but found nothing.

She checked the time again. It was past two in the morning by now. She rolled her eyes to the ceiling and shook her head, silently wincing at the thought of his nighttime activities with other women.

"Oh, okay. Umm. I got into an accident." Her face crumpled in shame, as if it were her fault.

"Oh, my god. Are you okay? Where are you?" There was panic in his voice, melting away Nora's annoyance.

"I'm fine, really, I am. But I'm going to need a ride out of here in the morning, and to be honest with you, I'm a little creeped out being in the hospital alone."

"Tell me where you are. I'll come right now."

She hesitated.

"I'm in...Woodbridge..."

"*Woodbridge?*" Eli sounded disgusted, like he had been forced to say a dirty word. "What the hell are you doing in *Woodbridge?*"

"Look, I'll explain when you get here. I know it's far. You don't have to come right now if you want to sleep until tomorrow morning..." She trailed off, not meaning what she was saying, knowing that he wouldn't let her sit in the hospital alone.

"I'm coming right now."

Nora smiled faintly, and she was sure Eli could hear how relieved she was, but she was too tired to care. "Thank you. Room 212."

Nora sensed a presence in her room. Eli was there - she knew it before she opened her eyes.

She peeled her eyelids open and let her vision adjust. Amber eyes smiled down sympathetically at her.

"*Hey*," Eli whispered softly. "How are you feeling?" He grabbed her hand in both of his, and she felt her face flush.

From how gently he was speaking, she assumed she must look pretty beaten up. The longer she lay in the hospital bed, the weaker she felt, but now that he was here, she wanted Eli to see her as strong, as a survivor.

She glanced at the clock. 4:30. She must have fallen asleep without realizing it. Philadelphia was over two hours away. She did the math in her head, smiling to herself as she realized that Eli must have left as soon as she called.

"I'm fine. I'm sore, and I'm exhausted. But I really am okay." She smiled meekly as she carefully hoisted her body back up to a seated position, the pain in her back steadily turning from dull to piercing.

"What the hell happened?" He laid a hand gently on the back of her head, fingers nestled in the thickness of her hair, but she wasn't able to enjoy the sweet moment. The hair on the back of her neck stood on end. She had momentarily forgotten what put her in the hospital in the first place.

"Oh, my god, Eli. This girl darted in front of me while I was driving!" she exclaimed, waving her hands excitedly as she spoke. "I had to swerve so I didn't hit her, and I went straight into a tree. Thank God I didn't hit it harder. I really think I could have died." She didn't know if that was true, but she needed him to understand the weight of what happened.

"Jesus. Is the girl okay?"

"No idea." She shook her head in disgust. "When I came to, she was gone. I tried to tell the cops about her and they didn't want to hear it. They were supposed to come talk to me here but they haven't yet." Nora started to realize that if they hadn't come by now, they weren't coming. She shook her head again in irritation. "Whatever. I'm sure they just thought I was drunk and making it up."

"Did they give you a breathalyzer?"

"No."

"Hmm."

Nora looked straight into Eli's eyes. She had already been written off by the police, and she wanted him to take what she was about to say seriously.

"Listen." She cleared her throat. "I'm pretty sure something happened to that girl."

Eli looked at her quizzically.

"What do you mean?"

She paused, leaned back in her bed and sighed.

"She was bloody."

"Are you sure?"

"Yes. I'm sure."

She did not want what she saw to be true, but she knew all too well how an inconvenient truth operates. It wraps its spidery limbs around your neck and suffocates you until you're forced to acknowledge its presence. She closed her eyes and took a deep breath.

"Eli...she looked like she was running *from* someone."

THREE

Nora's eyes slowly opened, her lids heavy with exhaustion. For a moment, she didn't know where she was. As her sight adjusted, she saw Eli to the right of her bed by the window, sleeping in a dingy orange chair with his head cocked, nestled on his fist. The prior night's events came flooding back to her and a knot instantly formed in her stomach. Her spine straightened, and a fresh jolt of adrenaline gave her enough energy to climb out of her bed, tugging along the machine dispensing fluids into her veins.

She padded quietly to the bathroom so as not to wake Eli. As she flicked on the lightswitch, she was taken aback at the face staring back at her. She leaned toward the mirror and winced as she gently touched her cheek, bruised purple with a gash in the center. Other than a mild concussion, the bruise and a small scrape dried with blood above her left eyebrow, she had gotten away relatively unscathed.

Well, that's something to celebrate I guess, she thought sarcastically as she combed her fingers through the tangles of her hair, a feeble attempt to return her appearance to normalcy. She splashed her face with cold water, rubbed the mascara marks from underneath her eyes. She had a wedding to go to in two weeks, and she wasn't sure she'd be able to cover her new battle wounds for it. This accident was slowly becoming a fiasco. What she had to do next was sure to take the entire day; she had to locate her car and inevitably pay a tow fee, and then she had to go to the police station to try and sort out what exactly happened the night prior. She shook her head at herself in disgust. She had no one to blame her situation on but herself.

When she emerged from the bathroom, Eli was awake and standing in the doorway, leaning casually with his arm up against the frame as he spoke a touch too closely to a young blonde nurse. She clutched a clipboard over her chest that Nora was sure was her own medical chart, and she was grinning at him in a way that made Nora feel like an outsider in her own hospital room.

Even on very little sleep in a hospital chair, Eli was strikingly handsome. His dark features kept his ethnicity ambiguous, though Nora knew he was Portuguese on his father's side. He leaned even closer as he spoke softly to the starry-eyed nurse, and she let out a laugh that people who knew her probably found endearing but Nora found irritatingly high-pitched. *Could she be more transparent? Take it easy, lady. You're supposed to be working.* Further miffed that the nurse, who was supposedly there to take care of *her*, hadn't noticed her enter the room, she interrupted their whispers.

"Eli. I thought you were sleeping." Her voice came off less casual and more accusatory than she had intended. She was usually careful not to resemble a demanding girlfriend, but she found it hard to restrain herself when she was this exhausted.

"Nori! This nice young lady was just telling me that you're ready to be discharged." Eli winked at the nurse, whose face reddened. Nora remembered how she had once been embarrassed by his unabashed flirtatious behavior, too. She was used to it by now, and she rolled her eyes at him.

"Great. Let's go then."

Though the late August heat was more than enough reason for air conditioning, Nora rolled the passenger window in Eli's car all the way down. She felt queasy at the notion of visiting the police station, and the fresh air, though thick, was making it slightly more manageable. She stuck her hand out the window, the wind whirring past the car as she rode the imaginary waves up and down with her hand. She thought of her parents in simple, quiet moments such as these. In her mind, she could see her father in the driver's seat of their station wagon, dark, tall and burly, every so often looking lovingly at her mother on the passenger side. Her mother's sun-kissed skin glowed in the daylight, her red hair long and wild as she moved her arm in waves in the wind. Nora watched them from the backseat, too small to reach her arm out the window, wondering when she would be big enough to ride the waves just like her mother.

It was in times of strife that Nora wished most that her parents were still around; she had no siblings, no support system, no family to lean on when the going got tough. When her mother had died in the accident and then a heart attack killed her father just two months later, she had been unable to get herself to finish college even though she was in her final year. Ironically, it would have been her mother who would have hunted down every teacher, insisting that they give her daughter more time to finish her studies, given the losses she had experienced. Now, she imagined her mother knocking down the door of the Sheriff, giving him a piece of her mind that his staff hadn't taken her daughter seriously after her accident, and why was it *her* responsibility to do *their* job? She had always admired her mother's tenacity but never felt comfortable being that forward. She had to channel her mother's strength and persistence today; she had only herself to rely on now.

Out of the corner of her eye, she caught Eli stealing a glance at her from the driver's seat. She wasn't sure if he realized it, but he had been the one who had gotten her back on her feet after her parents had died. He made her feel like she was a living person again and not an aimless zombie going through the motions of survival: eat, sleep, repeat. His mother had left his family when he was a child, and his father had long passed on. They had bonded over their orphan lives, and when they were together, she felt like she could breathe again. She held back a smile. *Well, I guess I have Eli.*

"So are you gonna tell me what you were doing all the way out here?" The break in silence startled her, and she felt her face get hot. She pulled her hand back inside the car and sank low in her seat.

"I don't want to tell you."

"Oh *reeeally*," he teased. "Now you *have* to tell me. I'm intrigued."

Nora covered her face with her hands, too embarrassed to watch his reaction.

"I had a date." Her voice was muffled, but she was confident he heard her when he burst into laughter.

"What!?" he cried, incredulous.

"Eli, stop it! This is so embarrassing."

"Who do you even know that lives in Woodbridge?"

"I met him online."

Eli hooted with throaty laughter.

"This is mortifying," she muttered.

"So how'd the date go?"

She kept her face in her hands but could tell in his voice that a huge smile painted his face. She paused and shook her head, wondering when the humiliation would end.

"He didn't show."

She expected him to laugh even harder, but instead, his tone turned contrite.

"Aw, Nori. I'm sorry." Somehow, his response was even more

17

humiliating than it would have been for him to laugh in her face. She snapped her head out of her hands.

"Don't act like you feel sorry for me." She looked at him with angry eyes, arms crossed, waiting for him to look back, but he kept his eyes on the road.

"No, I really am sorry. What a dick. Who wouldn't show up for you? Guy's crazy."

Nora lowered herself in her chair, tossed her arm back out the window and let herself gaze into the nothingness that surrounded them, and thought, *tell it to the mirror.*

Each mile road they reached, there was a pause in residences, and an old-fashioned drug store or rundown liquor store sat on the corner. Many of the street signs off the main road were hand-painted, faded and chipped from years of neglect. They passed a used car lot, decorated with multicolored flags strewn over a tiny brick building painted yellow. It was still 1975 in this lot, and the cars didn't look much newer. Nora half expected tumbleweeds to roll by as she chastised herself once more for agreeing to meet Ryan all the way out there.

By the time they arrived at the Huntingdon County Sheriff's Department, Nora welcomed the respite from the car, even if it was under such strange circumstances. The ride had been silent after Eli realized that Nora had gotten angry. Like every other argument they ever had, he had all but accused her of being too sensitive as he poked fun at her. She had turned her body to face the window, and he let her.

As she opened the door to the one-story, unassuming brown building, her focus immediately shifted. She had a job to do, and that job was to get the police to take her seriously and start looking for that girl. She took a deep breath, her heart pounding, and put her shoulders back to exert confidence as she walked up to the front desk.

The desk officer was slowly typing on an ancient computer as she approached, and he didn't acknowledge her presence. She cleared her throat.

"I need to talk to the sheriff," she began. She waited as he turned from his computer to face her. He looked close to her age but rougher around the edges, dark bags hanging beneath his eyes.

"Sheriff's not here." He seemed irritated, though they'd only just begun speaking. He turned back to his screen and continued clacking away.

She readjusted her shoulders to stand a little taller, took a harder tone, surprising herself with her assertiveness as she put both of her hands on the desk.

"Then I need to speak to Officer Crenshaw or Officer Mable."

"Whole department's out on a call." He didn't look away from his screen as he twirled his index finger in a circle, signaling her to look around. The cubicles were surrounded by empty, frayed chairs, and an office door was shut, the light off. Coffee mugs sat atop desks scattered with papers, abandoned for so long that the cream in them had started to congeal. She had been so laser-focused on getting her story out that she hadn't noticed that the entire office was a ghost town.

She let out an exasperated sigh, closing her eyes as she rubbed her temples. She wasn't going to leave the girl's fate in this guy's hands.

"Do you know when he'll be back?"

He sat slouched over the desk with his hand on his bearded chin, a bored look on his face, and gave her a hard look up and down before answering.

"No idea. But I doubt he'll have time to deal with anything else today."

"Can you tell me where he is?"

"Everybody's out dealing with a mess down on Bradner Road. Now, what can I help you with, little miss?"

"Nothing. Eli, let's go."

Nora threw the door open in anger and it slammed shut behind her as she stormed into the parking lot.

Eli jogged to keep up with her.

"Why are we leaving? You don't want to wait to see if the sheriff comes back?"

"We're gonna go find him ourselves. I know exactly where he'll be," Nora said bitterly. She felt her blood pressure rise, making her feel faint, like she was floating across the lot.

"What do you mean?" Eli asked, confused.

"Bradner Road is where I saw the girl and hit the tree. There's only one reason the entire department would be there. That girl is dead."

FOUR

"Okay, this is it. Just keep following this road." Nora nervously wrung her hands as she leaned her head toward the open window, searching intently for a sign of familiarity. Nothing stood out to her. She had led Eli to Jimmy's Bar - ignoring Eli's smirk at the choice of location for her date - then retraced her path from there. The elms were just starting to yellow, signaling autumn was on its way in. Everything looked different in the daylight - less foreboding, more picturesque, as the sun shone through the tops of the trees, creating a golden hue as they rustled gently in the wind. If the circumstances weren't so grim, Nora would have stopped to take some photos.

As they came around a left curve, her heart sank at the sight of police tape. She felt rage, sudden and intense, rise up in her chest. If someone, *anyone*, had just *listened* to her, had taken her seriously, things could have ended much differently. *Would* have ended much differently.

"Stop the car," she demanded. Eli abruptly pulled behind three white squad cars.

She spotted a short, bald man in a dark windbreaker marked POLICE in bright yellow on the back, camera slung around his neck, walking from an unmarked van into the woods inside caution tape. The brush shielded her view from seeing how many officers stood beyond the tape, and she tried not to imagine what it was they were photographing.

The car was still rolling to a stop when she threw open the door and slammed it shut, and marched up to a lanky officer in a sweat-stained polo smoking a cigarette just inside the caution tape.

"This area's closed, ma'am," he called as she approached, putting his hand up gesturing to stop where she was. She ignored his request and pressed on, her hands balled into fists.

"I know why you're here. I need to talk to the sheriff." Her hardened voice commanded attention, her fear of the police rapidly diminishing in the wake of her anger. The officer seemed to notice her tone and stepped outside the tape.

"What's your name?" he asked. Nora noticed his free hand resting on the gun on his belt, and slowed her pace as she approached, suddenly aware of who she was talking to.

She gulped before answering breathlessly.

"Nora Aberdeen."

The officer's eyes widened with surprise. He dropped his half-smoked cigarette on the gravel beside the street and crushed it beneath his boot.

"Ah," he said through an exhale of smoke, nodding his head. "We've been wanting to talk to you."

"Why haven't you been answering our calls?"

Nora sat at an uneven folding table across from the brawny, poised Sheriff of Huntingdon County. He wore a tan uniform and matching peaked hat like she'd only seen sheriffs wear in movies, his buzzed, greying hair showing his age, though it made him look distinguished. The hat cast a shadow over his face, keeping the expression in his dark eyes hidden, though it didn't scare her any less. It made it impossible to gauge his reaction as she answered his questions.

She didn't care for his accusatory tone, considering the police hadn't come to the hospital like they'd told her they would. He hadn't even bothered to introduce himself - only his badge revealed his status. Sheriff Townsend. King of the Garbage Heap.

She also didn't care for the dank room that she sat in, so small and dimly lit that she started to feel claustrophobic. She had to focus, though, to get all of the information out. Here was her second chance to convey just how serious this was.

"My phone is in my car, which I'm guessing is at an impound lot because I didn't see it where I crashed."

"Your car isn't at impound. It's here." He watched her closely, his expression unchanged.

She tried not to let her shock show on her face, and she wished she could control her pulse bursting from the side of her neck. The girl was most likely dead, though she didn't dare bring it up. If her car was at the police station, did that mean they thought she had something to do with it?

She swallowed hard. "Okay, well...can I look for my phone then?"

"No phone was recovered from the vehicle." He spoke slowly and intentionally, and Nora looked for some semblance of significance in his inflection or his choice of words, but found none.

They searched my car? Why? Do they think I'm lying about my phone? She wasn't a smoker, but suddenly felt the urge for a cigarette, realizing now why the room smelled of stale smoke. She imagined the number of stressed suspects trying to keep it together, or to muster the courage to admit what they'd done. At least it would have kept her hands busy; she was twisting them together under the table while working to keep the visible half of her body seem relaxed.

She blinked hard, clearing her throat before she began. She had to steer the conversation back on course.

"Well, you know where I was. I was in the hospital, waiting for you guys." She spoke slowly, but decided she sounded innocent enough. She raised her eyebrows, challenging him. "Your officers didn't seem very interested in finding a girl who was running alone late at night. Not even when I told them she was bloody. But I'm here now, so let's talk about it," she said, leaning back in her chair, shocking herself with her boldness. She liked the sense of control it gave her, though her voice shook more than she would have liked.

The sheriff didn't seem to notice her change in attitude and pressed on, ignoring her statement about the girl, leaning forward so she could finally get a good look at him, his rugged handsomeness surprising her, though now that he was closer the amber in his cologne made her feel slightly sick.

"What time did you get into the accident?" His voice remained gravelly and flat, like he was asking her what the lunch specials were for the day.

"I don't know exactly. Maybe 11:30? I don't know how long I was out before I woke up."

"You're not from around here. What were you doing in Woodbridge?" She detected a slight drawl in his voice, and she wondered if he was originally from the south or if it was just a local twang.

This time, Nora didn't allow herself to get embarrassed. *Just answer his questions, and get the hell out.*

"I was supposed to meet someone at that bar called Jimmy's, but they didn't show."

"Who were you meeting?"

"A guy I met online."

"We'll need his information."

She didn't even know if the information she was giving him was accurate, and she was becoming exasperated by the conversation.

"Ryan Williams. I don't have his number. I'd give you his username, but it's in my phone, which I do not *have*." She knew she should probably pull back on her sharpness, but it came so easily on such little sleep.

The sheriff let out an irritated sigh. He opened the file he had been holding and looked its contents up and down. Nora strained to see but quickly averted her eyes as he brought his attention back to her.

"Did you, or your vehicle, make contact with this...person you saw?"

Fuck. She could feel herself break into a sweat as a cloak of anxiety crept into her brain.

"No!" she exclaimed, her voice breaking. Her breathing became labored just at the thought of what he was insinuating.

He pursed his lips, cracked down the middle from incessant biting, and studied Nora's face for a moment. Feeling uncomfortable was an understatement; she felt as though he was peering right through her, like his gaze would never break. Then he stood up.

"Get yourself a phone. We'll be in touch."

Nora tried to conceal her surprise. He had asked such basic questions, like he was going through a formality that only called for the bare minimum. *Doesn't he want to ask me anything about the girl, how she looked, how she seemed?* She desperately wanted to ask if the girl was dead, but she didn't dare. She was getting off easily, so she opted not to rock the boat and moved on as he had.

"When can I get my car?"

"When we're done with it." It was clear from his brusqueness that the conversation was over. He held the door open for her, and she exited silently past him.

Eli was sprawled out on the wooden lobby bench, the length of him taking up the entire seating area, scrolling mindlessly through his phone.

"Eli. We're going."

"That was quick!" He popped up and slipped his arm gently behind her back, guiding her out the door ahead of him.

"We'll talk about it in the car."

She thought she'd be more relieved once she was out of that room, but somehow she felt even more anxious than she had sitting across from the burly sheriff. Nothing had been resolved. She had no car and no phone; the only thing she was leaving with was a feeling that she was in some kind of trouble.

As they stepped outside and headed toward Eli's car, she started fervently explaining that he needed to drive her home and that her phone was gone, but as an officer at the far end of the building strode inside, she trailed off.

She turned around to see if she could get a look at him, but he had already slipped behind the dark glass door.

There was no mistaking it though. His stature. His gait.

She couldn't place how, but Nora knew him.

FIVE

The smell of her house welcomed Nora as she turned the deadbolt and stepped into her foyer. It reminded her of a library book; the Victorian was old but warm, and the scent of the pink peonies she kept on the front table, as her mother had, was familiar and brought her instant comfort. She took a deep inhale as she tossed her keys on the table and instantly felt more at ease.

She passed the tennis shoes she kept neatly by the door in case she decided to ever get out and jog again. She ascended the stairs, the wood creaking beneath her stiletto heels. She groaned in exasperation and stopped to remove them, tossing them haphazardly down toward the foyer, where they rolled over the Persian rug and smacked into the front door. The floral wallpaper that lined the stairway was turning up at the corners, and the dark wooden banister looked like it was fit for a home belonging to a much older woman, but there it would remain; she feared changing anything may erase any memory of her childhood.

The quiet murmur of the television she'd left on in her room grew louder as she rose to the second floor, and by the time she reached it, it was so loud she couldn't believe she'd forgotten to turn it off. But she'd been in a hurry to make the long drive, and she'd been painfully nervous, changing her shirt and then her pants and then back to her original choice, her trusty V-neck, simple and classic. She scoffed at herself as she fished for the remote in her sheets, finally finding it with her fingers and clicking the television off as a housewife in an evening gown and too much makeup spoke forcefully to the camera.

She sat on her bed in the silence, and let the night weigh on her. She rarely allowed the house to become quiet; she kept the television on while she slept, and Coldplay or Fiona Apple flooded from her laptop speakers most of the day as she perused social media and wondered what she should be doing with her life. Her parents had each left her a life insurance policy when they died; in total, she had received $250,000. The house was paid off. She could have sold it and used the money to rent herself a swanky loft downtown like Eli had - mingling with others her age in the bar scene, making new friends and new memories and leaving her old life behind. And she'd tried. The nights in bars had been easy, even if she had been too shy to make friends. But the house was the last real thing she had that connected her to her parents, and those were the only memories she cared about. Leaving would be a form of betrayal - if not to her parents, to herself. This was where she had grown up.

In a fit of almost manic restlessness, she had decided on a whim to remodel the bathroom attached to her bedroom a year after her parents died. When the contractor had finished and she stepped into the room, her smile quickly diminished. She didn't recognize the room she stood in, though she'd spent every day inside its walls, and she had chosen the finishes herself. The yellowed shower tiles and bathtub had been torn out, replaced with the freestanding tub with bronzed clawed feet her mother had been eyeing every time they saw a home design commercial; the tired countertop was now a thick, white piece of Caesarstone; the walls, once a soft purple, now a deep ocean blue; the floor, which had been stick tile, now a dark cherry wood. It was beautiful, and it devastated her. She remembered her mouth dropping open, rushing the contractor out the door as she thanked him, then returning to the bathroom to sit on the floor and sob.

She felt a pang of guilt that her mother would never enjoy the luxurious tub. But more than that, she cried for the memories that she hadn't even realized were still nestled inside of her brain. The time she and Erica had fought so badly at her junior prom that she came home in tears and her mom sat with her on the floor, listening intently, every so often interjecting a "you're right" or "she'll apologize tomorrow" while handing her tissues to wipe her running mascara. She was right, of course. She always was.

She remembered wiping out badly on her bike when she was in second grade, her dad swooping her up into his big arms and flying up the stairs to clean her knee with peroxide. His voice was steady, telling her she was fine, that she'd be okay, but his brow had furrowed with a look of panic as the blood kept coming. He held a washcloth over it until it stopped, and only then did he breathe a heavy sigh of relief. She still had the scars.

Now the room was unrecognizable, as if those moments were wiped away with the construction. That was it for her, as far as renovations were concerned.

Instead, she used the money she'd received to live on and not much else. Before the end of life as she knew it, she had wanted to be a journalist. She gathered from the comments on her articles from her professors - phrases like "astute observations" and "clean, unbiased copy" - that she had a knack for it. But that dream died with her mother. It felt nearly treasonous to move on, to keep living her life as she had when her parents were with her, as if their absence meant nothing. She knew they would want her to get it together. Finish school, get a job. To become something. But she was rudderless without them.

She often logged into her bank account, staring at the number that ticked down the tiniest bit each month, wondering what she should do with such a significant amount of money. Her parents were always good with money, and they lived in an upper-middle class neighborhood with a good school system that was close to the city. But they'd never sprung for outrageous purchases, never had vacation homes or fancy cars like some of her classmates' parents did. She had been only twenty-two when her parents had died, and her newfound wealth overwhelmed her. It would have been her parents she'd turn to for advice on what to do with it, and now that they were gone, she was stuck in limbo. When she was a child she'd dreamed up what she would do with her money if she ever became rich, how she would buy a big house and fill it with dogs who needed rescuing. Now that she had it, the money made her feel inadequate, like she'd been given the key to something for which she was not prepared. So she tortured herself with guilt over it, and opted not to touch the majority of it until she was sure it would go to good use.

The ride home with Eli had been quiet, but he'd rubbed her thigh every now and again and shot her a smile to put her at ease. She wasn't sure if it was friendly or something more, and thought less of it than she normally would have, had her mind not been spinning. As he pulled into her driveway to drop her off, he'd insisted she stay at his place, nearly pleading with her that she shouldn't be alone while she was injured, and the concern in his eyes and the dimple in his cheek nearly convinced her to grab an overnight bag. But she knew she couldn't. She needed real rest, and she was never comfortable in his apartment. His neatness was almost sterile compared to her sloppiness. She often left her clothes strewn across the floor and her bed unmade; that was how she preferred it. Besides, she just wanted to feel the comfort of her own home, to sleep in her own bed, to not wonder if they were going to have a physical interlude. And her number one priority was a shower.

As she lathered up, steam rising around her, hot water struck her back like tiny knives, and she realized she was a bit more banged up than she initially thought. Her left shoulder was bruised and tender, and she couldn't remember the last time she'd felt so worn down. Despite the fragile state of her body, the heavy, dense condensation felt heavenly, cleansing the remnants of Woodbridge and its malaise from her skin, but she couldn't wait to get out and go to sleep.

The moment she turned off the valve, she knew something was off. She heard a slight creak that sounded like it was coming from the stairs, and there was a change in the energy of the house. She'd left the bathroom door cracked open to let the steam out. As she tiptoed past the shelf of towels she grabbed her floral silk robe, wrapping it around herself without drying off. She stood behind the door as it clung to her, its bright colors going darker as it dampened, peering out the slit next to the wall silently, and waited.

There. Footsteps. Her heartbeat quickened, and she could feel the pulse through her entire body. She fought through instant lightheadedness trying to calculate a plan of action. She had no phone to call 911, no exit because she was upstairs. Should she run down the hall, barricade herself in her room? Try to scale down the gutter pipe in her robe? What would the neighbors think? She imagined running wildly, screaming for help as onlookers locked their doors to shield themselves from the crazy woman down the street. She prepared herself to dash across the hallway and out the bedroom window, counting to herself as she shook with adrenaline. *One, two...*

"Nora?" A familiar voice called, floating up the staircase.

"Holy shit, Erica!" Nora cried as she clutched her chest. She finally took a heavy breath, releasing the tension that had stiffened her body.

Long, dark legs rounded the corner, and Erica popped her head in the doorway, hair black and shining, hanging loose as she smiled broadly and leaned into the door frame.

"Don't tell me you forgot? Date that good?" Erica teased with a wink. Nora clutched her chest in relief, chastising herself that in the flurry of unexpected activity, she had completely forgotten about a lunch they'd planned to gossip about her date.

"You know, you were supposed to text me when you got home last night. I almost drove my ass all the way out there and looked for you." Erica tsk-tsked as she hoisted herself onto the bathroom counter.

Nora shook her head, breathing heavily as her adrenaline came down, drops of water falling from her tresses as she let herself collapse against the counter.

"You don't even want to know."

Erica shook her head as she sipped an iced coffee through a metal straw, bewildered by the events that Nora described.

Nora watched her eyes widen with every detail. She had always envied Erica's skin, her perfect brown complexion a result of inheritance from her Latina mother and Thai father, supple and clear with a dewy glow that Nora could never achieve, no matter how many special creams she rubbed into her own pale skin. Nora would find herself focusing on Erica's skin in the midst of many of their conversations, sometimes tuning her out as she yearned for a tan that seductive, but today, there were more pressing matters to focus on.

"Holy shit. When you said it was bad, I thought he catfished you or something. I wasn't expecting a fucking MURDER." Erica spoke quietly but forcefully, her head leaned toward Nora, resting on her palm as her fingers wrapped the side of her face, her other hand gripping her cup.

Nora quickly pressed her finger to her lips to hush Erica, her eyes darting nervously to be sure no one was listening to them. "I don't even know if she's dead. I'm just assuming. I could be way off. And if she is, that doesn't mean she was murdered...necessarily." She didn't believe her own words, and neither did Erica. She picked at her sandwich, barely eating but pulling the bread apart so she could busy her hands.

"This is crazy, Nora," Erica said, shaking her head. Her demeanor, normally cool and laid back, had turned slightly frantic, her dark eyes distressed. It made Nora's stomach churn. She'd seen that face only once before, and she shuddered as she let herself remember the first time - a chilly day in November, when Nora's melancholia had reached its peak.

Two months after her father passed away, Nora slowly sauntered home from the drugstore. She swirled a bag of wine as she strolled, studying her street. The large colonials were filled with families who had already started to put up their Christmas decorations, tinsel and twinkling lights and neighborly warmth. A light dusting of snow covered the frozen ground, creating a gentle sparkle that Nora used to find captivating. She barely noticed it now. People told her that it would get easier with time, but so far, two months had felt like two years, and loneliness had engulfed her. Thanksgiving with Erica's family had been a distraction, but she'd felt out of place and unable - or unwilling - to keep up with the table conversation. Christmas this year would be spent waking up alone, for the first time. Once her favorite holiday, a day full of laughter and sharing stories and gifts and love, was over now. She could barely stand the thought of it.

The dust had settled. The casseroles that distant cousins dropped off had all been eaten in silence in her room as she mindlessly flipped through television channels, never able to concentrate on a storyline. The only family she had left was her mom's estranged brother David, but to Nora, he may as well be dead. The texts from friends checking on her had stopped coming when their messages weren't returned. She had no energy to hold up her end of a relationship, and so she let most of them go.

Every time she came home with something to say about her day, the conversations of the mundane she had taken for granted, she had no one to tell. She knew deep down that that had been part of the reason she stopped going to school, that she couldn't bear continuing to live her life like nothing had happened and then come home to the constant reminder that life wasn't the same. Time was cruel; it refused to stand still for her grief. She was alone, and now she felt the difference.

The ache in her heart had overtaken her thoughts until she could feel it manifesting in her bones. All she wanted was to feel better. Or even to feel nothing at all. Her thoughts had turned decidedly morbid, and she felt consumed by them. Would her skin still prune in the water, after she was dead? She imagined her body sitting in water for days, bloating until she became unrecognizable. She didn't love the idea of someone finding her looking like that, but couldn't even muster up the strength to concern herself with something so trivial.

She took four Xanax that she had been prescribed by her doctor for anxiety and headed up to her bathtub, the one her mother had envied, dragging her bottle of wine with her. She thought she'd drift off to sleep, and maybe she'd drown - she'd probably drown - but she didn't mind; she'd be too relaxed to care.

She didn't really consider it a suicide attempt - it was easier to swallow that way, even when she knew she was lying to herself - but she was keenly aware that she didn't exactly have a firm grasp on life, either. She'd left no note in case she did die. Only Erica would have found it, and she didn't have the strength to explain to her, even on paper, that everything she'd done for her still wasn't enough to save her.

At the time, she thought she had been thinking clearly. It seemed like a natural next step, to fade away with the rest of her family, to be free of the pain that seemed like it would never dissipate. The way she remembered it now, a cloudiness had enveloped her mind, settling like a fog, gripped into her brain like a parasite that refused to leave before it had taken everything she had to give.

She didn't remember much of what happened after that. She didn't remember Erica calling, or slurring her words trying to respond when she asked her what was wrong. She didn't remember their conversation, which Erica described as "messy." She vaguely remembered her pulling her out of the tub, wrapping a towel around her hair as she vomited all over the speckled bathroom floor.

What she remembered most clearly was Erica's face the following morning, her brow furrowed deep in thought as she pressed a cool washcloth over Nora's face. She never pushed Nora when she said it had been an accident. Nora lied, telling her she didn't know you couldn't mix Xanax and alcohol. Erica had simply stated "okay", but the look in her eyes, such genuine concern that seemed lined with hurt, made Nora feel incredibly guilty. It was obvious that she knew what really happened. Erica had been the only friend left who consistently checked on her, and Nora had even stopped responding to her. Erica had felt in her gut that something was wrong, and she'd called before Nora slipped into unconsciousness, flooring it when she heard Nora speaking gibberish until she peeled up the cement drive and sprinted inside. When Erica went out to grab them lunch that afternoon, she returned with three therapists' business cards and firmly stated, "You have to go. Pick one."

And there it was again. That face.

"Why didn't you call me to pick you up?" Erica's voice broke through Nora's daydream.

"It's such a far drive. I didn't want to wake you up and make you go all the way out there," Nora said. She'd told herself as much when she dialed Eli's number instead of Erica's, when she knew the truth lay somewhere in between that she knew Eli would be awake, and that she wanted him to be the one to see her, hurt and lonely in a hospital bed.

"Mmhm." Erica nodded slowly and stared at her, knowing Nora was lying but assessing that it wasn't worth the argument. "Well. I'm glad you're all right. Next time, call me."

SIX

She had brushed it off at lunch, but Erica's catfishing comment nagged Nora as Erica drove her home. It *was* weird, how Ryan hadn't shown up; they had messaged each other confirming their date that afternoon. And weirder still, that something so strange and terrifying had happened on her drive home, just miles from where they had planned to meet. She rubbed her temples. Exhaustion was setting in, and the only thing she could focus on was crawling into bed.

After lunch, Erica had come with her to purchase a new phone, and she was thankful she could keep the same number. She texted Eli that she had access to a phone again, and after reassuring Erica that she was okay to be alone, she felt herself hurrying her out the door. With every passing moment it became harder to be on her feet, and she could focus on little else but lying down.

But as the minutes ticked by, Nora found it impossible to sleep. She groaned at her mind's inability to meet her body's needs, and hoisted herself up and over to her desk. She opened her email, skimming past an e-vite she still hadn't responded to about her friend Charlotte's bachelorette party. She combed through the messages looking for the final one she'd received from Ryan, expressing his nerves and his excitement to meet her. All of his messages had come through her dating profile on a very basic dating site called Cupid's Arrow, a name she thought sounded stupid, but the romantic in her had won that round.

She opened the message, then stopped, puzzled. The message was there, but the name attached to it was blank, and the photo was empty. She logged into the site directly, and found that her account inbox no longer had the messages from Ryan saved. She shook her head, heart racing, and logged out of her account and then punched her mother's birthdate back in. There were old messages from guys she'd spoken with who had never panned out, but her conversation with Ryan - the only man who had seemed interested in a real relationship and not a one night stand - had been starred at the top of the page. Now, it was nowhere to be found.

They had exchanged nearly a month's worth of messages before they had decided to meet in person. Long-winded stories about their favorite movies and songs: they both loved 80s movies and new wave; their wishes for the future: they both wanted a family, once they found the right person. Sometimes they'd chat for hours, until he relented that he had to get up early for work and had to get some sleep. But he always said he couldn't wait to meet her, and she'd blush thinking about someone being so excited over her. But he hadn't met her, and now the messages were gone.

She searched within the site for his name. Nothing.

Okay, this is getting weird.

She drummed her fingers on her desk and considered the options. He could have gotten spooked and blocked her so she wouldn't come looking for him after he stood her up. But what if somehow, it had something to do with her accident? The sheriff asked her if she hit the girl before hitting the tree. Had someone run her over?

Her mind wandered to the girl in the road. *Who was she?*

What was she doing out there? Is it possible she's connected to Ryan? Is he the one who hit her?

She shivered, but realized she was spinning out and went back to trying to put together the pieces of what happened. She googled "woman dead Woodbridge PA". Her results yielded nothing of relevance and she let out a slow sigh of relief, scanning obituaries of women much older than the one she had seen.

As she searched, she learned that Woodbridge events were covered in a local paper with its surrounding towns, a publication called *The Huntingdon County Chronicle*. It seemed like kind of an interesting story for a small town, a young woman, not much older than a girl, really, in obvious distress. It seemed unlikely that a reporter for a paper wouldn't know about every single body making it to the local coroner. Maybe she wasn't dead, after all. Nora pushed aside thoughts of yellow police tape and let herself believe that. But it still didn't make sense that she was running alone in the dark, so disheveled she'd ended up in the street. She'd been running from something. From some*one*.

She tried "missing woman Huntingdon County PA."

Nothing.

She rubbed her hands over her face in frustration. Her stomach lurched, surprising her as she remembered she hadn't eaten dinner. She tore herself away and padded downstairs to the kitchen, waiting a beat before rounding the corner from her stairs to listen for footsteps. Nothing this time.

She ran her hands over the cool steel of her fridge, using the entire weight of her body to muster the strength to open its heavy door. She looked over the pathetic offerings, making a mental note to get to a grocery store. She tried the freezer but found only a half-drunk liter of vodka. Her hand hovered over it, the breath of the open drawer making her fingers go cold, and she thought better of it, reopening the fridge and opting for a sad-looking apple, before retreating back upstairs.

She rested her fingers on her forehead, thinking about a new approach to gain answers as she bit into her apple, grimacing at its taste and tossing it into the trash. She wiped her hands down her shorts and tried "missing women in Pennsylvania".

A site indexed by decade came up with a long list of women. She started at the top and worked her way down, studying each face intently, feeling the weight of each woman's absence as she considered them.

Nora nearly jumped out of her skin when her phone buzzed, breaking her concentration from her research. An unfamiliar number appeared on her screen. She was puzzled that someone would call so late before noticing the time. Hours had passed - it was already 7 a.m. She remembered the sheriff's stern message, that he'd be calling, and she'd better answer.

Her fingers shook as she answered, trying and failing to keep her voice steady.

"Hello?"

A deep voice she hadn't heard in years, one that she'd long forgotten, invaded her ears.

"Hi...Nora? It's your Uncle David. We need to talk."

She paused in shock for a moment before letting out an uninterested laugh.

"Why are you calling me?" Nora skipped the pleasantries, feeling no need to fake a relationship that didn't exist. It was the only thing she could think to say.

"Listen, I know we haven't talked in a while."

"Uh, yeah, I'd say it's been a while. Not even when my parents died." Her icy demeanor was as she'd played it out in her head time and again; she'd fantasized about her uncle calling her to make amends while she rebuffed his every attempt, and now was her chance to play it out exactly as she'd planned it.

Truthfully, Nora hadn't given half a thought to David until she saw a commercial for a rehab facility several months after her parents died. The days following her mother's accident all seemed to be under a hazy spell that could not, or would not, ever become clear. She had no trouble slipping into seemingly banal memories from her childhood, but from this, she could only remember fragments of her distress. Feeling as if she was hovering outside herself, watching as she lost all control of her body and falling to the floor as her dad choked out through tears and clenched teeth that her mother had been in an accident. Walking calmly through her backyard and into the woods that butted up to them on the morning of her mother's funeral, waiting until she was surrounded by trees to unleash a primal scream, and then another, wailing into a vastness that seemed more like a mirage than a place she'd grown up. She grabbed hold of a white birch and used it to steady herself, pressed her chest against its trunk to keep her balance, but still, she fell, crumpling into the fetal position, where her father eventually found her, crying silently. Without a word, he'd scooped her up into a bear hug, squeezing her so tight that it almost hurt but somehow made her feel safe, and they both dissolved into quiet, desperate tears, surrounded by the sounds of the forest. That was the last clear memory she had of her father, just the two of them. She imagined the lack of memory was her body's way of protecting itself from heartbreak strong enough to kill her. But even if she hadn't yearned for David's presence, he should have been there. He had no semblance of an idea what she'd been through since.

He paused before answering. "Well, that's complicated. I want to talk to you about something a bit more pressing."

"More pressing than my dead parents?" Anger washed over her. That he thought she owed him anything was a joke, and that included her time.

"Nora, I'm really trying here. I shouldn't even be calling you, but I'm sticking my neck out because you're still my family."

Nora faked a silent gag and shook her head, smiling condescendingly for her own amusement.

"Yeah? Mmmk, but I'm kinda busy. Why are you calling me this early? What do you want?" She was already half-listening, absentmindedly scrolling through google results for Ryan Williams in Pittsburgh, Pennsylvania, something she realized she should have done before agreeing to meet him in person.

"Did you get into an accident the other night?"

Nora's hand stopped cold on her mouse as the other gripped the phone tightly. *How the fuck does he know that?*

Then it hit her. The familiar presence as she walked out of the parking lot after she spoke to the sheriff. It was David.

She declined to answer him, and instead asked, "Do you work at the police station?"

Her tone was accusatory, but what she was accusing him of, she wasn't sure.

"Yes. I'm a deputy for the Huntingdon County Sheriff's Department."

Nora let out a cruel laugh. "You? *You're* a police officer? Okay..." She shook her head in disbelief.

"I've changed a lot. Cleaned my act up. I've worked really hard to get...to get where I'm at now. But I need you to confirm if you were in an accident on August 18th."

Nora let out a tired sigh. "Yep, and I'm pretty sick of talking about it. So now you know, it was me. Is that all?"

"I need you to meet me." He lowered his voice, underlined with urgency.

Nora scoffed at his audacity. After all this time, after she had planned her parents' funerals alone, she hadn't received so much as a phone call from him to console her, and *now* he wanted to talk?

"I'm not kidding. It's important that you meet with me. I know about the girl in the road. I need your help, and I think you need mine."

SEVEN

Nora snagged a corner booth at the Windfall Diner, the only restaurant within walking distance from her house. She ordered a Coke, suddenly wishing she had chosen a place that served alcohol. She'd agreed to meet with David if he came to her in Philly, and he was all too eager to oblige, saying that it wouldn't be wise if they met near Woodbridge, which didn't exactly sit well. She'd busied herself all day with laundry, the first load she'd done in weeks, and poring over job listings at newspapers that she'd never apply for, before fully committing to working herself into a frenzy about their meeting. She texted Erica before she left that she was meeting with her Uncle David and where they were heading, just in case things got as strange as he was acting on the phone.

Her legs shook nervously under the table as she fiddled with the plastic buttons on her tank top. Her heart pounded harder and harder as she waited, the minutes ticking by at a glacial pace. She considered deserting the meeting, but then she saw David walk through the door, bell chiming as he entered. He was off duty and in plain clothes. His blue eyes were striking, piercing through her in a way that made it hard for her to make eye contact with him, even from afar. He'd gained some weight, in a good way; the last time she'd seen him, he was rail thin. He looked much more mature than he had before, like a real man. It was still hard for her to imagine, but she could see in his posture that he was a cop - chest out, hand grazing near his beltline.

She reluctantly put her hand up to show where she was sitting, but her face remained stoic and she didn't rise to greet him. The fact that he had some information about her accident didn't mean that all was suddenly forgiven.

He gave a slight smile and put his hand up, hesitating for just a moment, then slid across from her in the tattered booth.

"Hi. How are you feeling? Are you...are you okay?"

His voice came out uneven, his eyebrows raised in apprehension as he ran his hand through his copper hair, which she realized hadn't thinned at all yet. He still looked young, though years had passed since she'd seen him. She tried to place his energy and realized that he was nervous, too. She'd been ridden with anxiety since they'd spoken, but she hadn't considered how he was feeling about their meeting. She remembered very few conversations with him since she'd seen him last when she was in junior high, and she assumed he didn't remember any of their conversations from that time in his life, either.

"Yep. So, what's this all about?" She desperately wanted to cut to the chase, not wanting this to become something that it wasn't, wishing that she could keep her voice a little steadier as she spoke. She wanted information; she didn't want this to be some overdue bonding experience, trying to reminisce about an old kinship that he'd concocted in his head.

She could see in his face that he was hurt that she hadn't softened, but he didn't address it.

"What did you see when you got into the accident?" he asked, pulling a notepad from his back pocket and unclipping a pen from his button-down.

"I assume you read the report. I saw a girl, she ran out in front of me," she said matter-of-factly, her legs bouncing beneath the table, still refusing to meet his eyeline.

"That's all the report says. Can you describe her?" His tone had turned methodical, as if he were questioning someone he'd never met.

Nora sighed, exasperated, her hand at her temple.

"Well, that's ridiculous, because I told them she was wearing a nightgown, and that it had blood on it."

She narrowed her eyes as David began taking notes.

"Are you working this case? Isn't that a conflict of interest or something?"

Now it was he who wouldn't meet her gaze. He glanced behind him, then at the patches in the ceiling as he said, "I'm not...I'm not here in an official capacity for her death." He cracked one pasty knuckle after another.

"So she's dead," she said flatly. She'd known in her heart that her intuition had been right, but the confirmation made her feel hollow.

David pursed his lips, dropped his head once he realized he'd broken it to her.

"Yes. She's dead."

"So what does that mean, that you're not here in an 'official capacity'?"

"It means...it means that I'm not here for the precinct. I'm here in spite of them."

"Okay, before we go any further, I need you to tell me what the hell's going on." She felt a surge of anger as she flopped back against the booth and crossed her arms. She wasn't in the mood for games, especially now.

There was a long beat of silence before he answered.

Finally, he said softly but definitively, "It would probably be better if you didn't know."

"I don't care. Tell me or this conversation is over," she said. She couldn't remember speaking so curtly to anyone the way she was now, but she noticed that it got her results with the police when she'd taken a harder stance. And it rubbed her the wrong way, that he waltzed into her life for some unforeseen reason, and now wouldn't even disclose that reason to her. How dare he invade her space when she was already grappling with what happened that night. That was just like him. She should have guessed the meeting would go like this. She decided she'd reached her patience threshold and grabbed her purse to leave.

"Don't go." David sighed, then nodded, hanging his head in defeat. "Okay. I'll explain. This has to stay between you and me, though." He paused as the waitress came bearing coffee and filled his mug to the brim, smiling kindly at her, watching her disappear behind swinging doors at the counter before continuing.

"We've been having...we've been experiencing a few suicides in our town."

Nora stared silently, but confusion flooded her face.

"The opioid problem is really bad in Woodbridge."

Nora snorted at his gall, and David's face reddened.

"Look, I know you're angry at me, and I understand. I did some horrible things to your mother when I was at my worst. But I've straightened my life out. That's why I joined the academy. I'm a different person now." He blurted everything out, like he had rehearsed what he wanted to say, but now that the conversation was happening he wanted the words he'd practiced out of his mouth as fast as possible.

Nora just stared at him, unsure of how to react. She watched the tiny scar below his bottom lip move as he gesticulated, evidence of a former lip ring that Nora guessed no one else knew about. Most of what she heard about her Uncle David growing up was negative - how he stole from her grandparents and her mother; how he never showed up for family events, and when he did, he made a scene; how he only ever called when he needed some money to score drugs, including when her grandparents had died and left their estate to her mother. She'd had limited interactions with him growing up. He'd always been kind to her, but she had never trusted him. She knew better.

As if he could read her mind, he said, "Look, I know you don't trust me, but I really need your help." He had gone wild-eyed and slightly frantic as he began to lose grip on their meeting, and Nora felt guilt creep in. His words seemed earnest, and she suddenly felt the need to keep him at arm's length dissipate. While her gaze remained unchanged, she softened her attitude.

"Go on." She dropped her purse back in the booth and sipped her Coke coolly as she watched him. He seemed so different from what she remembered. He looked much more put-together now, though she couldn't determine if it were his age or that this was the first time she'd seen him dressed in anything other than old t-shirts and torn jeans. She couldn't recall any meaningful conversations with her uncle, if they'd ever had any. She did remember spending a lot of time worrying about him. Her parents had tried their best to shield her from specifics, but she could hear their conversations about him as they talked in the kitchen on nights when she couldn't sleep. She was filled with panic that he would wind up dead, and she'd have to see her mother fall to pieces with guilt over cutting him off from their family. Things had ended up much differently than she'd expected.

The scent of fresh pancakes flooded the diner though it was well past dinner time, and Nora's stomach rumbled with hunger. She refused to order, knowing it would extend their meeting and invite small talk. *Get in, get the information, get out.*

"Okay. We've had a few cases that haven't...they haven't sat well with me. Once in a while they're legit, but a few young women have turned up dead, and they didn't exactly seem like typical junkies to me."

"Okay?" Nora shook her head, wondering what his point was.

"On the autopsy reports, they're all showing heroin use. But these girls aren't from Woodbridge. We haven't even been able to

ID three of them. So my question is, why are all of these young women from out-of-town coming to Woodbridge to die?"

"Maybe you have a kingpin selling bad drugs," she said dryly. She thought it was clear that she was making fun of him; she was fairly certain there were no drug lords in a town like Woodbridge, where the cows out-numbered the people. He didn't seem to notice.

"Maybe, but I don't think that's it. I've been asking around and all my CIs are coming up with are low-level dealers. If the major source was selling laced drugs, we'd be seeing way more deaths than just these girls." He lowered his voice, checking over his shoulder to make sure no one was in earshot, before continuing. "And they're not taking enough to overdose, but manner of death is always listed as a suicide - or natural causes, due to heroin - on the autopsy report."

Nora's eyes began to water and her nose tingled the way it did when she was facing real fear. She realized now, why David was here.

"Are you telling me that the girl I almost hit - that they ruled her death a suicide?" She forced down tears as they stung in the corners of her eyes. She didn't want to look weak in front of David.

David lifted his eyebrows and pursed his lips in acknowledgement, sitting back in his seat and throwing his hands up before resting them on the table.

"This is why I need your help. I assume you don't think she killed herself."

Nora shook her head and let her eyes wander as she thought.

"I mean, she did run out in front of my car...." she trailed off as she thought about it, before continuing, "No. I don't think she killed herself. There was blood on her gown, and she looked scared. They're saying she overdosed?"

"Her jugular was slit, and a razor was found next to her body."

The tingle was back.

"That's impossible. Her hands were empty." She felt her heart begin to thunder in her chest.

"Are you sure about that?" He wrote furiously in his pad.

"Yes, of that I am sure." She ran the memory over and over in her head every time she had a moment of silence; she knew exactly what the girl looked like, what her nightgown looked like, and her hands had moved frenziedly, but they were empty.

"Could she have had something in her pocket?"

"She didn't have pockets."

They sat silent for what felt like minutes before she carefully began, "I don't know if this is relevant..."

David perked up. "Don't try to determine what's relevant; that's my job. Just tell me everything you know," he nudged her encouragingly. Something his job had taught him to get people to open up, she was sure. She had to remember that.

"Well, it's about why I was out there." She hesitated.

"Tell me."

"I was supposed to meet this guy."

"Mmhm. Name?"

"I don't know if it's his real name, but he told me it was Ryan Williams."

"How do you know him?"

"Well, I don't really. We met online."

He stopped writing and looked at her sternly.

She rolled her eyes. "Oh, please. I didn't even use my real name. All he knows about me is I'm from Philly and I like sad music." *And my parents are dead.*

"What are you doing meeting strangers in person?" he asked, and there was a note of anger mixed with fear in his voice.

"Don't try to get paternal on me, David. That's not what I need from *you*." The inflection rolled off her tongue crueler than she'd intended, and she could tell that it stung him. She felt sorry, but didn't apologize; she just pressed on.

"Anyway, we were supposed to meet at Jimmy's Bar, but he didn't show."

"Did you speak to him after he...didn't show?"

"No. I tried to message him, but I didn't have internet service out there. I waited for a while and then I left. I didn't think much of it besides that I was pissed that I drove all the way out there to meet him, and he didn't even tell me he was canceling. But when I got home...the profile had been deleted. Or maybe he blocked me. I don't know."

"What do you know about him?"

"He said he's 32, works as a sales guy in Pittsburgh. No kids, never married."

David rubbed the stubble on his chin, pondering what he could do with the vague information he'd been given.

"Well, it could be nothing. Could be that he was lying about who he was and got spooked when it came time to meet."

She sensed that there was more.

"Or?"

"Or, could be he's involved. It is a coincidence that this happened right before the girl died. You don't come up with a whole lot of coincidences that *stay* coincidences in murder investigations."

"So you think she was murdered." She stared into his eyes, refusing to look away even though she found it difficult to keep them locked onto his.

He opened his mouth to speak, then shut it.

"I can't talk about too many details with you. Standard procedure," he said, shaking his head.

"I thought you said you weren't here for the department."

He smiled wryly.

"You don't miss a thing."

"Why *aren't* you here for the department?" Nora asked, with a note of suspicion.

He shifted his weight nervously before he began.

"Well, I'm not Homicide. I'm just a deputy. And basically since these girls have turned up, I've been thinking how it's been so strange...it just didn't sit right. When I brought it up to the detective working these cases, he brushed me off, so I went over his head to the sheriff. *That* was a mistake." He shook his head as he stared off blankly, and she determined there was more to that story but that now wasn't the time to discuss it.

"So why did you want to talk to me?"

"I wanted to see if you saw anything that would indicate that this was a suicide, or if you had seen anyone else in the area. The report taken is pretty bare."

"Uh, yeah, they didn't even come to the hospital to talk to me like they said they were going to." Her irritation lingered over how the situation was handled, especially now that the girl was dead and that they had ruled it a suicide without even following up with her about it.

"Not surprised. Not surprised at all," he said, more to himself than to her as he stared off. She imagined he was calculating his hidden grievances against his co-workers.

His eyes seemed to come back to the present and he looked her over.

"How are you feeling since the accident?" His eyes showed genuine concern.

"Honestly, I'm fine. Just a little sore." As she mindlessly rubbed her arms up and down, she looked back at him, really looked at him for the first time since he'd walked into the diner - and she was startled by how much she realized he reminded her of her mother. When she was younger she didn't think the two looked much alike, but now that she was face to face with him after all these years, the familiarity was there. Her mother had aged better, even though she was older when she died than he was now. She calculated that he was probably forty by now. Time and hard living had given him rougher looks, but he was still handsome, and his facial features were unmistakably like her mother's. The straight, broad nose, the high cheekbones - even the way he spoke, half-finishing sentences before starting them over. Peeks of grey peppered in at the temples, but the fiery red hair remained - the family heirloom, her mother used to call it, as she'd laugh and tousle Nora's hair. She felt tension melt away as she remembered that he was family, and that was something she thought she had lost altogether.

She didn't feel comfortable allowing him to bring her guard down so easily, so she brought the conversation back around.

"So, any news on my car?"

"I think you should call on it. They might be done with it by now. They don't know we're related, so *don't* mention it," he said, stressing the importance.

She felt her shoulders release from an imaginary girdle hold at the prospect of getting her car back. She hadn't realized how tightly wound she'd been since her accident.

The moment was fleeting; she wasn't satisfied with how things were unfolding.

"What do you know about the girls who died?" she asked, impersonating David's line of questioning.

David sighed. "Not much. Only one we've IDed was Rebecca White, about six months ago. We found her near the bridge by the river a few miles from where you had your accident. She was from just north of Philly, actually...from Abington. Her parents have no idea how she ended up in Woodbridge."

"How'd you ID her?"

"Her mom had a google alert on dead girls found in Pennsylvania. Can you imagine that? She'd been missing for months before we found her. They came to us when our local newspaper picked up the story."

Nora made a mental note. Rebecca White from Abington.

"And the others?"

"Not much. They're all Caucasian, roughly 18-25 years old. All of them were found in relatively close proximity to each other, in wooded areas. Very underweight, but that's typical...that's typical for addicts. They all had bruises along their arms and legs, which again, the coroner attributes to drug use."

"But you don't think that's it?"

"The bruising looked a little severe for it to be from just shooting dope. I'm no doctor, but it looked more like restraint bruising to me. And one of them - her fingernails were broken and bloody. Seemed more like defensive wounds. Again - I'm not a doctor." He ran his hands up and down his thighs nervously.

"Can't the coroner tell what it's from?"

"Look, Woodbridge isn't Philly. We're low on resources, and the coroner is married to the sheriff's daughter. If the sheriff wants it to be a suicide...it's gonna be a suicide."

Nora shook her head, not understanding.

"Why would he want it to be a suicide?"

He sighed, took a long sip of ice water, set it back down and swallowed hard before answering. "Because the alternative is a huge fucking nightmare."

"That being...?"

David's face turned pale, lowering his voice to just above a whisper, before his eyes pierced right through to her soul, sending a cold shiver down her spine.

"That there's a serial killer in our town."

EIGHT

Casey threw her long, golden hair into a bun as she knelt beside her old Volkswagen, frowning at the back right tire that had gone completely flat. If she drove on it any more, she'd bend the rim. She pulled her phone from her back pocket. *Fuck*. No service, and nothing in sight, save for a long, lush forest. Why hadn't she paid more attention when her mother tried to show her how to change a tire? She was always preaching to Casey about being an independent woman, and she was more irritated that this moment proved her mother right than she was about the tire. Her mother was incensed that she had decided to take the scenic route home from a preliminary visit to her college campus, and it had instigated a fight between them before she slammed the door on her way out. *Of course this had to happen*. She wasn't looking forward to the conversation that awaited her when her mom came to pick her up. *That's what I get for trying to get some time to myself to think*.

Shielding her eyes from the setting sun, she calculated how long it would take her to walk back to the tiny bar she remembered passing before she started to feel like something about her car wasn't right. She figured it was probably six or seven miles, possibly more, but they had to have a phone, and she didn't have much choice. With an exasperated sigh, she grabbed her camel-colored crossbody purse from the passenger seat, locked the car from the inside, slammed her door shut in anger, and began the trek backward.

As she hustled past the woods, taking in the tall shagbark maples with only slivers of light peeking through the breaks, a shiver went down her spine. It was extremely quiet, without so much as a bird chirping nearby, and she didn't particularly like it; she'd longed for space and silence to think about whether she was truly ready to leave her friends and go away to college, but this wasn't what she had been hoping for. Her flip flops smacking back and forth against her heels jostled against the silence as she power-walked down the road. The wind picked up and she shivered again, crossing her arms and rubbing the goosebumps that had formed along the backs of her arms as she traversed the side of the road. She checked her phone for service once more. No luck.

How did she even get a flat tire? She put air in her tires before the three hour ride up to State. She figured she must have run over a nail when she stopped for gas. Where was she again? She struggled to remember the name of the town before the dilapidated wooden sign she saw as she passed through, with its faded paint and crooked stature, came to her mind. Welcome to Woodbridge - Population: 739.

She had been walking for about 20 minutes, darkness nearing and no end of the woods in sight, when she heard a familiar sound - yes, it was crunching over gravel. A car.

"*Yes*," she whispered to herself as she closed her eyes in relief. Now she just needed to convince them to stop and help her.

Casey figured they'd take her for a hitchhiker and perhaps not want to stop for her, but she thought she looked pretty unassuming in her tank and short shorts, skin golden from a summer's worth of beach days. She thought they'd feel okay about giving her a hand if she flashed them her big, warm smile - it had gotten her out of trouble many times in the past.

A beat-up pickup truck slowly approached, and she threw both of her hands in the air. The truck slowly pulled to the side of the road and stopped, granules of cement growing louder. An attractive man rolled his window down to greet her. Maybe this was her lucky day after all.

"Everything okay?" he grinned, and she felt her face flush. He was noticeably older than she was, but she didn't mind.

She leaned in toward him, bottom jutted out so she could feel her hip was in his peripheral, resting her arms on the bridge of the door where the window had returned to its place inside.

"Actually, my car has a flat, and my phone has no service. Is there any way you could give me a ride to the bar a few miles up?" She pointed north, putting on a sweet, fragile-sounding voice in an effort to entice him to help her.

"No problem." He swung the passenger door open for her.

Casey breathed a sigh of relief and revealed a slightly flirtier smile, now that she could see him more clearly.

"Thank you *so* much."

Casey hopped up into the seat, legs, hips, arms, and then shut the door, the weight of its closure carrying a pang that bounced off the trees and back to them.

The second it clicked shut, she felt uneasy. She hadn't thought about how she'd feel being in such a small space with a man she'd never met, their bodies so close she could smell tangerines on his fingertips. She smiled faintly at the stranger next to her. He smiled back, and then he reached behind her seat.

A sudden, unexplainable feeling of dread filled her body. She'd made a mistake. She heard her mother's voice in her head. *"Listen to your intuition. It's the most powerful tool you have."*

She reached for the door handle, but it was too late. In one smooth motion, like he'd done it many times before, he wrapped one arm around her body and forced another over her mouth and nose. She felt a wet cloth against her skin as the man jerked her roughly towards him, holding her body tightly against the dirty passenger seat, pushing the cloth so hard into her that it spilled into her mouth as she tried to get something, anything, out. She writhed as violently as she could, flailing her body in every direction she could muster, but her small frame was no match for a muscular man. She struggled to breathe as she wrestled against him, jabbing her elbows and kicking her feet, and managed to choke out a scream when she got him in the side and he loosened his grip. It was in vain - no one was around to hear her, and as quickly as she'd gotten her shriek out, he'd forced the cloth back over her face, pressing harder, with more venom this time. She blinked hard once, twice and then felt even that was too much to try anymore. She did her best to conquer the drowsiness, to force her mind to stay alert, though she knew what was coming. She felt her vision slowly tunnel, and then completely disappear.

NINE

Nora couldn't deny to herself that she was shaken leaving the meeting with her uncle. The week had been a rollercoaster, that was for certain, and she wondered when she could raise her hand to get off the ride.

She and David had left the table amicably but awkwardly. She thought he might try to hug her, so she ducked out of the diner quickly, giving a short wave as she power-walked through the doorway. He had offered to give her a ride, but she did her best thinking on walks. She longed for privacy to sort through her thoughts, even if that meant looking over her shoulder every few steps. She zig-zagged through the back alley of the strip mall just beyond the diner until she reached the edge of her neighborhood. The end of summer had families out on their last hurrahs before school started again, out toward Cape Cod or the Jersey shore, and the traffic was bare. She crossed the main road easily, walking briskly onto the grassy median at Holloway Street, into an historic neighborhood full of soaring colonials with generous porches and lanterns already aglow for the evening against shades of pink and purple. She cut through the edge of Mrs. Thistle's vast corner property to get to her street, the same way she'd done since she was a teenager, hustling across the dewy grass before the sun disappeared for the night.

Her mind buzzed with questions, and she felt herself get lightheaded. *What if it was Ryan? What if she had set up a date with a murderer? Was she supposed to be his next victim? Why hadn't he shown up, if he intended to kill her? If it was him, why did he kill the other girl instead? Who was the girl? Was the girl really murdered? Was I out while it happened? Is there really a serial killer on the loose in Woodbridge?*

She decided to let her uncle take on looking into Ryan. He had more resources than she did to figure it out. She would focus on finding out the identity of the girl she'd narrowly avoided crashing into. She'd seen what she looked like while she was still alive, if only for a moment.

The phone in her hand buzzed as she slipped her key into the deadbolt, a text from Erica checking up on her. She shook her head and replied, "What a nightmare." The tin mailbox that hung on the brick by the door had begun to overflow, the bills jammed inside pushing the cover open. She rolled her eyes and sighed, gathering the stacks of crushed envelopes, wondering if there was such a thing as a service for taking care of one's meager day-to-day tasks that she found too daunting.

"Drinks???" Erica's attempt at getting her mind off of things, though she had no idea how cumbersome those things had just become.

Nora smiled as she typed. "Not tonight. Gonna try to get some sleep. Talk tomorrow."

She slowly climbed the stairs, leaning heavily on the railing for support. The night was still young but she was finding it harder and harder to function. As she finally made it into her room and sunk into her bed, she covered herself with every blanket, despite the warm weather. She smiled as she opened her texts and found a message from Eli encouraging her to come over that night, and with heavy eyelids, she told him she'd think about it.

She worried that she was so overtired that insomnia would kick in, as it often did, but it was a matter of seconds before she drifted into a deep, dreamless sleep.

Nora's eyes burst open. Disoriented, she tried to get her bearings as she rubbed her temples to ward off a headache that she could feel was setting in. As her haziness lifted, she realized that she had been in such a deep sleep that she would have kept sleeping well into the next morning if not for something waking her.

She heard something shut downstairs. It sounded distant and hollow. A cupboard softly closing. Her body sprang to a sitting position as she gripped her blanket tightly.

"Erica?" She called, though she may not have heard her over the murmur of her TV. She hastily grabbed her new phone from her bedside table and nearly dropped it. She hadn't yet purchased a case on the off chance that she would eventually find her old phone, and the unfamiliar curvature was slick over her fingertips. 1:03 A.M. She shot up from her bed in the darkness, goosebumps covering her from scalp to ankle. She tried to recall the day's events. Had Erica decided to stay over? No, she always slept in the same room with her when she spent the night. She crept carefully behind her door and once again peered through the slot in the doorframe. As her eyes adjusted to the darkness, she made out the large vase in the hallway, the arrows on the rug on the floor in the bedroom across the hall. She stood silently and waited.

Silence. Heavy and still. After a few long minutes of her heart feeling as though it would burst in her chest, she gingerly stepped her left foot into the hallway, body still planted behind her door, and winced as a subtle but audible creak filled the silence.

She froze as she heard a soft pattering of footsteps, then the gentle closing of her front door.

TEN

Nora sat at her family-sized oak kitchen table for the first time in over a year, shoulders draped in her thick lilac comforter, staring blankly as two police officers searched her house. She was suddenly aware of the mess that her home had become. She thought about picking up the heaps of laundry in the living room and rearranging the plush blanket and crinkled pillow that she used for napping on the couch, but she decided against touching anything before they were finished. One of the officers, a bumbling, overweight, middle-aged man with his blond hair freshly buzzed, ambled into her family room like a bull in a china shop. Her heart dropped as he picked up her favorite photo of her parents, the one on their wedding day where her dad's arm rested comfortably around his new wife, looking adoringly at her mother in her sleek white gown as she tossed her head back in laughter. She winced as the officer carelessly placed it back on the mantle above the fireplace, two inches off from the center of the room where it belonged.

Erica sat beside her, skin-tight sweatshirt with the hood up and the zipper to the seam as if to protect her from what was lurking in the dark, and gently rubbed Nora's arm. Nora could tell she was nervous, a foreign feeling for both of them.

Nora looked like she was in shock. But her mind had never worked faster. The timing had been too suspicious; there was a connection between the accident and the break-in, and she was determined to figure it out. She felt as though her mind was floating above her body and she was watching the scene unfold, like it had happened to someone else and it was her job to solve the riddle.

"You're sure nothing's missing?" A second officer, as generic-looking as the first, called from the living room as he meandered toward her. A sweep of the house had not furnished anything odd or broken.

"Not that I can tell. There were some papers that were rearranged on this table, but that was it," she said, motioning to the table where she sat. Truthfully, she'd been too exhausted and too scared to look around much. After she called 911, she'd sprinted to the safe in her parents' bedroom, where her personal documents and her mother's jewelry that held only sentimental value sat behind the safety of a lock. She imagined an intruder dressed in black, prying the door open with a crowbar. But as she frantically ran her fingers over its edges, searching for scratches or loose pieces, there were no signs of anyone attempting to break it open. She crept down the stairs next, slowly and quietly, just in case whoever it was hadn't really left. Her purse, a large and noticeable tote, had been sitting on the front table, in clear view of the front door. Her heart pounded fiercely as she closed her eyes and reached for her wallet. Relief washed over her and she let out an audible sigh, realizing her driver's license, twenty dollars in cash, and her debit card hadn't been touched. *What were they doing here, then?* Her laptop sat on her desk in her room, closed, where she'd left it. *Maybe they were here for...something else.* She shuddered as she imagined an intruder in her room, rummaging through her things, watching her as she slept...

"Well, there's no sign of forced entry." He stood with a bored look on his face, hand resting comfortably on his gun. "Anyone else have a key?"

"Just her." Nora motioned with her head to Erica, who straightened her spine as she gave a hard look toward him, daring him to question her. He barely noticed as he scribbled in his pad.

"I'd suggest staying somewhere else tonight so you can get some sleep."

"She can stay with me," Erica said, shooting her a soft smile and squeezing the arm she'd been rubbing.

"I'm okay. They're gonna patrol outside for the next 24 hours." Nora faked a smile back as if she weren't frightened, though she was terrified. She felt violated and unsteady. But more than that, her adrenaline was pumping. She had work to do.

Erica hugged Nora hard and told her to call immediately if anything seemed suspicious. She barely had her foot out the door before Nora raced up the stairs to grab her laptop from her desk, slapping the cover open as she hoisted herself into bed. Back to the missing girls.

She searched for hours, tongue pressed against the back of her teeth as they clenched. She found the original *Huntingdon County Chronicle* article on a young woman's body being found in the woods, followed by a local article in Abington once she had been identified as Rebecca White. Pictures of her in the Color Guard in high school, bits of information about her being a Dean's List student at Carnegie Mellon. Lots of quotes from her distraught parents. They wanted to know what happened to their little girl. *The Chronicle* alluded to drug problems. Her parents furiously denied it. Nora shook her head, imagining how her parents must have felt reading that about their daughter.

Her mind wandered to David, and whether to trust that what he told her was real. She found herself even jumpier than usual as she thought about the subject matter she was investigating, and how just an hour ago an unknown person was inside her house.

She got up from her desk and peeked through her curtains at the street, sighing a heavy breath of relief when she saw the patrolman at his post.

She moved back to the list of missing persons, disbelieving of how many were on the list. All ages and races. Some photos were mugshots, where the women looked rough and drug-addled, and Nora felt sorry for them, that no one had thought to provide a better photo, that they'd be judged and that people might be less likely to help identify them if they knew they were criminals. Others couldn't have appeared more All-American. She pored over each face, thinking about how each and every one of them had a family that was looking for them. Some were smiling and looked happy but had been missing for years. It seemed likely that most of them were dead. Nora felt incredible sadness as questions raced through her mind: *Where did all of these women go? What happened? Why are there so many missing? Isn't anyone doing anything about this?*

Her eyes grew heavier as she scrolled through the site, but she was determined to look at every photo before letting herself go to sleep. As she neared the date of her accident, she stopped cold. Caroline Barone. Nineteen years old. Missing from Allentown, Pennsylvania. Long, dark hair. Thick eyebrows, a symmetrical nose, full lips. The girl she had seen was much thinner, but it was unmistakably her. The girl who had run wildly into the road, like she'd been frightened. The girl who Nora knew wasn't missing anymore. She was dead. Nora's eyes welled with tears at the beautiful smiling girl with sparkling green eyes that lit up her screen. She could barely reconcile that now she was sitting in a morgue, dead and alone, and that Nora had been the last person to see her.

Well, second to last, Nora thought bitterly, and she shuddered as she tried not to imagine what happened to her.

Wait a minute. Nora's face tingled, her eyes growing wet. Her disappearance date was listed as April 17th. Four months before she'd died.

Nora sprang from her chair and called David, her hands shaking with adrenaline as she dialed.

"Nora? You okay? It's the middle of the night..." David said, and she could hear him stifling a yawn.

"David, we need to meet again." Nora spoke fast and brusquely, commanding his immediate attention. "Tomorrow. I'll come to you."

ELEVEN

Nora arrived ten minutes late to Dr. Wexler's office, a small, unassuming brick building covered in moss shielded by a magnolia tree. It sat at the corner of a neighborhood, and looked like it belonged with every other house on the street, save for the fancy "Psychological Counseling" sign in cheery script planted on the lawn. The facade of the building was just about the only thing Nora liked about going to therapy.

"Hi Nora," Diane the receptionist squeaked, as Nora sauntered past the sign about leaving judgments of yourself at the door. She saw the mousy woman looking just a touch too long at the atomic clock that hung to her left, and then she looked right back at Nora, and Nora's neck squeezed into her shoulders.

"Sorry I'm late again." She'd gotten caught up watching from her window as the handyman she'd hired climbed his ladder and installed a new surveillance system, one camera above her porch and one above the door leading to the deck. She cast her eyes down from Diane and took her seat, the one with the divot in the middle that was furthest from the front desk, making herself small as she fiddled with her phone.

"Hello, Nora." Dr. Wexler, a tall, slender man in his mid-fifties, opened the door and stepped aside, and Nora forced a tight smile, as she always did, and slinked past him and the orchid on his desk, the tranquil art on the walls, over to her chair, tensing as soon as she hit the seat.

He settled into the leather chair that sat across from hers, leaning into its high back as he opened his legal pad and jotted the date.

"So, what's happening this week?" He smiled his warm, fatherly smile, his cheeks turning up where the dark hairs at his temples were greying.

Nora cleared her throat, weaving her story together carefully so as not to reveal more than she wanted to.

"My Uncle David called."

"Your mother's brother?"

"Yes."

He scribbled a note, flipping through her file.

"Why do you think he called?" He put a hand to his mouth thoughtfully, staring at her over his wire-rimmed glasses.

Nora shifted, rubbing her hands through her curls before releasing them in front of her face, until the pieces stuck to her lip gloss.

"He seems like he wants to...get to know me, I guess? Help me?"

"Help you, how?"

Her eyes went to the ceiling as she plucked the strands from her lips.

"I don't know. I guess he probably feels sorry for me. Like I can't take care of myself. Like I haven't *been* taking care of myself."

Dr. Wexler looked at his pad and pursed his lips. He was wearing a hunter green sweater that he wore often, and Nora found herself memorizing the tiny spots of ink that speckled the front of it.

"We met. At a diner. He's sober now. So he says."

"You met?" Dr. Wexler clicked his pen, his thick eyebrows adjoining.

"Yeah. I figured I'd hear him out."

"And how did you find that meeting?"

Nora shook her head. "I didn't find it anything. He's a cop now. Which is just...bizarre. The last time I saw him, he was strung out."

Dr. Wexler nodded. "That was many years ago, yes?"

Nora bit her lip, her eyes wandering as the memory came to her.

"I wasn't even a teenager. I remember he looked sick. He was nice, but it felt like he was faking it. I don't know how to describe it."

"Try."

"He seemed like he wanted something. My mom was angry. She didn't say it, but I could tell. She wasn't herself."

"How was she?"

"She seemed very stressed. I guess she was probably more hurt than anything else."

"And how did that meeting end?"

"I don't know. They told me to go upstairs. I tried to listen, but I couldn't hear what they were saying. Then I heard my dad yell. I felt the door slam. And that was it. I never saw him again." The fear she'd felt that day rose to the surface as if she were still twelve years old, trembling as she felt the vibrations of the door.

"What was the discussion like between you and your parents, after he left?"

"We never discussed it. I think they were trying to protect me."

"Did you feel protected?"

Nora paused, shooting him a hard glance before snidely saying, "No, Dr. Wexler," the way she always did when he asked her difficult questions. He ignored her disdain, because it meant she was telling the truth.

"How *did* it make you feel?"

She took a deep breath.

"Like...an outsider. They always told me everything, except when it came to David." She balled her hands into fists and squeezed, then released. "I'm supposed to go to his house," she continued. "To talk."

"What do you expect you'll talk about?"

She shook her head.

"I don't know him anymore. I really don't know."

"Why do you think you accepted another meeting?"

Nora shrugged.

"Are you looking for an apology?"

"He did apologize."

"Do you accept that apology?"

She avoided his eyeline and instead watched her hands running along the burgundy velvet of her chair, creating streaks as they went against the grain, and then smoothed back over them.

"I'm not sure."

"Are you interested in fostering a new relationship with him?"

She rubbed her temples.

"Again, I'm not sure. I don't know if I can trust him."

He uncrossed his left leg and repositioned it over the right, his corduroys swishing as he moved, and held his pen at his lips for a moment before speaking.

He used the pen to shake toward her, a new spot of ink falling onto his sweater, and said, "I think you owe it to yourself to find out."

"This place is a dump." Erica spoke matter-of-factly as she passed the sign welcoming them to Woodbridge, arm hanging out the window of her black Impala, while Nora nervously ran her fingers up and down the passenger seatbelt as they headed toward the police station.

"I know," Nora said. *It's also probably home to a serial killer*, she thought. She hadn't told Erica much about her conversation with David. She'd said only that he was an officer and wanted to reach out when he saw her name on her paperwork from the accident. She knew she was about to get invested in this mess, whatever it was, and she didn't want Erica, the perpetual voice of reason, trying to talk her out of it.

The houses they passed each sat on a large parcel of property, but most of the homes were derelict. Each house seemed to be broken in its own way; a bent gutter lining the bottom of a caving roof; cockeyed siding that looked like it was ready to be ripped directly from its structure during the next storm; a hole big enough for a family of raccoons to seek shelter under a crumbling cement porch. Every so often there would be a man sitting on a porch stoop or watering the grass manually with a hose, eyes narrowed and suspicious of the girls driving by that were clearly out of place. With each passing home beside its watchful owner, Nora wondered, *Is that him? Does he live here?*

She had noticed when she'd driven through the first time that Woodbridge was mainly rural, but in the daylight, now that she was focused on its residents, it was clear to her that the town was decaying. She wondered if the people who lived there years back had thought it would be something better one day, or if everyone in its clutches had followed it into disrepair without much of a fight.

She shuddered as they passed a handmade sign with a shaky arrow pointing east for the Woodbridge Cemetery. She would forever associate the town, its stale air and the morose feeling attached to it, with death.

Erica dropped Nora off at the police station, waited for several minutes until she saw Nora pull her SUV around from the back, grimacing at its new markings, then floored it without giving the police cars in the lot a second thought. Nora had to smile as she watched her peel out - a flash of black, hand still swaying in the wind, and then she was gone. Erica had never had any real respect for authority, stating with vigor and a smug grin on her face to teachers and officers alike, "Status does not equal righteousness." Nora's face would burn hot as she stood in Erica's shadow, not wanting anyone Erica was verbally assaulting to associate her with that point of view. Now that she was in a dicey situation with the police herself, she began to understand what she'd meant all this time.

She watched Erica leave and then hopped down from her seat to inspect the damage. She closed her eyes and shook her head at the twisted frame, the marks in the silver paint revealing a black bodice, and ran her hand over the mangled bumper, quickly recoiling as it moved over a sharpness that was imperceivable. The entire bumper would undoubtedly need to be replaced, but it was driveable, though she shook ever so slightly as she climbed back behind the wheel.

She'd told Erica that she was stopping at David's, but failed to mention that before she headed to his house, she wanted to revisit the scene where she'd hit the tree, and she wanted to do it alone.

She traversed the familiar, winding pathway, past Jimmy's Bar. She shuddered as she slowed by the tiny, nondescript building, with its muddled brown exterior and its handpainted, red, worn sign placed next to the road, like a tourist attraction. The bar was somehow creepier in the daylight where she could see just how tattered it was, and she realized that this could have been the place where people last saw her before she herself went missing. She imagined her face plastered all over the local news, everyone she'd ever met talking to police about their thoughts on her whereabouts, even though no one had even the slightest clue where she would have gone missing, except for Erica. She'd have to be the one to provide a photo, and she'd also be the one leading the search party. The thought made her deeply uncomfortable, and she pressed her gas pedal to the floor until the bar was out of her sight in the rearview mirror. She put her focus back on the road in front of her until she recognized a thick-trunked oak tree that was slightly closer to the road than the others, with a brand new scar etched into it, and pulled her car over several feet in front of it. She sat for a moment before exiting, reliving the scene of the girl she now knew was Caroline Barone, remembering the sickening squeal as she avoided connection with her, the thunderous crash before she blacked out. She squeezed the wheel so tightly her knuckles turned white, focusing on her breathing and looking at her empty console.

The outside of her car was unsightly, but the interior was much neater than it had ever been. An elderly officer had hobbled to a place she couldn't see in the back of the precinct and returned with a plastic bag with some kind of numbering on it. The few belongings that had been strewn throughout her vehicle were inside, so she assumed they must have checked it for some kind of evidence. He'd handed her the keys and the bag without so much as a second glance, and when she'd said, "That's it?" he raised his eyes to her for the first time, his forehead crinkled, and asked through a condescending smile and yellowed teeth, "Did ya want us to keep it?"

The bag held only strawberry-flavored lip gloss she thought she'd lost a year ago, a recreational pass to a state park from a hike she'd been on with Eli, random receipts from gas stations, and the not-so-occasional trip to Taco Bell. No phone. The police had told her more than once that there was no phone found in the car, but she'd secretly hoped that she could do a better job than they had, perhaps finding it lodged in a nook somewhere between the seats. She did a sweep herself, jamming her fingers between the back cushions and pushing the lever to the front seats all the way back, to no avail. She could feel that something was off about it being missing. She knew she didn't leave it at the bar; she'd checked her account one final time for a message from Ryan before she pulled out of the parking lot, though there'd been no internet access, so she'd have been none the wiser had he tried to reach her. She swore she'd tossed it in the console in front of her shifter in frustration after several attempts to get service. But the console was empty, save for scattered dust and old, sticky soda that had settled there long ago.

She told herself that she was returning to the scene of the crime - *was* it a crime? - to see if it had been flung from the car. But she knew deep down that more than that, she was here for Caroline.

She thought more than once about asking Erica to accompany her. She knew she would do it, but she'd relied on her enough already, and maybe, for once, she could stop being a burden. She didn't know how long she'd be out there, or what she was even looking for. She held her hand above her eyes to keep the sun from obstructing her view into the woods. She considered the road in front of her and realized that the scene had been released, and the police tape was gone. Now anyone could walk through these trees, tramp through the place where Caroline had died, and they'd never know that a soul had been lost in their path. Guilt crept into Nora's brain as she hopped down from her car; if she had just woken up sooner, if she'd protested more to the police taking her statement, maybe things would have turned out differently. She pushed the thoughts out of her mind and grabbed her notepad, fishing through her purse for a pen before realizing she didn't have one on hand. She shook her head, exasperated with herself, slamming the door behind her.

The tape had been strung on the north side of the road, to the right of where she'd crashed. She slowly approached the tree she'd struck and ran her hand softly over the markings. The roots were barely raised from the ground - the tree was older than she was and wasn't going anywhere. She could have died here, easily. Suffered the exact same fate as her mother had. But she hadn't, and she couldn't help but feel that there had to be a reason why.

She envisioned where she'd seen the man with the camera wrapped around his neck and attempted to retrace his path. The heat was heavy, but a chill still ran through her as she thought about what exactly it was she was doing, and she instantly wished that she had, in fact, asked Erica to join her. She pushed through her unease and started down the hill that declined from the road into the woods, a place where two weeks ago she would never have ventured alone, but now felt compelled to visit. After a few feet she came upon a small patch of grass that looked worn, like a trail of people had moved in and out. She assumed this must be the route the police had taken to and from the body. From Caroline. She took a deep breath and followed it, through a thick shroud of trees. She was surprised at how dark the forest became once she found herself just past them and into their territory. The sunlight only came through sparse openings between the lush greenery, making it seem like it was already dusk though it was early afternoon. She noticed right away that there was no marked trail in the vicinity, nor any signs pointing where a hiker should continue their route. She pushed through some branches as she followed the traffic footpath for hundreds of feet, then found that it ended abruptly at a clearing, where a fallen tree covered in moss had created an opening in the brush long ago. Her eyes circled her surroundings for more signs of a path before sucking in sharply once she concluded that this was it. This was where she'd been found.

She turned around for the first time since she'd descended into the forest and realized she couldn't see her car. She couldn't even see the road, where it ended or began, and she guessed that from the street, you couldn't see where she stood, either. She felt a small sense of relief once she realized that even if she had woken sooner, she wouldn't have been able to see Caroline, or what happened to her.

Still, she felt uneasy. It was deathly silent, save for a lone bird chirping in a distant tree. There was a heavy stillness where she stood, where she presumed Caroline's body lay for hours before she was found. She'd already fought through her apprehension to get herself into the forest, and as she realized she'd have to follow the path to even find her way back out, her mind went slightly panicky. But she felt like she couldn't leave without properly examining the area. She reminded herself that she owed Caroline this much.

She knelt down to the grass, examining the stems carefully. She went instinctively to run her hand over the blades before yanking it back, suddenly aware that there may be blood amongst the earth. She pored over the fallen tree for any sign of recent disturbance, but it looked like the only beings that had touched it were the squirrels and chipmunks that used it to take cover from the summer rain.

She stood back up and smoothed her gym shorts, running her hands over her thighs in self-assurance as she moved her sights to the branches that surrounded her. She looked at each tree individually, which proved difficult in such a lush area. But she took it one trunk at a time, looking for signs of struggle as she ran her hands over smooth bark.

Then she saw it. It was almost indecipherable against the dark grain, but it was there. She threw her curls into a bun to keep them from shielding her vision, straining her eyes to confirm what she was seeing, her heart pulsing quicker and quicker as she moved closer to the tree trunk. Amongst the untamed wilderness, just past the clearing, there it was. Shielded from the outside world, as Caroline's body had been. A streak of dried blood.

TWELVE

Casey had been described as a firecracker more than once in her life, but she barely recognized that girl now. When she'd first woken in the cabin, the memory of her abduction was so hazy that she couldn't remember if it had actually happened or if it was a vivid nightmare. As she lifted her lids, heavy with the type of exhaustion only a chemically-induced sleep could create, the horror of what happened to her came flooding back. Her eyes fought to adjust to the darkness, and with a heavy breath, she reached her arm out and used them to gain information. Her hands rolled back and forth over bumps and itchy fabric, until she realized she was on a twin-sized mattress with no sheets. It smelled like trees and fresh dirt, but she was completely encapsulated. She did not know this place.

She immediately began to hyperventilate and she hugged her knees, her head on a swivel, taking in the dark, damp room. She listened for any signs of her abductor as her eyes finally began to adjust. She struggled to breathe in through her nose and out through her mouth, tiny, hurried gasps escaping her, though she tried to remain silent. The pieces of the room started to come together, a picture that needed time to paint itself. A closet full of women's clothes. What looked like dead animals on the top shelf of the closet, that she later learned were wigs. And the man, whom she was now ashamed she had been attracted to when she'd first seen him, sitting very still in an old rocking chair in the corner by the door, staring at her with a gleam in his eye, as if he had been waiting for hours for her to wake, and now it was finally time. She'd screamed, a primal scream that came from a new place within her, but the sound reverberated back to her. The man never flinched.

For the first few days after she'd been taken, she'd scream as loudly as her body would allow, her throat burning, lungs quaking. She would wait until the man had been gone for several minutes before gearing herself up for a new cry for help. She tried at different times of the day, using the tiny beam of sunlight slipping under the door to judge the time difference. With each passing day, her screams became less urgent, less impassioned, until one day she finally stopped. She could hear birds chirping every morning, but no matter where she stood in the room, she never heard the sound of cars, never heard a hiker in the distance, even though the room where she was cordoned off was deathly silent.

She first attributed the smell of pine to the shoddy woodwork that surrounded her, but the more she thought about it, the more it made sense that she was in the woods somewhere, maybe near where her car had gotten a flat. If that were the case, no one would ever know where to find her.

He seemed almost tired when he arrived, always smelling slightly of sweat and the outdoors, as if it had taken him a great deal of time to get to where she was. But as soon as he saw her, his eyes lit up, as much as such darkness could. She envisioned the scene of her abduction from above like an audience watching a horror movie, knowing how the story would end but helpless to do anything about it.

She'd fought him those first few days, grabbing at anything on him she could, tufts of his hair and his dampened shirt as she

Her mind had raced for days looking for a way out of the room she'd been confined to, but she had no tools at her disposal, and escape seemed less likely as days passed and her mental and physical state began to wither. Her brain had forced itself to adapt; it was easier to get through the day if she sedated her emotions, as foreign a feeling as that was.

As the days slowly passed, she resigned herself to the fact that no one was coming for her, and it was becoming more and more likely she would be spending the rest of her life - however long that was - in isolation. Her spark had faded, and she'd never known it was possible to feel so weak. She was only given a meal once, maybe twice a week if she was lucky, and the lack of nourishment had begun to take a toll. Her skin had dried so much it was beginning to flake even in the humidity, and it had gone grey with dehydration. She didn't mind much anymore; less water meant less peeing in the bucket he'd provided for her in the corner of the room. She could feel her eyes become sunken, the bones in her face becoming more prominent as she held her head in her hands.

What refused to adapt was her memory. Casey's last conversation with her mom played on a loop in her brain. She remembered every word.

"You're eighteen years old. I know you're under the impression that you know it all, but you're not as smart as you think you are." Her mother's voice going shrill, the way it only did when she was truly angry and speaking with condescension quicker than she could stop herself from saying it.

Casey's face went red in anger and humiliation. Nothing made her more upset than someone talking down to her and questioning her intelligence, and her mother knew that, so she hit her back where she knew it would hurt.

"I'm sorry that when *you* were eighteen that you screwed your life up and got pregnant and never went to college, so you don't really *get it*, but things are a little different for me," Casey shot back, calculated and snide, though her heart sank a little when she saw her mother's face fall.

"Wow. This is exactly what I'm talking about. Really mature, Casey. You really proved me wrong." She rolled her eyes and Casey felt a resurgence of anger at her dismissiveness, deciding she was done with the conversation. If her mom didn't want to treat her like an adult, she didn't owe her anything.

"Are you really going to walk out in the middle of our conversation?"

Standing in the doorway, her fist on the handle, always one foot out the door.

"Yes, I *really* am, and I'm an adult, so there's nothing you can do to stop me," she'd screamed. Her face scarlet with anger. She'd slammed the door behind her, sealing her fate.

Why did I get in the car. Why did I get in the car. She taught me so much better than that. The shame of it was crushing.

The worst part of it all, no matter how much it made her skin crawl as he whispered *Mommy* into her ear and hugged her from behind - the worst part was the guilt. She imagined her mother, strong but sensitive, putting on a brave face to the public, crying before bed when no one is around to see her break down. Did she even sleep anymore? Sometimes she felt like her mother's pain was washing over her, and she willed an extrasensory connection to form between them, so that at least she could communicate to her that she was still alive. Was there a search team? What did she think happened to her?

"Please don't stop looking for me," she whimpered softly into her musty pillow as thick tears spilled from her eyes like a faucet, rolling down her hollowed cheeks faster than any time she'd cried before. Now, when a memory would come to her and she would feel the tears well in her eyes, she would brush them off as quickly as they came. She didn't feel better afterward; there was no release of tension like she used to experience from a good cry, so it was better to preserve her energy. Now there was just a vast hole within her soul that she assumed would be void until the day she died, and that felt like it would be coming much sooner than later. She felt sick to her stomach as her mind wandered and she thought about what the end game was for all of this, but she had to push the thoughts away along with the tears. There was no room for that now. Right now, there was only room for survival.

THIRTEEN

Nora rolled her car gently over the dirt driveway to the address David had given her. His modest ranch home sat in another tiny township called Three Springs, just a few miles outside of Woodbridge. To the untrained eye, the two towns may have looked identical, as if one was an extension of the other, but Nora could tell Three Springs was a definite upgrade from its neighbor - most likely due to its proximity to the interstate. Like Woodbridge, there were few shops, and the ones that stood hadn't been updated for years - if ever. But she'd passed a McDonald's, a sign of travelers passing through, though its arches were worn and the design hadn't been updated since the '80s. The neighborhoods were dotted with petite homes that were well-cared for, perched on manicured lawns. When she passed into town, she felt nostalgic for Old-town Americana, in direct opposition to the discomfort of a place teetering on complete ruin, manifesting itself under her skin every time she crossed into Woodbridge.

She had thought long and hard about it being David who'd broken into her home and had nearly canceled their meeting half a dozen times. It wouldn't be the first time, if it was him. When she was nine, she'd awoken to her mother, frantic and screaming, tether couldn't reach, and the best she could identify were more bags and some clothes on velvet hangers he would sometimes rifle through for several minutes before landing on the one he wanted her to wear, turning his back to her while she changed.

She was desperate for information. If there was a way in, there was a way out. She pushed her hand against every wall she could reach, remembering what he'd done as her fingers burned where fresh nails began to pierce through her skin again. Her hands ran over the rough grain to feel for loose boards or even a popped nail she could attempt to pry out and use to unchain herself, or that she could utilize as a weapon against him. The man had made sure to keep the chain around her ankle tight, and the links short. She couldn't reach the door, its choppy edges and brass knob mocking her, a means to escape so close yet so far - but she tried anyway. She readied herself, *Come on Casey*, mustering strength through her anger, before sprinting the short distance she could from the mattress on the floor toward the door, yanking her ankle as hard as she could. She yelped out in pain and then furious sobs as the chain kept its place. Her body was a hapless victim to its inflexible, cold anatomy as it forced her down, to the thin, brown carpet that lay atop more wood, hard and unforgiving as she pounded her fist against it, asking aloud to the empty room why this had to happen to her.

She daydreamed about what it would be like if she did find a loose nail; stabbing him straight through his pupil when he leaned close and whispered to her, just when he seemed most comfortable, most fragile. It would please her, to bestow upon him an ounce of her pain, to blind him, to make him have to explain to people in the outside world how he came upon such an injury. But she knew that even if she ever got the opportunity, it wouldn't make sense to hurt him, because it wouldn't kill him. It would only anger him, much more than any scratch marks could, and she'd learned the hard way how easily he could physically overpower her. She might not make it out of another fight.

screeched, but she knew she was in trouble when he didn't even try to silence her. On the third day she'd scratched his arm pretty deeply, blood pooling almost instantaneously, and as a result he'd pried her nails off one by one, the weight of his body pinning her down without flinching as she shrieked in pain, begging for him to stop. He'd only let out a gentle "shhh" as he plucked each nail from its adjoining finger, as if the sound, normally reserved for a parent comforting their baby, would calm her.

This was her life now, sitting in what she imagined as a torture chamber, shackled to the floor, hair dyed to an unnatural dark brown sometime before she'd come to. She watched herself in a murky, oblong mirror that sat across from her mattress, as her life slipped out of her fingers more and more each day. The Old Casey, who was getting ready to go to college and had a family and friends and a life, seemed to become less attainable and less real. Memories of parties and boys and secrets between girlfriends seemed like a mirage she'd once seen whose image was beginning to wither.

Now, all she had were these four walls. The wood seemed thick, her own voice bouncing back at her any time she screamed, like no sound she made would escape. The room's construction looked shoddy, like it had been put together by someone with only basic carpentry skills. A lone, flickering light bulb overhead provided her with light, but it was artificial, and she could feel confinement getting harder on her body. No fresh air, no sunshine.

There wasn't much in the room, for utility nor entertainment. She'd rummaged through every drawer of a tall vanity that sat adjacent to her bed, but he'd taken care to be sure every drawer was empty, save for a pale peach soft-bristled brush he combed softly through her hair every time he visited. She tried once to push the vanity and darkly laughed aloud at the sheer weight of it against hers, her shrinking muscles now unable to even scooch it an inch. She could see an aging duffel bag underneath the wigs in the makeshift closet, its contents unknowable, but nothing else. Her searching for cash she'd set aside for their family vacation that she knew had disappeared into the abyss of David's arms. The window pane had been broken in so he could unlatch the back door. It was the first place Nora had checked before the police arrived after the break-in the night before, and she breathed a heavy sigh of relief when she found that the back of the house hadn't been disturbed. The timing of David's call had certainly been coincidental, and even though he did appear to be sober and was now an officer himself, she didn't know him anymore. Now was not the time to start trusting him.

But this time, there wasn't anything stolen. In fact, she had some loose cash on her dad's desk in the den, and it hadn't been touched. The timing was strange, but she couldn't think of a reason for him to do it, if the motivation wasn't financial. He hadn't asked her for anything - not yet, anyway. But the thought of being close to a cop gave her a sense of protection. If it was him, he was a loose cannon. If it wasn't, then he didn't need to know.

Maybe it would have been better if it had been David, she thought to herself, twisting her car keys in her hand. She would have a get-out-of-jail-free card, without being forced to reconnect with him. Plus, that would mean that there wasn't a stranger in her house, looking through her things. Looking for *her*...

She saw the shadow of a woman looking through the bright curtains in the bay window and furrowed her brow in distrust. She'd assumed she was meeting David alone.

She hopped down from her car, eyes watchfully on the brick facade, when the front door opened, and David, looking slightly distressed, hurriedly approached her outside as she closed her door.

She hadn't noticed the silver band at their first meeting, but she noticed it now amongst his freckled fingers. She had no idea he was married. What else didn't she know about him?

"Hey, listen," he began carefully, rubbing the nape of his neck, avoiding her eye line. "My wife is home today. I thought she was going to her book club, but...but I guess not." He stared into the clouds as three ravens passed overhead.

"What, you don't want me to meet her?" Nora said. She meant it as a lighthearted joke but it came out harsher than she'd intended, more of a challenge than a question. Distrust was still at the forefront of her consciousness; he hadn't earned anything better than that from her yet.

"Well, yeah, I want you to meet her. It's just...in her condition, I don't want her to stress, and yesterday you were a little...aggressive." He looked down at his feet sheepishly. Nora balked at him calling her, of all people, aggressive, but felt her face burning hot. Anyone who really knew her would say quite the opposite, and it was slightly humiliating that he found her any sort of threat. Maybe she did have the upper hand between them.

"Condition?" Nora looked at him quizzically, but just then, a stunning, brunette, and very pregnant woman appeared in the entryway.

"Honey? Aren't you guys going to come in?" She smiled and lifted her hand to greet Nora as her other hand cradled her belly, and Nora felt her heart fall into her stomach.

She smiled back, faintly, at the woman holding the door open for her, and she found herself climbing the cement steps up to the porch. A complete stranger, yet someone with whom she was intrinsically linked. A woman bearing a cousin. Something Nora was certain was out of the realm of possibility.

She suddenly felt foolish, and contemplated turning and running away, back into her car, and driving back to Philly, leaving this entire mess behind. She had no obligation to do this. David was the cop. She'd gone the last decade of her life just fine without him. This was tough work, physically and emotionally. She didn't need to put herself through it anymore. But her feet felt locked into place as she stood at the doorway, not sure how to interact with the woman standing before her. The woman moved to the side for her, and Nora stood there as if she were a vampire awaiting a formal invitation. The woman smiled at her again, a patient, inviting smile, and said, "Come on in."

Nora entered but lingered in the doorway until David came up behind her, and she was forced to step into a quaint living room that resembled a lakeside cabin, complete with beachy pillows and dark wooden accent tables.

"You want some tea, Nora? I can make a fresh pot." Her smile sparkled as she put her hand on her burgeoning hip awaiting an answer from the edge of the kitchen. Nora was vexed that this woman knew her name and presumably much more than that, while Nora never knew this person existed.

"I'm okay. Thanks," she stammered.

"Okay, well you just let me know if you need anything. I'm Briana, by the way, but I guess you knew that. I put some cookies out for you guys in the kitchen. There's a bathroom right down there if you need it." She pointed toward a narrow hallway and then fixed her eyes on Nora before letting out a cheerful sigh. "It's so nice to finally meet you, honey. Can I give you a hug?" Before Nora could think of an answer, she was wrapped up in a long, warm embrace. She was surprised as she felt herself melting into it, her abdomen connecting with Briana's substantial belly. She'd left the forest shaken and skittish, and Briana's maternal energy remarkably put her at ease.

Nora broke from the hug first and looked to David to shoo Briana away so they could talk. She noticed a dreamy smile cross his face as Briana embraced her, but it quickly faded when he caught her eye line. He cleared his throat and began, "You guys can talk later, honey. I have some stuff...some stuff I gotta go over with Nora. Okay?" He smiled and kissed her forehead as she leaned into him. Nora shifted uncomfortably, feeling entirely out-of-place.

"Okay, honey. I'll leave you to it." She grabbed hold of Nora's hands and squeezed, locking her bright blue eyes into Nora's.

"Let me know if you need anything." Nora knew she meant

more than just cookies and tea, but she brushed it off, looking away as she thanked her.

"She's really sweet." Nora said as Briana breezed out of sight.

David's eyes lit up and he smiled proudly, watching the doorway where Briana had departed. "Yes. She sure is."

Nora took a deep breath, readying herself to upheave the mood entirely.

"I found something," she began.

David looked puzzled. "What do you mean?"

"In the woods. I went down to where I think Caroline was found."

David's face turned dark.

"Caroline?"

"That's the other thing. The reason I'm here. I found her, David. The girl from the accident."

David jerked his head back to make sure Briana was out of earshot before raising his hand to his forehead, excitedly asking, "How in the hell did you do that?"

"I spent some time - well, a lot of time - going through missing women's cases in the state. She's from Allentown. It's her. I know it is."

"You should not be going into those woods alone," he said, and Nora heard a hint of anger in his voice. He took a throaty exhale, then followed it with, "That's really great that you ID'd her. That is going to help tremendously."

"I don't know how to tell the police without making myself seem suspicious. What should I do?"

"Let me take care of it. I'll tell them I figured it out. Maybe they'll - they'll take me more seriously."

"She's been missing for months, David."

His jaw twitched.

"And you just saw her."

"Yes."

He rubbed his chin, his stubble making scratching noises that cut through the thick silence.

"So she was being held somewhere, most likely. Interesting." He leaned back against the counter and crossed his arms. "Now. Tell me what you were doing in the woods by yourself."

"I wanted to see if I could find something the police overlooked, since you said yourself they aren't taking these deaths seriously. And it's a good thing I did, because like I said, I found something."

His eyebrows raised, his voice lowering an octave.

"What did you find?"

"I think I found...I think I found some blood. On a tree," she said nervously, finding herself anxious to relay the information to him.

David stared at her doubtfully. "How do you even know where her body was found?"

She dragged a heavy oak chair to the dining table and sat down, ringing her hands out of sight. "I don't know, exactly. I followed a path that looked like it was from everyone's boots going in and out, where my car hit the tree. And over near where the path stopped...that's where I found it."

"What were you doing there? Why didn't you wait for me to go with you?" His anger melded into offense as he took a seat across from her at the table.

"I had to go. And I felt like it's something I had to do alone. I can't explain it." She left it at that, not feeling the want or the need to discuss it further.

He noticed her agitation and decided not to press her, for fear of scaring her into closing off completely.

"Okay. Well, next time you get an idea like that, let me go with you. I'd like to see this blood and get a sample to be tested. If it belongs to Caroline or to...someone else, then that's really important."

"I can show you where I found it."

"I know, but now you might have contaminated a crime scene..." he trailed off. Nora felt like she'd been struck, panic rising in her chest.

"Not any more than any other person who could have trounced through there. It's open for anyone, David. *Your* police force opened the scene," she said, knowing deep down that she had to convince herself that she hadn't done anything wrong more than she had to convince him.

His eyes softened. "It's okay. If what you saw really is blood, it should still be there when I go. I'll check it out this afternoon."

She sat silently, her eyes falling to the floor.

"Is there...is there anything else you wanted to talk about?" He hoped for a mention of his wife. How it was obvious she'd make a good mother, that Nora was excited about a baby cousin.

"Look. I bought a map of the county from City Hall. Can you mark where each of the girls were found dead?" She grabbed the scroll from the gym bag that had been turned into a makeshift investigative kit, taking it upon herself to move the candle centerpiece to the kitchen counter as she spread the enormous paper map over the table.

David was floored that she was taking this so seriously, and felt a sense of pride in her investigative skills. He'd had no part in them, but it seemed to come naturally for her. Maybe it was in the genes. She could tell by his expression that he was impressed with her investigative process, and she found herself stifling a smile.

"I don't know exactly, I only know approximates. I was only there for two of them." He pulled a red Sharpie from a drawer, popping the cap off with his teeth, and marked an X on each spot.

"And is this area protected? Government-owned, anything like that?" Nora asked as she traced her fingers down the crinkled page.

"The township owns this area, which is where the girls were found," David said, circling a large portion of the southern woodlands, closest to the road, with a separate black marker. "This area up here is owned by an investor who's, like, eighty years old.

Harold Robinson, I believe. He bought the property, I don't know, thirty years ago? Thought it...thought it might be worth something one day." He shook his head.

"And what about this area? Who owns this property?" Nora pointed to the northeast quadrant of the forest.

"No idea. You're looking at hundreds of miles of forestry here."

Nora reached for a pen from a carousel full of office supplies on the counter, then pulled her moleskine notebook out and jotted a note to research all of the property owners - the first note of research she'd penned to herself since college. It put her right back in the moment of her first journalism class, where her professor taught her how to take notes, and she felt a familiar rush at the thought of getting back at it. This was real. This was going to make her time in school worth something, even though she'd dropped out.

"Are there any structures anywhere near where the bodies were found? Public bathrooms, cabins, empty buildings, anything like that?"

"Not anywhere in the general vicinity."

Nora frowned.

"That doesn't make any sense."

"Well, none of this makes sense...but what's on your mind?"

"Why would a bunch of addicts..." she trailed off, wincing at the term. It seemed too harsh a term for dead young women, especially in David's presence. She began again.

"Why would these women randomly go into the woods to do drugs? There's nowhere to hide if someone walked by."

David chuckled.

"This isn't exactly a family park. We're talking about wild forestry. Bears are the only thing they'd have to watch for."

"So why are they here at all, then? Did they walk miles and miles from wherever they came from just to get to the woods? It doesn't make sense. It's too hard to get here on foot from any of the houses or buildings in the area. Unless you found a car?"

"Baby? Can you help me for a second?" Briana's voice, sweet as honey, drifted into the kitchen from a room at the end of the hall. David jumped up, rushing down to her. Nora found herself taking note of every inch of the kitchen in which she sat to avoid the realization that she was spending time with her uncle for the first time since her parents died, in a house that he owned with the wife she never knew about.

It was clean but warm, mixing modern and traditional aesthetics, the way Nora envisioned she'd like her house to look if she ever bought another. A glass bowl full of fresh apples. Candles lining a rustic wooden shelf. Nine lemons in a cylinder vase. *Very zen.*

David emerged from the hall and Nora jolted back and tried to look busy sweeping her pen over her pad, as though he could read her thoughts.

"Everything okay?" she asked without raising her head.

"Oh, yeah. She's putting together a rocking chair."

Nora nodded, remaining silent.

"Well. Where were we?"

"I asked if you've ever found a car."

"Oh, yes...nope, no car." He ran his hand through his hair, the same way Nora did when she was nervous. She ignored it.

"Okay, then. So this is not an opportunistic area to come and do drugs," she said, gesticulating at the map. "Wouldn't you agree that there are a million better options? I'm pretty sure no one would look twice in the bathroom at Jimmy's." She rolled her eyes as she thought about what she'd seen in there. CALL JANICE FOR A GOOD TIME, accompanying a phone number on the wall next to the sink. An unemptied trash bin. Everything had felt wet and gross. One look at it and she'd turned and walked right back out.

David nodded. "You're right. And if this were a known area for people to come and do drugs together, we probably would have heard about it. We never get calls out there, except for these bodies. Makes sense, why we rarely ever find drug paraphernalia in the vicinity. The first call I went on, I found a needle on the side of the road. Much more likely for someone to just pull over, shoot up, then chuck the needle out the window and be on their way. So it could be that they were dropped off here. Maybe...maybe they started to OD, and whoever they were with left them there so they wouldn't get charged..." He trailed off, doubting his own scenario.

"That doesn't make sense, either. I'm telling you, the girl - Caroline - she was running *from* something. She looked...afraid. Something wasn't right. And someone dropped her off so she could go kill herself? No." She shook her head definitively, one hand on her hip, the other trailing the map. "That's not what happened."

David looked her over, a sense of gratification filling him as he took note of her attitude. She was strong-willed, just like her mom. And she was smart. He remembered her being a good student when she was younger, but he hadn't been around for the teenage years to see what she'd made of herself. He hadn't known what to expect when he'd walked into the diner. Maybe addiction ran in the family and she was a mess after her parents died. It was possible she was under the influence of something when she got into the accident, that maybe that had been part of the reason she'd been so defensive on the phone. But he'd found her apprehensive but clear-headed, and much more put-together than he had ever been at her age.

Nora saw him looking at her strangely from the corner of her eye and jerked her head up. David looked away and moved toward the fridge.

"Want something? Water?"

"No thanks. Did you find anything on Ryan Williams?"

He sighed. "Well, it's a very common name. Nobody in Woodbridge popped up, so I tried Pittsburgh, and it brought up quite a few results, but it's only gonna show guys with a record." He waved her over to his laptop in the adjoining den.

"Anybody look familiar to you?"

Nora leaned past him and scrolled through the results.

She shook her head, somehow relieved and disappointed at once. "Not at all."

"Well, he probably wasn't using a real photo. Do you have any pictures of him?"

"Yes, actually." She'd taken a screenshot of his photo to text it to Erica for approval, who had acquiesced that she "mildly approved."

She flicked her camera roll open but found it empty; all of the photos were on her old phone.

"Shit. I don't have it anymore. Let me ask my friend if she has it." She fired off a text asking Erica to send it to her, knowing a barrage of questions was sure to accompany it.

"Can you describe him?"

"Nerdy glasses, like Buddy Holly." *A rugged, handsome face underneath them.* "White. Sandy brown hair, blue eyes." A tight-lipped, lopsided smile that she'd found charming. The photo was slightly muddled, like it had been taken years ago. She'd thought it was the result of a photo filter, but now she wasn't sure.

As expected, his photo came through, along with a paragraph of text in all caps that she didn't bother to read. She would deal with Erica's wrath later.

Her heart had fluttered the first time she'd laid eyes on him, but this time, her heart pounded in fear. She hadn't looked at him since she realized he, at the very least, wasn't who he'd said he was, and in the worst case scenario, was responsible for murdering several women. One of which could have been Nora.

She lifted the photo to David, who squinted at it. "Text it to me. Is this the only photo you have of him?"

"Yeah. That's all he had on his profile."

"Just so you know, it's not a great sign when you meet

someone online and they only have one photo," he chastised, an attempt to keep things light.

"Okay, *Dad*." The word caught in her throat. The last person she had called Dad was her own father, and she hated herself for throwing the word around so carelessly now, like it didn't mean anything to her. Her demeanor immediately turned icy.

David noticed her expression instantly change. Her eyes, which had resembled a curious baby deer since she was born, had turned cold. She'd put a wall up, invisible, but palpable. He shifted in place uncomfortably before changing the subject.

"Do you think you can reach out to the dating app? See if they can tell you anything...anything about him, if he canceled his profile or what."

"I'll see." Nora made another note to herself to call Cupid's Arrow, thinking it was a good idea that she wished she would have thought of first, but unwilling to give him the satisfaction.

FOURTEEN

Nora stepped into Jimmy's Bar purposefully, channeling a different woman than the one who had meekly sidestepped for men to saunter in and out the door as she had just days prior. She found it hard to shake off the thought of the place she'd been meant to meet with her would-be date/murderer, and thought, *Maybe I'll find something there.* She was defying what came off as a direct order from David, to stay out of Woodbridge completely until they figured out what was going on, but she couldn't help herself.

David lived only about ten or twelve miles from the bar, but the shifting, winding roads that broke through woods and past old farmhouses and more liquor stores made the drive much longer than she'd expected. It gave her time to think about the information she hoped to gain, and the best course of action to get it. The sun was beginning to set, the familiar haze of gold fading to pink before it disappeared behind the trees, and it was enough to make her rethink venturing there at all, in the opposite direction of the highway that promised salvation. But she knew it would nag at her until she went back, so she ignored her shaking hands and carried on.

She recognized a heavyset, grey-haired man hand-drying glasses with a stained rag behind the bartop. His eyes looked her up and down, appraising her. He had been behind the bar the night of her accident.

She waited for him to address her as she approached the bar, but he only stared, so she began. "Hi. I was here last week..."

He didn't answer, but he continued to hold her gaze.

She cleared her throat and put on a more authoritative voice. "Are you the owner of this bar?"

"Yep. I'm Jimmy." He motioned to a plaque sitting behind him, tarnished with age, that read *Jimmy's Bar* in the same cursive font as the sign out front. He looked wary of her question, but his voice remained aloof.

"Oh. Hi, Jimmy."

He set the glass down, leaned over with his hands on the bartop. His bloated belly grazed the bar, keeping him from getting too close, but she could still smell beer on his breath.

"What can I do for ya, little lady?"

Nora held back an eye roll.

"I was wondering...do you know anyone named Ryan Williams? I was supposed to meet him here the other day." She went to pull out her notebook from her shoulder bag, then thought better of it, and instead pulled out a lip gloss.

"You from the newspaper or somethin'?" His eyes narrowed, and his body language turned rigid.

She noticed his demeanor change and revised her approach.

"Oh, God no. I just wanna know who stood me up last week!" She forced herself to chuckle as she slathered on her gloss, hoping to bring down his defensiveness, but she was sure she was coming across as inauthentic.

"Never heard of 'im. Sorry." He turned his attention to his glasses once more, lining them up in rows of ten. She couldn't decipher if he was lying, or if he was just wary of her line of questions.

"Oh, that's okay. I just wanted to pop in for a drink, figured I'd ask while I'm here. Can I get a whiskey sour?" She smiled at him sweetly as she took a seat at the bartop.

Jimmy looked her over once more, then silently poured her a drink in a lowball glass, sliding it down the slick bartop to her. She caught it carelessly, smiling shyly before taking a sip as she glanced at the television in the corner, marveling over the girth of the ancient, clunky unit. The drink was bitter and strong, so she sipped slowly. She didn't want to push him, so she waited for Jimmy to begin the conversation again, and a few minutes later, he obliged.

"You from around here?"

"Just down the road in Three Springs," she lied. He didn't look convinced, but said nothing.

She waited for him to grab a beer for a man dressed in trucker's gear sitting adjacent to her at the bar, then began again.

"You know, the night I was here, there was a car accident down the road. Did you hear anything about that?"

Jimmy faced the sink as he washed his hands, but she could see the side of his face twitch.

"Folks get into car wrecks all the time out here. Deer runnin' in the road and such." He didn't look at her, kept his eyes transfixed on another glass as he began to towel the rack dry again.

"Oh. I passed it and it looked pretty bad. Just wanted to make sure the driver's okay." Sipping her drink nonchalantly through two straws, like she had all the time in the world and didn't actually care about what she was asking. She could feel that they were in a delicate dance, both careful not to step on each other's toes.

"Didn't hear anything about it."

Nora seriously doubted that in a town this small with the entire ambulatory team checking on her that word wouldn't have gotten to the owner of a bar just miles down the road. Why lie about something like that? She shifted gears.

"You must get to know your customers pretty well. This is just about the only place in town to grab a drink." She forced a laugh.

He set down the glass he'd been drying a touch too hard and turned to face her, dropping both of his hands on the bartop, turning his full attention to her for the first time since she'd arrived. He smiled at her, but it gave her pause. It wasn't the type of smile that invited more conversation. He'd seemed like an old drunk at first, but now he seemed clear - somehow more capable, more menacing.

"You ask a lot of questions, little lady." His smile - if she could even call it that - didn't wane, and his eyes, seemingly darker now than when she'd first arrived, bore into hers.

"That wasn't a question." She smiled back at him, holding her breath as she braced for his reaction. He looked at her for a few seconds, and she nearly jumped as he burst into laughter from a place deep in his gut.

"Touché."

Nora had overstayed her welcome, that much was clear. She took one last drink before leaving cash on the bartop, tipping generously, careful not to leave any trace of her name. She stood up, pushing the battered stool back under the bar, then before turning to leave, casually draped her arm on the bartop and asked, "Oh yeah, one last thing, and I'll be out of your hair. Did anyone find a phone here in the past week?" One last-ditch effort, though she knew it was pointless.

"No idea." He pulled out a plastic green basket from beneath the bar for her to sort through, but the basket, consisting of a stale package of Marlboro Reds and some faded papers, was shallow enough that she could tell right away that there was no phone inside.

"Okay, thanks anyway. Nice to meet you."

He watched her as she passed through the door. She clung to the handle to let it ease shut, leaving it ajar less than an inch, peering through the slit at Jimmy. He had been watching her too intently, had made it clear he wasn't comfortable with her questions. It could have been that she was an outsider, someone he didn't recognize, but it felt to her like he knew more than he was saying, and she wanted to know why.

She watched him amble toward the back of the bar, pick up a corded phone located beneath the bartop in the corner. She couldn't make out what he was saying, but his voice had gone hushed. He glanced around the bar as he spoke, though there were only two other patrons in the entire place. He hung up the phone with a heavy clang, and she softly let the door close, hustled to her car and peeled out of the lot like her life depended on it.

"Some out-of-towner was just here. Couldn't tell if she was a reporter or what. Askin' a lot of questions about the other night."

"Was it Nora Aberdeen?"

"Didn't say what her name was. Little thing with big red hair."

"That's her. Okay, I'll take care of it. Thank ya Jimmy." Sheriff Townsend slammed the phone into its receiver. He rubbed his face in his hands before abruptly pounding his fist on his desk.

What was it with this particular case? He was starting to feel out of sorts, like he didn't have a handle on things, and that was unusual for a man of his stature. He wasn't easily fazed - not when they found the first, or the second, or the third bodies. But whatever happened here seemed to be putting everyone a bit more on edge. Even Parker Crenshaw, his most loyal deputy, had stared at him just a little too long when Bill declared he'd ruled the girl a suicide, but he'd moved his eyes to the floor as Townsend's eyes bore into his. He knew better than to question his sheriff. He was probably just worried because of the Rebecca White case. Shit, what a mess. The parents had made life a living hell for all of his officers, returning to his station for days on end, asking questions that they just didn't have the answers to after that *Huntingdon* framed photos and knick-knacks filled every corner, as if an open space would dismiss that there was a young woman who used to live here.

Nora felt it would be rude to look away, so she slowly, carefully inspected each photo as she passed the front corridor into the living room. Rebecca had shared the same long, dark hair as her mother. A family photo revealed a much younger and happier-looking Maria, arms draped over her husband and her daughter at the beach. They smiled brightly and looked happy. Nora found it heartbreaking, then wondered if people felt the same way when they looked at the photos of her parents in her own home. It wasn't the reason she kept the photos out. On some level, she wanted to show her parents, wherever they might be, that she still loved them, still thought of them every day. She also wanted to see them every day as she once had, never wanting to forget an inch of their faces the way she was starting to forget some of the times they'd shared. In this strange way, she felt connected to Maria, understood that she wanted her daughter's presence around all the time.

"Can I offer you some tea? Water? I baked some cookies." Maria seemed nervous but eager to have another young woman in her home as she placed a white serving tray on the coffee table, full of enough cookies to feed a party, though it was just the two of them.

"I'll take a water, thanks." Nora settled into the floral sofa in the family room and smoothed out the most professional-looking skirt she could drag from the back of her closet. She wasn't hungry but grabbed a cookie anyway. The more she could put Maria at ease, the more information she'd be willing to provide.

"I hope you don't mind, my husband couldn't make it. He's...still not comfortable talking about her." Nora caught a glint of moisture covering Maria's eyes as she spoke, but they were gone as quickly as they had appeared.

She smiled apologetically, shaking off what she'd just revealed, and clasped her hands together in her lap. "So. What can I tell you about my girl?"

Nora held her breath for a moment and then let it out before beginning, giving herself a tiny pep talk in her mind. *You can do this.* She grabbed her pad and pen and began, easiest questions first, nice and slow.

"Tell me about Rebecca. What was she like?" She wanted to look away from Maria as her eyes teared up again, but she knew she couldn't.

"Well, she was a parent's dream. Honestly, she was. I'm not just saying that because she's...gone."

"How so?"

"She never got into any trouble. We never had to worry about her. Some parents, their hair turns grey when their kids become teenagers." She chuckled. "She never drank, never smoked. She was very shy, but she was extremely intelligent. She got an academic scholarship to Carnegie Mellon in Pittsburgh to study Mathematical Sciences."

"That's great."

"She was so bright. She really could have done something wonderful." Maria turned her eyes to the ceiling, shaking her head.

"What were her friends like?"

"Truthfully, she had a hard time making new friends, even in college. She really only spent time with a couple of people. She didn't have a ton of spare time with her studies. The person she really hung around most with - her *best friend*, I guess - was Tricia." Maria continued to stare off, wrang her hands absentmindedly.

"Do you know Tricia?"

"Oh, I know her. She's nothing like Rebecca, we'll just say that." She grimaced as she sipped her tea.

"What's her last name? I'd like to maybe get a quote from her." She intended on getting much more than that, but Maria didn't need to know.

"Burke. The two of them have been friends since grade school, but she lives in Philadelphia now."

Perfect.

"So, I know this is difficult to talk about, but in *The Huntingdon County Chronicle*, there was an article stating that Rebecca...had an issue with narcotics."

Maria scoffed.

"Oh, I know about the article. Piece of rag trash." She shook her head, trying to continue to sip her tea carelessly, but her hand shook.

"So, you're certain that she never took drugs of any kind?"

Maria seemed put-off by the question, giving off the vibe that she was on edge.

"I'm her mother. I would have known. There was no chance of it," she said coldly, placing her delicate teacup on its dish just a touch too forcefully, wringing her hands together harder as she leaned forward on the couch.

Nora knew trust was essential, so she leaned in and lightly touched Maria's hands, clenched together over the coffee table.

She proceeded cautiously. "You know, when I read that, I thought the same thing." She smiled warmly and she could feel tension releasing from Maria.

"Thank you. I appreciate you saying that."

"Rebecca was such a beautiful girl. Did she have a boyfriend?"

"She'd hate me for saying this, but she never had a real boyfriend. Just kid stuff when she was very young. Never anything serious."

"Do you know what she was doing in Woodbridge? Could she have been meeting someone there?"

"I highly doubt it. She left to spend the night at Tricia's and she never came home."

"Did she say anything before she left?"

Maria's eyes welled. "I told her not to forget that we were going to the farmer's market the next day, so she shouldn't be late coming home. I told her I loved her, and she said 'I love you more.' And then she was gone." Her voice shook as tears spilled over her eyelids down hollowed cheeks. "Tricia claims she never saw her that night. I don't know if she made it there or not." She wiped the tears angrily from her face and dabbed her nose with a tissue. "I'm trying to make peace with the fact that there are some things I'll never know."

Nora found herself pushing down tears of her own. She felt awful for this poor woman, a woman who had a close relationship with her daughter, who worried for months wondering what happened to her, and then when she finally found out what happened, it was the worst possible outcome. And the press hadn't made it any easier on her. But she had to try to gain as much information from her as possible.

"What did the police say to you when you went to Woodbridge?"

"Ha," Maria scoffed. "Not much. That she overdosed - which, I can't see how that's possible. I asked when she died. I waited for them to say that her body was so badly decomposed that they couldn't tell, thinking she'd been dead the whole time she'd been gone, that I'd been looking for my dead daughter since the day she disappeared. But they said she'd only been out there a few weeks before she was found." Silent tears fell down her face as she stared past Nora's shoulder, her eyes distant as she recalled the details with great clarity. "They called her a 'runaway', which was such a ridiculous notion that I actually laughed in the sheriff's face." She brushed the tears from her face and slid her fingers beneath her lashes to collect the dripping mascara.

"I got to see her one last time, when I didn't think I would. And they said there was no sexual trauma. That is the *only* thing I thank God for, in all of this."

Nora scribbled furiously in her pad, doing her best to keep up with Maria as she spoke.

"Please don't put that in your article."

Nora looked up and saw Maria's eyes pleading with her. She'd said more than she had intended to say, that much was clear.

Nora put on her best reassuring smile. "I'm not going to write about anything you don't want me to write about." *Because there is no article.*

"Anything else strange? Do you have any thoughts about what happened to her, since you...disagree with what the police think?"

"Tricia is very different from Rebecca. She's disrespectful. A troublemaker. So I don't know if she ever saw her that night or not. She could have been with her when she went missing, for all I know." She snorted, but she didn't seem convinced of her own accusation.

"Rebecca's car was found fifty miles from Woodbridge, at a gas station in Newport a few weeks after she went missing. I think she may have been abducted there. Or maybe someone had her car, and put it there...after." Her body involuntarily shook as she choked the words out, allowing the scene to play out in her mind, as it had nearly every day since Rebecca had been found.

Nora's head swirled. *Fifty miles. Someone took her to the place where she was found.*

"Was there anything suspicious about the car?"

"The police wouldn't know. They never even took samples for forensic testing. An investigator we hired looked it over, but there were no fingerprints we didn't recognize. No...no blood. We pored over that car. Every tiny receipt, every inch of the carpet. For the longest time, I thought that was the key to finding her. But it wasn't."

Nora asked some banal questions to lighten the mood before she left, meaningless to anyone but Maria, and found herself rushing to get out of the house, where the air seemed to have somehow gotten thicker.

Nora floated out the doorway as Maria held the door, barely registering the people walking down the street who waved to Maria as they strode by. She could hardly grasp the depth of what Maria was telling her, and it left her feeling breathless and almost faint. Rebecca had likely been held somewhere - for many months - before being found. It fit the narrative she'd put together for Caroline. She was right. She was held somewhere, and then someone had killed her. The events were sounding more nefarious, more connected, and they swirled, heavy and nauseating, in Nora's core.

SIXTEEN

Part of survival, Casey learned, meant interaction - and she had to take what she could get. She hated the man with every ounce of her being, that he had taken her against her will, taken her from her family, for an agenda that she still didn't understand. But she found it hard to admit to herself that as time passed, she realized the days he didn't come were the worst. Staring at the wall with nothing to look at, nothing to do but imagine her family moving on without her, was unbearable. Living in isolation was not something a social creature like Casey had ever thought she was capable of for any period of time - much less...*indefinitely*. But she soon learned that when it came to surviving, she was capable of just about anything. And that included looking forward to time with him.

The first time he'd brushed her hair, she'd winced as if she'd been punched. He seemed puzzled at her reaction, pausing the song he'd been whistling, but said nothing and kept brushing. As the days turned into weeks, her longing for human touch outweighed her repulsion toward him, and she sat motionless as he ran his fingers through her hair. She disgusted herself, that she didn't mind it much anymore. If she ever made it out of here, she'd keep that to herself.

Over time, she came to know his schedule. *Their* schedule. She'd wait, her head spinning with nausea, for the man to arrive to give her the drugs that her body, against her own will, had come to rely on. He'd smooth his hand down her face, whispering, "Good morning, sweet Virginia", but she was afraid to ask him why he called her that. After her nails were gone and she had no other weaponry, he'd sometimes plant a kiss on her cheek, his moist lips sending repugnant shockwaves down her spine. After a fresh injection of the poisonous liquid, she'd fall back in her bed, letting warmth wash over her as tension released from her belly. He'd chatter on about his day, as if they were old friends. She tried, the first few days, to remember everything he was saying. To look for a clue as to who he was - a name, a hometown, a friend - and what he was doing with her. But she couldn't make sense of what he was saying - it seemed like he was talking to her like they knew each other, referencing times they'd spent together when he was younger, though she was more than certain they'd never met. Her confusion mixed with the haze of the drugs made it impossible to concentrate, so instead, she closed her eyes and let her mind wander into strange euphoria, the only time of day her pain could dissipate.

Some days she got food, a bagel or a muffin, whose first taste she could immediately identify from Zuckerman's Coffee & Bakery in the city. She'd broken into heavy sobs at the realization, startling the man as he screamed through heaving breaths at her to stop. But she couldn't. It was a place she had visited every Saturday with her mom. The only place she ever really had soul-baring discussions with her. The weight of it was unbearable, and the emotional pain was more than he could ever do to her, so she continued crying, and he stormed out of the room, slamming the door behind him, waiting for days to return.

She never revealed to him what caused her upset - she didn't want him to stop bringing food altogether - and the man, clearly avoiding another emotional scene, didn't ask. He continued to bring the same food each week. Was it Saturday? Would they cross paths? She wondered if her mom would keep their tradition alive in her absence.

After she'd come to accept her new surroundings, he'd brought in books for her to read to him aloud, mostly old children's picture books she'd never read before. The first few times her voice shook in fear, dreading the thought of what he would do to her if she didn't read the way he wanted her to. But as the days went on, she realized he was listening intently on the edge of the bed, and he never seemed to get angry so long as she did what she was told. He seemed quite relaxed after her nails had been taken and she'd shown him no other signs of resistance.

She secretly enjoyed the reading. Though the books were elementary, they provided a gateway to a world outside. When he was gone throughout the day, she'd peruse through the yellowed pages, smoothing her hands over the paper as she read. The only time she could envision herself away from her desolate world was while she thumbed through those pages - a vacation, if only in her mind.

SEVENTEEN

She hadn't known it at the time, but Nora had done herself a favor to give herself a day after meeting with Maria. It gave her time to process the information about Rebecca before going to meet Tricia. It allowed her a better idea of how to approach her, of what questions to ask. She cleared any preconceived notions about Tricia that Maria had instilled from her mind.

Tricia was living alone, a fact that unsettled Nora as she began to notice a shift in the neighborhood nearing her apartment downtown. Restaurants and shopping malls gave way to liquor stores and strip clubs, and hordes of people gathered on nearly every street corner, to do what, Nora could only guess. As she pulled into the soaring, aging apartment complex, street level windows yellowing behind steel bars, she felt her hands reflexively tighten against her wheel. She heard a catcall in the distance as she descended from her car but couldn't make out if it was meant for her, and she didn't care to find out, so she kept walking, nearly jogging now. She hustled into the door and down the hallway, over the weathered carpet, past maroon doors of apartments and paper-thin walls barely shielding loud televisions and aggressive arguments until she finally arrived at the silent door harboring Tricia.

She knocked swiftly, watching the people milling throughout the halls carefully as she waited. Tricia called to her to come in, and Nora was baffled at the invitation without Tricia knowing who or what was outside of her unlocked apartment. She opened the door and hesitated as if waiting for a guard dog to blindside her, then stepped inside when she found no movement.

"It's Nora Aberdeen," she called, her voice cracking. She looked around the connected kitchen and living room, at a dated television on a bare wall facing a stained couch, a heap of dirty dishes in the sink, and not much else.

"No shit. I'm back here."

Nora followed the voice to a sole bedroom, silently appraising it as she crossed the threshold into a teenage haven. A shrine of photos circled her bed, leaving behind memories of Rebecca, proving that in some ways, they'd both forever be eighteen. Bunched tissues covered in wet mascara littered the floor surrounding an overflowing garbage can.

Tricia sat huddled on her bed, hugging her knees over sheer dark leggings, fingers interlaced though chipped black polish. Not exactly the picture of a welcoming invitation, though she'd sounded eager when Nora had called to tell her she was writing a story about Rebecca's life. Nora stood awkwardly, not knowing where to set up shop since there were no chairs in her room.

Tricia looked directly at Nora through heavy black eyeliner, then abruptly asked, "So are you gonna sit down?" Her husky voice didn't match her tiny body, a smoker's thick inflection.

Nora's face went crimson before taking a seat at the very edge of the duvet. Tricia was much younger than she was, but still commanded the room, even huddled on her bed in the corner in an oversized sweatshirt. Nora pushed her shoulders back, closed her eyes and took a breath. Her eyes were only closed for a moment, but when she opened them, Tricia was staring at her blankly through unkempt black hair, an obviously unnatural color under long roots of light brown. Nora reminded herself that this girl was grieving, and that was something she knew all too well. They weren't as different from each other as it would appear on the surface.

"What do you want to know?" Tricia demanded. She was already growing impatient, and they hadn't yet begun.

Nora felt her hands start to shake, but she forced herself to smile.

"I'm interested to know about your friendship with Rebecca. I know she was a great loss in your life, and I'd love to understand how you guys bonded, and what she was really like." She pulled her notebook from her bag, uncapped the pen she'd clipped to the front, and waited.

Tricia's eyes watered but she quickly wiped them away, leaving smudges of makeup beneath them.

"We've known each other forever. She was the nicest person I've ever met. I was a bad influence on her." Tricia smiled slightly.

Nora smiled back at her encouragingly.

"I'm sure that's not true."

"No, it is. She only ever drank when we were together." She stopped and looked at Nora seriously. "*Don't* tell her mom I said that."

"I won't. Promise." Nora held her hand up in scout's honor, and Tricia gave her a confused look before continuing.

"Anyway, we went to parties once in a while, but she was always really busy studying and with her music."

"Did she ever have time to date?"

Tricia's body stiffened.

"I don't know." She fiddled with a silver hoop circling her left nostril.

Nora reached her hand across the bed and placed it on top of Tricia's, mimicking the movements she remembered people using on her when they reached out after her mother had died.

"You're not going to get into trouble."

Tricia's body relaxed, but only slightly, and nodded silently.

"She's gone, and I'm just trying to make sense of it. I know she was a good person, and I know you are, too. Nothing you tell me is going to make me think differently." Nora looked into Tricia's eyes but kept her expression soft, and she saw her tear up again.

Tricia flicked her eyes away, and stared at the wall as she answered.

"She met someone. Online."

Nora's ears pricked.

"Do you know where, online?"

"Some site having to do with Valentine's Day, or something?"

Nora worked to keep her body from wretching.

She cleared her throat. "Did she ever show you a picture of the guy?"

"Yeah, she texted it to me. I don't really remember what he looked like, but I remember he was cute."

"Do you still have that picture?" Nora tried to mask her intense interest, but her hunger for the information was clear.

Tricia looked at her suspiciously. "I delete all of my text conversations."

She tried to stay expressionless, but she could feel her face fall.

"That's okay. Did she tell you what his name was?"

"Tom, somebody? I don't remember if she ever told me his last name."

"It was a long time ago. I understand." Nora said casually. Tricia was the perfect person to extract information from. She just needed her to open up. She took a moment to look around the room. Heaps of laundry piled on top of a broken handled basket. An ashtray full of stubbed cigarettes on a gold-handled nightstand and a faint smell of smoke and incense to accompany it.

"Did she ever have any other boyfriends?"

"Nope. That's why she was so excited about this guy. Honestly, I was a little surprised the guy messaged her so quick."

"Why do you say that?"

"She didn't have a lot of boyfriends. I think guys thought she was nerdy. Once you knew her, she was really fun. But guys are dumb."

"Was she shy?"

"Oh, yeah. I'm really outgoing, and she was the opposite of me. That's why I liked her so much." She smiled wistfully, seemingly reflecting back on their time together.

"So, I want to ask you about her disappearance. She said she was going to your house the night she went missing, but then I talked to Mrs. White, and she said you told her you never saw her. Was that out of character for her, to say she was going somewhere and then really go somewhere else?"

Tricia shrugged.

Nora tried a more direct approach.

"Was she going to meet a guy that night? The guy she met online?"

Tricia closed her eyes hard, like it was painful for her to get the words out.

"Do we have to talk about this?" Her voice shook, showing weakness for the first time since they'd spoken.

I'm blowing this, Nora thought, annoyed with herself. She started to panic, and then remembered that she was the only person who could get this information. She had a duty. To Rebecca. To David. To Caroline. *Calm down. Think about how to say this.*

She took a deep breath before answering.

"We don't have to talk about anything you don't want to talk about. I just want to do Rebecca justice. I want to get everything right. For her. She deserves that."

Tricia nodded and kept her eyes low, her fist on her cheek, waiting an excruciating minute before answering.

"Yes. I covered for her. Her mom is a lot different from mine."

Nora's stomach tightened. "How so?"

Tricia laughed sarcastically.

"My mom kicked me out when I was 17. She doesn't give a shit what I do. Mrs. White is really overprotective. *Too* protective. They're exact opposites."

"Did you tell the police that you covered for Rebecca?"

"Her mom freaked out. When she didn't come home, she rolled up to my house. When Becca wasn't here she started screaming." Tricia started to cry and pulled her knees back to her chest as she recounted the day, her voice shaking, tears rolling down her cheeks faster than she could brush them away. "I kept texting Becca that she needed to go home, but she wouldn't respond. I didn't want her to get in trouble, so I told her mom she spent the night at my house and she must have stopped somewhere before she went home. But she knew something was wrong. She could tell I was lying."

Nora handed her a tissue so she could blow her nose before continuing, though judgment moved its way through her. Tricia had vital information about her missing friend and she had kept it to herself. *How dare you*, Nora thought. It wasn't her place to decide what Maria could know. *You couldn't check on your friend?* She remained silent, listening intently, but began to feel the disdain Maria had for Tricia.

"She just kept screaming. She was so upset. Finally I couldn't take it anymore and admitted she never came over. I told her I didn't know where she went. And that's true, I didn't know exactly where she was going. She just said it was at a bowling alley, kinda far away. But I never told anyone that, because I didn't think it mattered. And then she turned up *dead*, and it was too late." She was sobbing now, her shoulders heaving.

Nora reached her hand out and placed it gently on Tricia's back, felt the rise and fall of her breath with every sob, and her anger began to wane. She whispered gently, "It's okay, it's okay, you're okay." It was true that Tricia had withheld crucial information from the Whites. But she had to remind herself that this girl was eighteen when her friend disappeared. She was afraid to tell the truth. She didn't want her friend to get in trouble for meeting a guy. Erica probably would have done the same for her when they were younger.

She allowed Tricia's sobs to relent before she continued.

"Now, I want to ask you a question, and I'm not going to judge you, no matter what you say. But did you and Becca do any drugs together?"

Tricia snorted.

"I'm dead serious - I offered Becca a joint *one* time. She'd never smoked weed before, so I had to show her how to do it. She took three hits, got super paranoid, and said she was never doing it again." Tricia laughed, her nose stuffy. "Don't tell her mom that, either."

"I won't. So she never...took anything else?"

Tricia shook her head in disgust. "If *I've* never done heroin, then Becca *really* hadn't. I saw what they were saying about her in the newspaper. I've heard rumors around town. They're not true. Literally, none of them are true."

"What are people saying?"

"That she was a junkie. She went to Woodbridge to score. She didn't know her own limits, and she overdosed," Tricia mocked. "It's so frustrating. They don't know her. If they did, they would never say that. She was the nicest, smartest girl I've ever met. She was a good person. The fact that people talk about her like that...it makes me sick."

Nora nodded. "Listen, I want to thank you for being open and honest with me, because I know how hard it is," Nora began softly. "I've gone through what you're going through. I want you to know that what happened to Becca isn't your fault, okay?"

"I know."

"I'm serious. I know you think you would have done things differently, knowing what you know now. But you didn't know. And you didn't do this to her."

Tricia nodded silently and looked away.

"I'm gonna leave you my number, and if you think of anything else, you can call me any time."

"For your newspaper story?"

"Just, anything. Anything you think is important for someone to know. Or if you just want to talk to someone. I'm here." She scribbled her information in her notepad and ripped the page out, handing it to Tricia. She knew she wouldn't call, but she felt compelled to give it to her. "Thank you so much for meeting with me, and for telling me about Becca. I really appreciate it."

"Sure." Trisha stared at the page as if it were written in a language she didn't speak.

Nora gave a little wave as she walked out of the room and let herself out.

Tricia stared for a few more moments at the paper Nora had given her after she'd left, then crumpled it into a tiny ball and tossed it into the sea of tissues beside the garbage. She slunk back into her bed and pulled the covers to her chin as she laid facing the wall, resuming the position she'd been stuck in for months.

EIGHTEEN

Nora nearly jumped out of her skin when her phone started to buzz. Every time she worked on the case - which, if she were being honest with herself, consumed most of her days - she was on edge even more than usual, and it was no different as she pored over Rebecca's old instagram account. There were few photos, but they provided some insight that seemed to prove what Mrs. White and Tricia had said about her. Two photos of her tabby cat, who Nora had noticed watching her while perched in her bay window before flopping on her back to bask in the sunlight. A photo of her playing clarinet, with a thoughtful poem as the caption. Pictures with friends, one of them being Tricia, with a small string of playful conversation between them in the comments. Her last photo was the Carnegie Mellon insignia, titled "Dream come true." There were no photos of her partying, and she seemed excited and proud to begin her college life. Nora let her thoughts wander into darkness, closing her eyes to stop tears from falling as she let the weight of Rebecca's death fall on her. Her eyes shot open at the sudden vibration on her desk, her nerves jolting her body from sadness to instant anxiety. She assumed the dim light of her laptop and the lack of sleep wasn't helping, but the subject matter proved hard to work through without her stomach curling into itself, no matter the time of day.

"Jesus Christ." She put her hand to her chest and steadied her breathing before looking at the screen. Unknown number. She answered, assuming it was David.

"Nora Aberdeen?" A gruff but familiar voice flooded her ear.

She froze, attempting to steady her breathing once more. *Is this who I think it is?*

"Yes?" she choked out.

"This is Sheriff Townsend of the Huntingdon County Police Department."

She faked surprise.

"Oh, hi Sheriff! How are you?" She knew it was obvious she was putting on a front, because no one would ever be that cheery to speak with him in her situation, but she found that she had no idea how she should sound. *What does he want. What does he want. What does he want.*

"I wanted to talk to you about your accident. We've made some progress and think we've identified the girl you said you saw. Can you describe her again, for me?"

Nora's eyes narrowed. He seemed overly interested in something he hadn't cared about in the least when they spoke in person. And she could swear he seemed...kinder?

"Oh. Okay. She was white, maybe late teens, early 20s. Dark hair. Wearing a nightgown." *I know exactly how old she is, but I'm not fucking telling you that.*

"That seems to match up with a body that was found less than a mile from where your accident occurred. The deceased has been identified as Caroline Barone."

So David had done it. He'd called in the information as he'd promised he would. It was over.

"Did you know her?"

Nora's eyes widened.

"No."

"She lived in your area."

"It's a big city."

A heavy pause, both of them weighing their next move.

"You don't seem surprised that her body was found."

"I saw all of the cop cars the next day where I had my accident. I had a bad feeling."

"You're sure your vehicle didn't make contact with her?"

Nora could feel beads of sweat begin to form at her temples.

"No!" She cried incredulously. She couldn't help herself. "Can't you tell a car didn't hit her?"

"There were no injuries that would indicate a vehicle was involved. We just have to follow protocol."

"Okay..."

Nora stared at her phone doubtfully. The conversation was starting to feel suspicious - if this were protocol, he would have asked her much more when she was down at the station. What game was he playing? And why?

"This guy you were meeting...did you get his information, like I asked?"

Nora fumbled with the pile of notes she'd been jotting down about the case before relaying his username, which consisted of seemingly meaningless letters and numbers. She'd thought a hundred times about creating a new account and trying to send him a message. Now she was glad she hadn't.

"What happened to her?"

"Like I said, she's deceased."

"I mean...do you know how it happened?"

Another long pause.

"We have a pretty clear picture of what happened," he snipped.

Nora's face scrunched.

"So...I didn't know her. Is that all? Are you looking for... anything else?" Nora's attempts to keep her voice steady were faltering, putting her in a hurry to end the conversation.

"What do you do for a living, Nora?"

Nora sat for a moment, not knowing how to answer. *Why is he asking?*

"What do you mean?" Nora asked in a feeble attempt to stall, then slapped her own forehead.

"Young lady, I'm asking what you do for *work*. How do you make *money*?" His condescension cut through her, razor sharp. "Are you a reporter?"

"I...I have an inheritance. I don't work." Nora stammered, embarrassment washing over her as she said the words out loud for the first time since her parents died. Her joblessness was never intentional. Her parents hadn't wanted her to work while she was in college so she could focus on school. After she dropped out, she hadn't mustered the energy to look for anything resembling a job. She'd considered volunteering at the municipal animal shelter, but the rigorous schedule they'd required had put her off. She wasn't ready to commit to that, and feared letting the animals down on the days she found it impossible to get out of bed. She thought about telling him she *was* going to be a reporter, *actually*, before her life went to shit. But she thought better of it, because he didn't exactly sound like he was asking because he wanted to discuss the latest column in *The New Yorker*.

Silence for a moment, before his gruff voice snorted, "Huh. Must be nice."

Nora didn't answer, putting all of her energy into keeping herself from breaking into tears.

"Just know that we're still working on this case," he said brusquely. "I'll be in touch."

NINETEEN

As Nora approached Caroline's mother's house, she noticed that it better reflected a state of mourning than Maria's did. Overgrown weeds surfaced through cracks up the sidewalk and surrounded the porch stoop, and the grass hadn't been cut in weeks. It looked as though it had been abandoned, save for the car behind the steel fence in the drive.

The state of the home immediately put Nora on edge. She'd already been anxious about meeting Caroline's mother face-to-face, about having to explain to a stranger her daughter's last moments. It was clear now that this meeting was going to go much differently than it did at the Whites' house.

She took a deep breath and rapped on the door. Minutes went by, her breath quickening with each passing moment. Before she lifted her hand to knock again, she heard a lethargic thumping before the door slowly creaked open.

Behind the heavy green door lingered a shell of a woman, taller than Nora's five foot three frame, but somehow seeming much smaller than she. Her dark hair was disheveled, like she'd just woken up, though it was three o'clock in the afternoon. She stood with her eyes fixed on Nora, but said nothing.

Nora nervously cleared her throat. "Hi, Mrs. Barone?"

She didn't respond, but stepped away from the doorway, making way for Nora to enter.

As Nora stepped inside, she sucked in sharply. The home was littered with junk on every surface, corner, and seat. Piles of clothes, newspapers, and empty bags of potato chips surrounded them.

"Want something to drink?" Caroline's mother asked, making it clear she expected her to say that she didn't. That was fine with Nora this time. She didn't want to consume any of the dead energy she felt had attached to the house.

"No, thank you."

"Sit down." It wasn't a question. Nora awkwardly pushed over a pile of magazines on the sofa to make room to sit, taking up as little space as possible.

"Thanks so much for meeting with me, Mrs. Barone."

She put her hand up and shook her head. "Tess."

"Okay, Tess." Nora forced a smile. Tess fell beside her on the couch, leaning her back lazily against the armrest. Once she was nearer to Nora, she could see that her eyes, though the same green shade as her daughter's, looked dull and distant. It should have dawned on her when she'd been so monotone on the phone when Nora had called, but it was clear now that Tess was chemically aiding her grief. She guessed it was pills. In an instant, Nora remembered how she'd felt the day she ended up in the bathtub, which most of the time, felt like a lifetime ago. But all of her feelings came flooding back, filling her with compassion for Tess.

"I just wanted to start by saying that I'm really sorry about Caroline," Nora began delicately.

Tess looked away and nodded, but said nothing. She took a swig from a beer that had grown warm on the end table.

"I wish...I don't know. I wish things had turned out differently. I wish I wouldn't have passed out. That I could have done something more." Nora choked up, barely getting the words out.

Tess noticed and said flatly, "It's not your fault."

She didn't mean it; her mind had raged after Nora had called her and explained her accident, asking to come by to talk to her about Caroline, and she'd fantasized about slapping her in the face the minute she walked up to the door. But morbid curiosity about her daughter's last moments had consumed her, and before this had happened, turned her life upside down, it had been in her nature to make people feel at ease. There was still a piece of her alive, somewhere deep inside, even if she didn't know how to find it.

"So, what's this about?" Tess took a bigger swig, drips of liquid falling from the sides of the bottle down her lip, and sloppily wiped them away with the back of her hand.

"I guess I'm just here to gain some clarity on what happened. Do you know why Caroline was in the woods? Or why she was in Woodbridge?"

The gall of this girl, Tess thought, and she couldn't help but snort. But she answered her anyway, because she was dying to talk about her daughter. And the last person to see her alive was sitting on her couch.

"She was missing for weeks. I have no idea what she was doing out there."

Nora thought about asking if she'd ever done drugs, but decided against it. Tess was much icier, more guarded than Maria had been, and she wasn't giving off the impression that she was going to get personal with her. She wondered why she accepted Nora's idea to meet at all.

"Do you have any theories?" Nora's eyes met Tess's and they stared at each other for a moment.

"If I did, I don't know that you're the one I'd tell." Tess sat back casually, her tone anything but careless. There was anger under the coldness of her voice.

Nora's face burned.

"I'm sorry." She felt like crying, like leaving that moment, pretending like she'd never arrived at her door. But she knew she couldn't do that.

She cleared her throat, her hands clasped together over her knees, and gave it her best shot. "I'm just trying to gain some insight, because I do not believe she killed herself."

Tess's face showed her shock at the weight of Nora's statement. She sat silently for a moment, her hands shaking so slightly it was almost imperceptible, before slowly responding, "Neither do I."

"Did you tell the police that?"

"Sure did. They didn't want to hear it. Said the Medical Examiner had already recorded it as a self-inflicted wound." A sob caught in her throat as she imagined, for the thousandth time, her daughter's throat being sliced open. She did the one thing she told herself that day she wasn't going to do - she lost her composure, medicated as it was. She found herself weeping in front of a stranger, the last person to see her daughter, the last connection she'd ever have to her baby girl. "She would never do that. I know her. I *know* her. She was my whole life. It's always been just us two - we were best friends. She was everything that mattered to me." She used the arm of her sweatshirt to mop up her tears, but they refused to stop falling.

"Why are you *here*?" Tess cried between sobs, suddenly spewing vitriol as she rose up, towering over her, with a haggard finger pointed uncomfortably close to Nora's chest. This had been a terrible mistake. Tess had her under a microscope. She had never planned to give up information about Caroline. She wanted *Nora* to give up information about Caroline.

"I'm sorry. I shouldn't have come. I'm so sorry." She felt panic rise in her chest, the urge to flee now her main concern as she sprung from the couch, brushing off crumbs from her backside as she rose.

"No. Don't you fucking dare skirt out of here. What are you *doing* here?" Tess wailed, unable to control herself now. Tears still fell but her face had transformed to angry and bitter, guttural and howling, desperate for information.

"I think someone killed your daughter, and I want to know who it was." Nora blurted out, then covered her mouth in shock at her own lack of composure. Tess's raw emotion had blurred the lines, had put her back against the wall, making it impossible to keep it clean.

Tess stared at her, steadying her breath, then wiped her eyes once more with the back of her tattered sweatshirt, which had now become dark with moisture. She slumped back to the sofa with a thud and a crinkling of garbage beneath her.

"Good." Tess nodded, rustling a tissue from between the couch cushions to blow her nose. "Tell me what you want to know."

Nora felt dizzy, like she was viewing the scene outside her own body. She gripped the couch and did her best to clear her thoughts. She brought out her notebook this time, deciding it would be easier for both women if she kept her eyes glued to the pages.

"Do you know what Caroline was doing in Woodbridge?"

Tess sighed, closing her eyes as she answered.

"Yes. She was going to meet someone."

The lightheadedness grew stronger.

"Do you know who it was?"

"She told me his name was Danny. It was brand new. And then she went missing. I told the cops and they said they'd look into it. But here they are, still ruling it a suicide," she said bitterly. Tess stopped short of explaining that she had been in hysterics when she gave them the information, that they probably could barely understand her as she crumpled over her daughter's body to identify her in the morgue.

"You think this - Danny person - had something to do with it?"

"I don't think it's a coincidence. There's no way she was gone of her own accord for weeks without contacting me. We talked every day. I should never have let her go. I'll live with that for the rest of my life." Tess stared in her direction, her eyes glassy as they gazed past her, as she bit the stubs of her nails.

"I also don't think it's a coincidence *you* saw her right before she died." Suddenly Tess's eyes came back to the present and bore into Nora, so she slung her eyes to her notes. "Do you know him?" She asked coldly.

Nora looked up in shock. Tess stared right into her soul, and she could see her hands gripping her beer bottle tightly, her knuckles going white with each squeeze.

She vehemently shook her head.

"I have never met Caroline, and I have no idea who this Danny person is. I swear. The day of the accident...I only saw her for a second. Trust me, I'll never forget it."

Tess searched Nora's face for signs of deception but found only fragility. It had been needling her, that this girl may have run over her daughter and then lied about it to the police. Tess had assumed she was feeling guilty about it and wanted to make amends to free herself of the guilt. Her lips had curled during their call, knowing that Nora was the only person with real information since the police had proven to be useless. And if anyone was going to get it out of her, it was Tess.

But then, there was the problem of the knife. She watched Nora closely before taking a deep exhale, allowing herself to believe she was telling the truth. It was the first deep breath she'd taken since Caroline had gone missing, and her lungs ached. She tipped the back of her bottle up and nodded in acceptance.

Nora took a deep, silent breath before continuing.

"What was your daughter like?"

"Tough as nails. Like me." Tess smiled for the first time in weeks, and immediately she felt ashamed. It faded as quickly as it had come. "Strong." The word caught in her throat as she envisioned the slice across her daughter's neck, how cold and small she'd looked atop the steel table at the morgue. "Very smart.

Funny. Creative. You know, they say that about lefties." Nora's ears perked as she wrote down "left-handed" in her pad, starring it for later.

"Did she ever talk about anyone having any kind of vendetta against her? Anyone who would want to hurt her?"

Tess shook her head. "Never. And she told me everything."

"What did she tell you about Danny?"

Tess squeezed her eyes together painfully.

"Huh. I guess she didn't tell me everything."

"I didn't mean..."

She put her hand up.

"Please. Don't patronize me." She sat for a moment, mulling whether she wanted to tell her what she knew. But Caroline was dead, and there was no bringing her back, so there was nothing to lose.

"She said he was shy. They met online."

Nora's pulse raced.

"Had they ever met in person?"

"This was supposed to be the first time. And the place she told me they were meeting - some bowling alley called Spares and Strikes - wasn't in Woodbridge, but it wasn't far from where they found her."

"Do you have a picture of Danny?"

"Why would I have a picture of him?" Tess asked snidely, shaking her head.

Nora ignored her attitude.

"Anything else strange happen, or did she say anything weird before she went missing?"

"Nope. I would have known if something were off. She was excited to meet Danny, she said she'd call me the next day. I never spoke to her again." She shook her head, pushed back more tears.

Nora nodded, not sure what to say next. She knew there was nothing she could say that would ease her pain. The weight between them was heavy.

Tess broke the silence, her eyes looking toward the window, though the drapes had been drawn shut. "They told me they had to keep her nightgown for evidence."

Nora tensed, remembering the gown and its blood and its pale essence in her headlights. "Did they mention anything about it?"

"No. But that's not the problem."

Nora waited. Tess pulled a crumpled package of cigarettes from the back pocket of her jeans, a habit she'd kicked years ago but began again the day her daughter had disappeared. She sifted through papers and magazines and receipts on the coffee table before landing on a bic lighter, smacking the lever down as sparks flew, sucking in deeply as the flame ignited her, bringing her to life for just a moment.

"She didn't own any nightgowns," she said, her voice muddled through smoke.

Nora felt bumps form from her shoulders down through her thighs, unintentionally drawing away from Tess to huddle into herself.

Tess turned to face Nora. "You really think you're gonna figure out who did this?" A challenge more than a question.

Nora pursed her lips. "I don't know. I'm trying." It was the truth.

Tess nodded, leaning forward so her arms hung over her knees, but kept her eyes on Nora. Her face suddenly hardened, her voice steely.

"Well, you better do it quick, before this happens to someone else."

TWENTY

BEFORE

Everything in Caroline's body burned as she ran through thickets of trees. She tried to keep quiet, but guttural gasps escaped her as she ran wildly, away from the cabin, down the hill, past the rushing river, away, away, away, where he couldn't find her.

The ground was cold and unforgiving beneath her bare feet, but she didn't stop. This was it. This was her chance.

The man had left hours before, and he never came back twice in the same night. She'd had enough, and this was it. Tonight was the night she'd finally get home.

She'd been buttering him up for weeks, complimenting him, telling him how much she enjoyed his bedtime stories through gritted teeth, and he was so delusional that he delighted in her lies. Her plan to get him to trust her had worked, and he started getting less careful about putting things away. She'd waited in stillness before slowly, quietly rising from the dirty mattress on the floor. She pulled a bobby pin from the back of her hair, ripping it out so quickly it brought pieces of her hair with it. She'd found it in the bureau days earlier and studied its ridges, detailing in her mind the perfect placement she'd need to unlock the door. She slid it into the lock with a soft click, causing her to jump though he was long gone. She jiggled it around for minutes before using it to move the latch, and with each failed attempt, panic stealthily rose as her hand started to shake. She stopped and refocused, took a deep breath, and imagined in her mind's eye where she had to place it. She tried once more until she heard a metal clang. She grasped the brass handle, heart thundering in her chest.

She turned the handle and felt that there was no resistance. Slipped it open slowly. It creaked, which made her wince. She waited, heard only the heaviness of silence, and took a moment before forcing herself to step outside the room she'd been trapped inside for weeks.

When she saw that the lock on the front door was rigged so that it could only open from the outside of the structure, she panicked. She followed the only source of light to a window in the kitchen above the sink where a stream of moonlight poured through. It was the first time she'd realized there were other rooms in what appeared to be a makeshift cabin. She pushed and pulled and clawed at it before realizing that it didn't have the capability to open. Rage and panic, wild and heavy, told her to get out. Just make it work, somehow. She grabbed a wooden chair, so heavy she could barely lift it at first, and with incredible strength supplied by pure adrenaline, heaved it at the window. It smashed into hundreds of pieces, and she let out a small cry of disbelief and euphoria. She climbed over the kitchen sink, barely noticing as her bare feet stepped over shards of glass.

She heaved her legs through the window, which was even smaller than her body had become but she pushed her way through it, cutting her chest and back as she wiggled her way out. She hit the ground hard and fell to her knees, a wave of intense pain washing over her. Her body wasn't used to moving like this. But she knew she had more work to do. Stepping outside, the fresh air hit her in a way it never had before. It was almost foreign, experiencing the outside world. She'd forgotten what it was like to be outside.

She took only a moment to brush the shards from her chest and hands, wiping streaks of blood on the gown he'd forced her into. She thought briefly about ditching it and running naked, but knew she wasn't thinking rationally. They would need it for evidence when she got out of here.

She looked around the outside of the cabin and realized how dark and desolate a location she had been taken to. No one would have found her here. She tried to adjust her eyes, to decide which way to go, but there was no way to tell which path led toward any kind of civilization.

As she scanned her surroundings, something caught her eye. A tiny, blinking red light from the top of the cabin. She squinted through the black of night and realized it was attached to a camera. *Fuck.*

No time to strategize. *Time to run.*

Her long, raven hair fell wildly over her face, impairing her vision in the shadowy woods, but she didn't dare try to move it. Every millisecond counted. She didn't know how far she was from a road, or a neighborhood, or anyone at all who could help her. All she could see were hundreds of tall trees, their colors imperceptible, and the occasional puddle that reflected the moonlight.

She ran for several minutes, through bushes that scratched her arms, over sticks that stabbed her feet. Then her body started to give out.

She couldn't remember when her last meal was, but she hadn't thought about that when she planned her escape. Her vision had been cloudy since the day she had been taken to the house, and she had hoped that getting back outside would help the murkiness clear. Instead, the outside of the cabin seemed surreal, like something that was happening around her that she couldn't control. But she kept running, pushing, forcing herself on. When she felt like she couldn't go anymore, she pushed harder.

As branches scratched at her arms and tore at her gown, she saw lights breaking through the trees. A car.

She let out a cry of disbelief, of joy, of hope. *I have to make it, I have to make it, I have to make it,* she chanted in the wind breathlessly, nearing tears, as she pushed through the pain that ached through her body. But her brain was unable to process the dark surroundings correctly, unable to catch up with her body's movements, and before she knew what was happening, she had emerged from the brush and found herself in the middle of a street. The silver car she had been seeking whizzed past her as she heard a thunderous crash.

She stood in the road for a moment, blinking and trying to piece together what had just happened, before realizing that the car she had been running toward - her shot at escaping - had hit a tree. It had been so long since she had been in the outside world, and whatever he pumped into her veins each day made it impossible to focus.

Her heart beat furiously, her limbs going numb. She couldn't make it much further on her own. She needed help.

She slowly, nervously approached the car, creeping up the side and peering into the SUV using the side mirror. A young girl, not much older than she, was slumped over the steering wheel, her long, red hair strewn chaotically around her shoulders. She was breathing, but motionless, and a trickle of blood ran down the left side of her face, toward her closed eyes.

Caroline's eyes panned to the woods as she heard a sharp crack, distant but unmistakable. Her stare did not veer from the woods as she shook the girl's arm, lightly at first and then more desperately, but she didn't respond. She wanted to yell at the girl to wake up, but she stayed silent, for fear that he was somehow nearby, that he would hear her and take her away and she would never have the chance to escape again.

Her adrenaline pumping, she desperately looked for anything she could use as a weapon, anything that could help her escape from wherever she was. She spotted a phone with an aqua case, thrown haphazardly onto the lap of the driver, so close to the edge of the seat she feared it would fall out of her reach. She sighed with euphoric relief, hoisted her body up and stretched her hand over the slumped girl, and snatched it.

Another crack. Someone was nearby. From head to knees she began to shake, fear pulsing through her.

Her eyes darted wildly as she clutched the phone. She tried to stay still and listen as she punched in her mother's phone number, but all she could hear was her heart pulsing, the sound almost deafening. She knew she should call 911 but, more than anything, she longed for her mother - to hear her voice, to hug her, to know that she was safe with her. The number sat on the screen as the phone tried to connect, until moments later revealing that the call had failed. Her disorientation grew and she began to sob, but she knew she wasn't safe if she stayed where she was. She couldn't remember which way she had come from, so she just started to run, tears further blurring her vision. And then it came to her - her mother's voice, as clear as the last day she'd seen her, telling her that emergency calls would work anywhere, so she tried to dial 911 as she ran, but her hands were shaking so badly that she couldn't. She had to stop.

She slumped over as she took one long breath, gasping and desperate for oxygen. As she held the phone up, she had the chance to dial only a 9 before she felt cold steel at her throat as strong arms swept around her from behind. She was too exhausted, too famished, too disoriented to comprehend what was happening or to even fight it, but her hands instinctively clawed at her throat as she felt warm liquid spill from her neck and onto her hands. She tried to cry out, but a stifled choke was all that came out. She didn't understand, but she knew it was him. She could feel it. And then she felt nothing at all.

TWENTY-ONE

"Hey baby! How ya doing? Are you eating enough?" Briana held the door for Nora as she stepped inside. Nora marveled how their home smelled like a fresh bakery no matter what time she came by.

"I'm fine, thanks." It felt odd answering such questions for someone other than her mom. "How are you feeling?"

"Oh, let me tell you something about this little girl. She is keeping me up ALL night already! I thought that was supposed to happen AFTER she was born!" Briana giggled, not sounding at all like she'd missed a night's sleep.

"A girl." Nora said softly.

Briana's hand went to her mouth.

"Oh my God. I thought David told you already."

"Did you call me?" David popped his head in the entryway. "Oh hey, Nora!"

"I am so sorry, honey. I accidentally told Nora we were having a girl. I didn't know you were keeping it a secret!"

David shifted uncomfortably as Nora watched him.

"Oh. Umm. Well, it's no big deal you told her." He hadn't been keeping anything from her. Anyone with vision would have noticed Briana was pregnant, but Nora hadn't mentioned it. He figured she needed time to process it and opted not to bring it up.

"Congratulations," Nora said, attempting sincerity, but the words came out hollow.

"Thanks. Why don't...why don't we set up shop in the den. I have a white board out there we can use."

For the first time since she'd passed them, Nora looked at the photos on the mantle in the living room before she made her way through the kitchen. The couple on their wedding day at a courthouse, where Briana shone as much as any bride Nora had seen in magazines. A vacation at a lake with two friends she didn't recognize, David holding onto an oar. Maternity photos set somewhere in an open field, where David gently cradled Briana's belly. It was still so strange, seeing moments of her uncle's life that she hadn't imagined were possible.

"Okay, so what do we know?" David cut through her thoughts as he hustled past the kitchen, grabbing a cookie from a glass jar on the counter and wordlessly offering Nora one, stepping down into the den as he stuffed it into his mouth.

Nora thought about declining but he hadn't given her much choice, and her stomach growled with hunger, so she took a bite. Oatmeal chocolate chip, her mother's favorite. The sugar hit her almost instantly, and she willed it to assist them in putting together a profile.

She pulled out her moleskine and scanned her notes, taking a seat in front of the board on a weathered couch as David stood before her.

"He's finding his victims on a dating site. Some of them, at least," she began, her voice muffled with grain.

David quickly wrote down the details on the white board, tiny letters underneath photos from the deceased before they'd been killed.

"Is *that* your handwriting?" Nora grinned. Her first olive branch.

"Hey!" David whined, but he smiled broadly.

"They're all white, and around the same age, like you said. The picture he used with Rebecca is a white dude, so he's probably white."

"Well, we don't know for sure. But historically speaking, in cases like this - yes, he's probably white."

"If this is the same guy I talked to, then the picture, I'm sure, is not him. So we don't know how old he is."

"Correct. Basically we can weed out the elderly and the physically incapacitated, because the nature of the crimes and the location of the bodies are too much work for someone like that."

"So we're looking for a white dude, in decent physical shape, aged 18 - 60, who lives in Pennsylvania. That narrows it down." Nora shook her head.

"Well, I don't think he's 18. Unless he's some super genius. This is a complicated crime to pull off, to make a murder look like an overdose or a suicide. I think...I think he's had some time to practice."

Nora shuddered.

"Judging by the dates they've gone missing and approximate date of death, he seems to be kidnapping them, or luring them in some way, and keeping them for a significant amount of time before dumping their bodies. But no sign of sexual trauma on any of them. That's important. Speaks to...speaks to motive - or lack thereof," David noted as he wrote.

"At least they didn't have to deal with that," Nora said quietly.

David fidgeted with the marker, waiting until Nora was ready to continue.

She shook her head and stared out the window into the backyard, where a white peony bush was blooming next to an old birdbath. "It's so strange. What is he doing with them, if not...that?" she asked, using her hand to prop her head up on her knee.

David's shoulders dropped and he capped the marker, taking a seat across from her.

"Are you okay?"

"I'm fine. Let's keep going."

"I meant...I meant are you doing okay, just in general. Do you need anything? Do you...do you need anything from me? From Briana, maybe? She's really taken a liking to you." He smiled proudly.

Nora decided he was seeing things in a rosier picture than they were. Briana was just nice. They'd barely spoken. She didn't know Nora. And if she did, maybe she wouldn't like her, anyway.

"I'm good. Do I seem like I need something from you?" Nora had been on her own for some time, and he needed to understand that. But she hadn't meant for it to come out so harshly, and her words hung in the air.

David shook his head. "No."

Nora moved on.

"Sheriff Townsend called me."

David dropped the remnants of his cookie to the floor, cursing as he rushed to pick up the pieces.

"What did he want?"

"He wanted to know if I knew Caroline."

"Fair question."

"Yeah...but then he asked me what I do for a living. Isn't that a weird thing to ask?"

David looked at her and shrugged.

"I guess. I don't know why it would matter, but I'm sure he had a reason. Maybe to see if you work nearby, or if you guys used to work together."

"No, he didn't ask *where* I work. He asked my occupation. And that was it." She shrugged, putting her hands on her hips.

He rubbed his hand over his chin in thought, marking chocolate throughout the bristles of the rust in his beard.

"What are you smiling at?" It was the first time Nora had cracked even the slightest grin in his presence.

"You have chocolate on your face. Let me grab you a paper towel."

She leaped up the step from the den to the kitchen, surprising herself that she knew just where to find it, and wet it at the sink before handing it over to him.

"You're a mess. Good thing you have Briana," she said, snickering.

David nodded, happy to laugh at himself.

"You're right about that. Gonna have to get my shit together...before the baby comes."

They stared at each other in silence for a minute.

"Hey, Briana's making enchiladas for dinner. You...you gotta try them - I swear, they'll be the best you've ever had. Stay for dinner?" She looked like she hadn't had a proper meal for some time, and he longed for a chance to spend time with her in a normal setting.

Nora's knee-jerk reaction was to say no - no one could beat Erica's mom's enchiladas, anyway - but she stopped herself, slowly nodding, practically salivating at the thought of a home-cooked meal.

"Yeah. I can do that."

"Great! She's gonna be so excited!" David sprinted out to the living room, calling, "Bri! Nora's staying for dinner!"

"That's great, baby!" Briana called, her voice echoing from the front of the house.

Nora chuckled, her face flushing. She didn't see what all the excitement was about.

"Let's get to work, so we can be done before we eat," she said as David reentered, his face falling in disappointment as she got back to business.

"Okay, sure. Did you get anything useful from Caroline's mom?"

"Yes, actually. Caroline was supposed to meet this guy at Strikes and Spares in Carlisle."

David's hand moved like lightning, the marker squeaking as it swept over the dry erase board.

"Good work. I'll check it out, see if any employees remember seeing her. Anything else?"

"She's left-handed."

"Caroline or the mom?"

Nora rolled her eyes.

"Come on. Caroline."

David darted to his desk and opened up a manila folder. His eyes moved quickly as he shuffled through a pile of paperwork. He stopped and looked up at Nora.

"The weapon entered her skin on the left side. It moved from left to right and exited on the right." He mimicked the motion with his hand.

Nora's eyes watered. She'd always known, but this was confirmation.

"It wasn't her," she whispered.

"It wasn't her," David affirmed.

David bustled around his tiny kitchen, nearly running into Briana's burgeoned stomach as she lifted saucy enchiladas from the oven, the smell of onions and garlic and cumin surrounding Nora as her stomach growled. Her eyes darted from David to Briana to see if they'd heard it, but they were chattering to each other about nursery colors.

"What do you think Nora? Is yellow too much?" Briana put a hand on her hip in playful defiance.

"Oh...I don't know," Nora stumbled, unwilling to enter into familial affairs.

"I think it's just precious and perfect for our little ray of sunshine," she said, smiling at Nora as she used her oven mitt to slap David on the back.

"It's too bright!" David exclaimed. "Nora, help me out here."

"Can I see the nursery?" Nora asked, flinching as the words came out.

David's eyes lit up.

"That's a great idea. Then you can tell Bri how crazy she's being."

He waved Nora over and she rose from her chair at the table, her feet feeling as if they were suddenly attached to cinder blocks, but she drudged on and followed him, past the wooden door at the end of the hallway.

The walls stood eggshell white against fresh carpet, and a grey wooden crib, covered with a brand-new sheet full of baby animal prints, stood in the corner of the room, waiting stoically for its new occupant. A rocking chair sat beside it, stacked with freshly washed, tiny onesies, and a plush giraffe donning a pink bow. A changing table sat adjacent to the crib, boxes of diapers piled alongside it.

"This is really sweet," Nora said sincerely, suddenly feeling emotional as she imagined the infant who would eventually reside here, kicking her feet and cooing for attention until she was rocked to sleep. Maybe she could hold her, one day.

"Aw, thanks. We've been working on it for a while now. Once we settle on the paint color, we're...we're all done."

"You must be so excited."

David rubbed his hand over the nape of his neck, his eyes fixed on the crib. "Oh yeah, of course. Bri's meant to be a mother. She's gonna be great. It's...it's me I'm worried about," he said, chuckling, but his face looked solemn.

"I think it's normal to be nervous," Nora said, leaning to peer at the baby clothes but not wanting to dirty them with her hands.

"Yeah, I guess. Big change, ya know?"

Nora gently squeezed his arm, and he looked at her, surprised, as she smiled.

"Yellow is perfect."

TWENTY-TWO

The Woodbridge Township website looked like it had been put up when the internet first came to fruition and hadn't been touched since. It was the first place Nora attempted to gain information about the claimed, and unclaimed, property surrounding the areas David had identified as the locations where the victims were found. There was a list of points of interest on the site - old homes in town supposedly haunted by dead families of the Victorian age, drawing occasional visitors from neighboring towns, to the chagrin of the locals. Nora didn't believe in ghosts but had to admit that the photos did have a haunting quality; their stately, southern gothic styles had given way to ruin, and she was surprised to learn that most of the homes were still occupied, despite their eerie presence. Alongside them on the list were favorite hiking spots in Tuscarora Forest, though the spots on the list were not actually in Woodbridge but miles away. That was it. There wasn't a search function within the site, so it was obvious she wouldn't be able to find anything worthwhile.

Next, she tried searching by county land records, which prompted her to pay a registration fee, but asked for the address or the name for which she was searching. She had neither. She sighed heartily, realizing she'd be heading back toward Woodbridge once again.

She arrived at the County records office through sprinkles of rain, watching dark clouds carefully as wind whipped trees at its mercy, branches settling to the west against peacocked trunks. She rifled through her backseat, somehow full of littered papers and clothes and old bags of fast food, even though it had been mere weeks since she'd received it completely cleared out, and found a sweatshirt to cover her head. She sprinted to a nondescript building where township functions were listed on an ancient marquee upon entering. She read them off to herself as she flicked beads of water from her shoulders.

Dog Licenses
Marriage Licenses
Water Billing
County Clerk
Tax Assessment
Get married and find a killer, all in one shot!

She began at the county clerk, who referred her down the hall to tax assessments to find the liber and corresponding page where deeds would be listed on a map of Woodbridge. The size of the book overwhelmed her, its meaty pages filled with coordinates and numbers that she didn't understand. But she pressed on, taking deep breaths as she thumbed through each page, a fresh wave of must seeping into her nose with each turn. She knew this was the work real investigative journalists had to do, and now was as good a time as any to learn. She owed it to Caroline - and to Tess - to take the time. She jotted meticulous notes from each grid's corresponding parcel of property that fell anywhere in the realm of possibility of where Caroline could have run from.

She tore the page of numbers from her moleskine and brought it to an elderly woman with glasses resting at the tip of her nose sitting at the desk beneath the grayed sign marked DEEDS, who said nothing but frowned as she scanned the number of files she'd have to pull. She slowly rose from her chair and its wheels squeaked behind her, shooting Nora a dirty look before moseying to cabinets of documents that stood taller than she did, heaving a huffed breath as she reached, grunting with overexertion as she pulled each file down and slapped it to the floor.

Nora drummed her fingers over the counter as she waited, surveying the building and the dribbles of rain falling faster now down the murky window. As far as she could see down the hallways, she was the only patron inside. It was eerily quiet, even the rain remaining silent, the clicks of the cabinets echoing off the walls and bouncing back toward the old woman, moving with such lethargy that Nora feared she may enter rigor mortis.

She silently thanked her parents for moving to the suburbs before she was born. They had both grown up in rural towns, socking money away since they were teenagers until they'd made enough to open their own bakery downtown, where she'd spent many days ringing up customers and testing new frosting flavors. She'd never been in a town so vast in its backwoods and outdatedness, they'd made sure of it. David must not have had the same qualms.

They had always told the story with pride, how they'd put together a business plan with a lot of heart and little knowhow, leaving everything they knew behind to make the kind of life that fulfilled them, the kind that could only be achieved in the big city, the kind that would allow them to close up shop by the time their kids were done at school for the day while they still turned a hefty profit. Nora had ended up being the only child, and she'd always marveled over how her parents took a chance and built a successful business from the ground up while putting her schedule over everything else. Dance class, book club, even tryouts for the cheerleading squad in the 8th grade that she hadn't made, blushing as girls who made the list snickered as they watched her face fall. She'd been too depressed, too embarrassed to go to school the next day, and her mother had called an employee in to cover for them so they could spend the day with her. They'd taken her to lunch and told funny stories to get her to smile, and her mother had told a detailed, gregarious tale about how upset she'd been the day she didn't make the pom pon squad. She gestured frenziedly as she showed Nora how she'd thrown her locker mirror on the floor and it shattered, and everyone had pointed and laughed. Nora had gasped, saying, "That's seven years of bad luck!!" But her mother had scoffed and swatted the air, coolly stating, "No such thing as luck." And then Nora watched her dad's soft eyes crinkle, smiling mischievously toward her mother, giving away that she was lying about the whole thing just to make her feel better. It was just the kind of parents they were. Maybe now that she was actually doing something with her life, taking fate into her own hands as her parents had done, her survivor guilt could dissipate.

The woman behind the counter slapped the last file on top of the pile, startling Nora back to the present. She made copies of each file and charged Nora five cents per page. Nora stifled a giggle at the price, fishing through her wallet for quarters.

"Can I use that table over there to look this over, make sure I've got everything I need?"

"What do I care?" The words had barely left her mouth before she turned back to her seat, sighing as she plopped herself down in front of her desk.

Nora grinned.

"Okay then."

She rifled through the paperwork, disallowing it to overwhelm her. She started with the property David had told her about, belonging to Harold Robinson. He owned several parcels on both sides of the road, but as they'd determined, he was too old to commit the crime. She noted to check on any of his relatives who had access to his property.

As David had mentioned, most of the remaining parcels were township property, and most of what remained fell under the

Tuscarora Forest state park jurisdiction, though its outskirts that flooded over into Woodbridge didn't feature any facilities.

About ten miles from where she'd seen Caroline, there was a three acre property, deep within the forest, past a river that ran over the confines of her map. The only information listed for the owner was an entity called V.E.M., LLC.

What's VEM? Nora wondered. Something about it wasn't sitting right with her. Who would want to buy land in the middle of the woods for their business?

She shot David a text that she'd found this V.E.M., and that maybe it was worth looking into. He responded that putting property under an LLC wasn't something that was, in and of itself, suspicious. She rolled her eyes, wondering if he was going to question everything she ever said forever, as if she were his kid sister.

This was something worth looking into, she determined. So she starred the page, moving V.E.M. to the top of the pile.

TWENTY-THREE

"Seems a little far-fetched, in my opinion." Erica's tone was brash, her heart-shaped mouth crumpled into a frown, her slender shoulders hunched forward as she crossed her arms on top of the ceramic table at Joe's Brew, a tiny coffee shop at the far end of downtown Philly, their spot since their frappuccino days in high school. She threw the word 'opinion' in as a peace offering; she wasn't offering an opinion. She was telling Nora how it was, before this got out of hand.

Nora instantly deflated. She had been eager to share the news of what she had been working on with David, finally finding the nerve to say out loud what was going on to someone outside of their bubble. Now Erica was playing the skeptic, sacking the wind from her sails with one sentence. Brushing off hours of dedication and her excitement about putting her old journalistic skills to good use. She could solve a real crime. Get a killer off the street. Accomplish something with real meaning. Nora had been proud of her work, and it was immediately being dismissed.

She should have seen this coming. Erica was always truthful, no matter how brutal that truth may be. A realist almost to a fault. If it wasn't her idea first, it took seeing something with her own eyes to trust what was true. And Nora hated to admit it, but she was usually right. But she hadn't been there. She hadn't looked into a grieving mother's eyes, hadn't worked with the pieces of information like a puzzle that begged to be solved but didn't provide a front cover to work from.

Erica softened her gaze when she saw Nora's shoulders fall, her dark eyes offering sympathy. She absentmindedly braided her hair down her left shoulder as she switched gears.

"You look really thin, babe. What's going on?" she asked, her tone turning to concern. Nora was tired, and she didn't want to be analyzed, though she was sure what Erica was saying was true; she hadn't been eating much, not since she'd been in her accident and her world as she knew it came to a crashing halt.

"I'm fine. I've just been busy, working on *this*." Nora threw her hands in the air, exasperated, not knowing how to show Erica how heavy, how daunting this all was.

In truth, she knew that it would sound strange, that she had become engulfed in what could be a multiple-murder investigation. She didn't know how to explain that this could be life-altering, that it already *had* been life-altering. She hadn't woken up each day with this much fire in years, and she felt like she was getting somewhere. This *mattered*, as much as Erica dismissed it.

"Are you still planning on going tomorrow?" Erica asked, though it sounded more like a challenge than a question.

"What?" Nora was caught off-guard before she realized Saturday's date. September 1st. Charlotte's wedding.

"Oh, the wedding. Yeah. I still gotta figure out what I'm gonna wear, but I'm going." She thought about how ridiculous it all sounded, going from investigating a murder to worrying about what she would wear to an event that was supposed to be the happiest day of her friend's life. She remembered a dress she'd purchased months ago and hadn't yet worn and decided right then that she'd wear it. She couldn't be bothered with thinking about something so trivial. Then her thoughts moved to Eli, who had told her weeks ago that he would go with her as her date. They hadn't discussed it since.

"Ugh. I gotta make sure Eli's still coming." She pulled out her phone to text him.

"Oh, that's happening again?" Erica teased with a wry smile, but a twinge of annoyance lined her words. They had never openly discussed it, but Nora had suspected Erica had been jealous of her, maybe for the first time ever, when she began dating - or, whatever it was - with Eli.

Nora glanced up from her phone. "No. Just going as friends."

She could swear Erica looked relieved, that her rigidness had eased.

Hey, we still on for tomorrow?

He responded almost immediately in the affirmative, and she couldn't hide a playful smile as she texted back, *Pick me up at 5:30. Wear something nice. I'll be wearing blue.*

A rumble outside startled Nora. She leaned backward in her chair, craning her neck to peer out the window. The sky had been such a bright hue that it almost hadn't looked real as she walked into the cafe, but now she could see low, shadowy clouds forming, a darkness in the distance that would soon envelop them. Trees that lined the sidewalk bent and shook in the wind, promising a storm.

When she flicked her eyes back to Erica, she was still watching Nora, but her smile was gone.

TWENTY-FOUR

Rain pattered gently on the window pane of Nora's bedroom, signaling the end of August. September was Nora's favorite month; she admired how the leaves turned gold before drying and crumpling to the ground, the wind picking up just the slightest bit, the turn from unbearably humid to a much more tolerable temperature seemingly overnight. She welcomed the rain, knew that it meant a new month, a new beginning was here. She watched in her silk robe through the slits of her blinds as tiny drops hit the window, dripping down to meet other drops that sat waiting, twirling slowly before jutting down swiftly, the motions chaotic, never following the same pattern twice.

As she sipped her coffee, savoring each swallow, she mused over how different circumstances can alter lives from person to person, people who probably weren't all that different from each other before one fateful, defining moment. The purgatory Nora was caught in was not lost on her; two completely different worlds, and now she was tied to both. Charlotte, whom she had met in college before her parents had died, in a simpler time. Things Nora thought were important problems paled in comparison to what she would eventually face. Now, Caroline, whom she had locked eyes with for no more than a moment, whose life she could only piece together from the little bits her mother was willing to share, and from what she could find on her old social media accounts, because she was dead. Yet here they were, connected.

Nora had once found Charlotte's big Bambi eyes, her naiveté, her zest for life to be endearing, but she felt herself pull away from her after her parents died. Charlotte had remained the same person, but Nora hadn't. She could feel herself changing as the months went on, and with the change, the new Nora didn't necessarily *want* to see the good in things. Sometimes Charlotte's attitude would rub off on her and she'd feel good after a night out with her, and others, she would leave a meetup exhausted by her positive outlook. She'd let the friendship slip between her fingers over time. She was shocked by the invitation she'd received in the mail, covered with lace and hearts and a personal note from Charlotte, who'd written in perfect calligraphy "I really hope you can make it!" complete with a smiley face, compelling Nora to convince herself, and Erica, to go.

Charlotte had found her prince charming. She was probably going to cry tears of happiness as she confessed her love in front of all of her friends and family to Robert, who would stare back adoringly. They would kiss, they'd be married, they'd cut the cake, they'd dance, they'd head off to their honeymoon in Bermuda tomorrow. Caroline, whose own eyes used to shine brightly, who used to have a family, who probably would have gone on to get married herself, was robbed of the chance to ever experience these moments, the love in the room, the bliss of a romantic trip with a new spouse. Charlotte was getting foundation brushed on her pink skin and her long, chestnut hair curled, stepping into her gigantic white gown, full of tulle and rhinestones and promise, while Caroline lay, cold, alone, dead. Never coming back, no chance for redemption, no more memories to be made, no matter how much her mother willed it to be so. Charlotte was a good person, a person who deserved happiness.

But didn't Caroline deserve that too? Nora was bitter on her behalf.

She sighed, pulling herself reluctantly from the window over to her closet, gently running her hands over the satin fabric of her dress as it hung in the front of her closet. She smiled faintly, a jolt of adrenaline putting itself above all else as she realized that Eli would be over in less than an hour. Maybe one day she could have a day like that. *They* could have a day like that. He seemed to be the only person it might happen with. He was the only one who could pull her out of her own head.

The day after she'd found Nora in the tub, Erica had left to run some errands and promised to be back by dinner time. Nora was grateful for the kind of friend who would drop everything to be at her side, but after living alone she'd felt a bit suffocated. She knew Erica was just trying to comfort her as she braided Nora's hair while they watched rom-coms back-to-back, but she'd been constantly asking if she was okay, if she needed anything, if she wanted something to eat. After months without any mothering, she found it overwhelming to receive such intense attention that felt more like an overbearing babysitter than her best friend. The only mothering she was looking for was from the one who wasn't able to provide it anymore, but she never mentioned it. Minutes after Erica left, she sprinted out the door, clamoring to be anywhere else. There was one place that she knew wouldn't remind her of home, and she headed straight there.

When Eli opened the door in his sweats, his rugged, casual handsomeness had sparked something in her. She looked deeply into his dark eyes for a few seconds, time standing still. She wrapped her arms around his neck, his silver chain digging into her fingertips, and felt herself melt into him as their lips met. She hadn't planned it, but for that moment, she stopped caring about what might happen. She wanted to feel something, and when he met her intensity as he kissed her back, pulling her into the room as he kicked the door closed behind them, she did. She almost couldn't put her finger on what the feeling was, but when she realized it, it caught her off guard. For the first time in months, she'd felt alive.

Tangled in sheets after what Nora would later describe to Erica as the best sex of her life, Eli traced his finger delicately down her arm as they talked about their parents, and how things were so different without them. Nora rarely ever spoke about her parents, even now, and it had been nearly two years since they'd been gone. Once in a while she'd make a casual comment to Erica whenever she mentioned her own parents. Simple things, like when Erica bitched over her mom loudly playing Spanish music early in the morning as she fried eggs in the kitchen while Erica tried to sleep off a hangover, and Nora had smiled and exclaimed that her mom used to dole out the same passive aggressive punishment. But she felt Erica tense up at each mention of them, like she didn't know how to respond, even though there was no need to walk on eggshells. She knew that Erica didn't want to upset her, to say the wrong thing. That wasn't like her, and it made Nora uncomfortable, so she tried to avoid mentioning them altogether.

But she didn't want to stop talking about them, didn't want them to fade away like ashes in the wind. They existed only in her memories now, and they were memories she wanted to share, so that she could remember them more readily. She'd felt warm and safe in Eli's arms, and it surprised her how easily she could share her most treasured moments with him. He'd listened intently, interested in what she had to say without passing judgment, and she found herself able to reflect on her struggle since they'd been gone. She longed for a companion to share these intimate moments, and she found herself falling even harder for him.

Nora had wanted to stay over that night, but Erica had called to say she was on her way back to Nora's house, and she wanted to keep Eli interested without overstaying her welcome. She softly kissed Eli goodbye as he walked her out the front door of his apartment, coolly stating, "We should do this again." Her smirk was met with a wide grin, and he simply said, "Absolutely."

She remembered just how she felt that day, and in the weeks afterward, because she was feeling it again. The old but familiar flutter that she hadn't experienced since Jeremy Dawson, her high school crush. It had been a welcome feeling the first time around, the fresh hope that jittered some life into the stagnation. It had made her feel like she was finally back among the living. But it had ended before it really had the chance to begin.

Was it different this time? He'd looked so worried, had been so gentle with her when she woke in the hospital. He'd texted her every day since, checking on how she was doing. Maybe seeing her like that sparked something in him, the way he'd first sparked a change in her. Maybe the accident had the ability to bring some positive change. And there it was again, back in her head, dashing her dreamy thoughts of Eli. The accident.

Was it her fate, she wondered, to be surrounded by ghosts? She didn't think she'd ever be the same after this. The way she could feel it in her bones after she lost her parents, that she'd never be the same person. She sighed again, rubbing her face. She had to get Caroline out of her head, if just for one night.

She cradled her favorite mug, the one from her Hawaiian vacation with her family seven years prior, with Plumeria dancing across the front, forming an endless circle under a stamp that read HONOLULU. Of all the time they spent together on serene beaches, at outdoor restaurants lit by tiki torches, she remembered most clearly her mother bitterly telling her father on the plane, "If David could just get his shit together, he'd be coming with us." She let the steam from her coffee warm her face, sending a shudder through her body. The rain had brought much cooler weather with it, and though she welcomed the drop in temperature, she wasn't sure she was ready for the adjustment.

She sat at the oblong, antique vanity that she'd plucked from an estate sale, at the urging of Eli - *A classic beauty for a classic beauty*, he'd said with a wink - to begin applying her makeup for the night's events. She leaned close to its grand mirror to check out the damage on her face, gingerly fingering the bruise on her cheek, which only hurt now if she pressed on it. The swelling was gone and the bruise had shrunken and yellowed, barely noticeable unless you were looking for it. It was hard to believe she had been in a terrible accident - a life-altering accident - just two weeks prior. So much had happened in those two weeks that it felt as if months had passed. She could feel herself changing, again. Another defining moment.

She applied a thin layer of moisturizer to her face before using her brush to apply her foundation, something her mother had taught her how to do when she was eleven. The first time she'd tried makeup on, she'd casually walked by her mother reading a magazine on the couch, a sly smile over her face, and waited for her mother to notice. She had noticed, and her reaction had shocked Nora. Her mother sprung to her feet and screamed at her to wash her face off, and Nora scampered up the stairs before she could see the tears flowing down her rouged cheeks. Fresh-faced, Nora pushed her face into her pillow and shed more tears no one ever knew about, the way she preferred it.

Later in the day a knock came on Nora's door. Her mother gently opened it before Nora answered and she slunk through the door, Dior makeup bag that had seen better days in hand. She took a seat next to Nora on her bed and hesitated before softly rubbing Nora's back, saying, "I'll show you the right way to do your makeup." But it had only made Nora feel worse, because she didn't know she'd done it wrong. Nora didn't want makeup on anymore; the moment had been marred. But she nodded silently anyway, and let her mother work.

Her loose curls fell in Nora's face, tongue pressed between her lips as her brow furrowed and she gently patted moisturizer over Nora's swollen face from an expensive-looking bottle. The moment had been so confusing for Nora; she didn't understand what the big deal was about putting some makeup on, especially since all of her friends already wore it to school. And then there her mother was, taking time and care like an artist working on her greatest masterpiece, brushing foundation across her face, the bristles tickling her cheeks. She was worried she'd receive an equally explosive reaction if she asked her why she'd gotten angry, so she didn't say a word, didn't dare ask questions, as her mother finished instructing her. She wanted her to say she was sorry, but she knew that this *was* her apology. Now that Nora was older, she understood what happened. She didn't always handle it the right way, and this had been a prime example, but it seemed so clear now. She hadn't been ready for her girl to grow up.

Nora rose from the mirror and slinked into her dress, adjusting and pulling and smoothing until she got it to look right. As she moved in and out of her bathroom while she searched through heaps of eyeshadow palettes for the perfect shade of bronze and ran a flat-iron over her hair, she noticed that a fly she'd spotted that morning still stood on the bathroom mirror above the sink, its body perpendicular with the wall, its head facing down. She moved down the counter until the fly aligned on the mirror with her face. She imagined her face morphing into his, becoming a woman with an insect for a head, wondering what it would be like to live in such isolation, where no one would dare interact with the strange girl who was half insect. Each time she visited the bathroom, she took note that the fly had not moved. A zebra spider sitting in the right corner of the ceiling sat still, watching them, and would surely hunt him eventually. As she stopped in one more time before heading downstairs to wait for Eli, she leaned in closer, peering at it quizzically. She normally didn't look this closely at her own face in the mirror, the imperfections too near. But the fly had her curiosity piqued. Was it dead? No. She could see its antennae moving, registering her presence. Why hadn't it moved all day? It was making itself a sitting target, letting any lurking predators know where he was and that he didn't plan on relocating to a safer spot, or even moving at all. She was used to black flies that were impossible to catch, buzzing around her head as she swatted the heavy summer air, never coming close to actually killing one - they were too quick. This little guy seemed like he wasn't going anywhere. She felt a strange affection for him, and though she deduced that she could easily squash him with a tissue, she didn't. She kind of liked his being there. She killed the spider instead.

Eli looked even more dapper than he usually did when he arrived at her doorstep, clad in a tailored charcoal suit and a navy tie, hair gelled so it shone, perfectly complimenting his naturally tanned skin. She grinned at him, felt her heart flutter when she noticed he had matched his tie to the color of her dress. It was little things like this that made it so easy to forgive him for everything else.

"Hi gorgeous," he grinned, and she could swear her heart skipped a beat.

"I look okay?" She flashed him a flirty grin as she twirled in front of him.

"Stunning." He held his hands up like he was taking a mental photo of her, and she blushed, but she relished the attention. Maybe this night would be all right after all.

Eli strode to his Supra, a limited edition sports car that Nora knew was rare and therefore expensive, and he opened the door for her, gently brushing a loose strand of hair behind her ear as they locked eyes, and he grinned his goofy grin at her, and her heart pounded in her chest like it hadn't in months.

"You feeling okay, Nori?" he asked sweetly, and he rubbed her bare knee as he stole a glance at her as he drove.

"Yeah, I'm feeling okay. A little tired, but I'm all right."

"Your head's okay, though?"

She grinned.

"Yes, Eli. I'm fine."

"I'm excited for tonight." He raised his eyebrows playfully.

"Oh, yeah?"

"Yeah." He winked at her, and she turned to the window so he couldn't see her blush. "We haven't been out together in a while. We're due for some fun."

She hadn't been inside a church since her dad's funeral, but she didn't realize it until they arrived in front of the looming, ornate structure. She felt her body stiffen, considering yet another thing that reminded her of her parents. She wondered if one day that would change, or if she were destined to live in this purgatory between her two lives, the before and the after, until she eventually joined their ashes. The rain had cleared in time for the wedding, the grey skies suddenly parting. She took Eli's arm as her heels scuffed over the wet pavement, the only indication there had been a storm. She sucked in a deep breath and held it while Eli opened the heavy ligneous door as she walked inside, the bell tolling for six o'clock. She smoothed her satin dress down the sides, clutch in hand, as she scanned the church for Erica. She spotted the little black dress before she saw Erica's face, the short length elongating her legs even more than they already were, her olive skin even darker than usual from working outside for the parks and recreation department that summer. Nora had thought she'd looked good, maybe even *hot*, until she saw Erica's low-cut minidress that hit her in all the right places. Once again, she was shrinking in Erica's shadow, even with Eli by her side.

Erica's eyes met hers, and she waved them towards her. Past the pink bows on the ends of the pews, Nora and Eli huddled into the wooden bench. Nora subconsciously pulled her dress down the inch it had ridden up when she walked down the aisle as she took her seat next to Erica.

"Thank God you guys are here. I don't know anyone else," Erica whispered as she surveyed the room.

Relief washed over Nora once she realized that Erica was glad to see her. She wasn't sure how they had left things at their last meeting, and there seemed to be a stiffness between them that hadn't occurred since an argument over Eli years ago.

But today, Erica seemed back to normal. She opened her purse and lifted a silver flask from inside, shaking its contents back and forth with a smirk as she lifted her eyebrows playfully. It reminded Nora of their high school days, when Erica would look back at her over her shoulder, smiling naughtily, as she climbed out her window onto her roof, six-pack of beer in hand. Nora would always follow, cautiously, and they would sit and drink and smoke cigarettes as they talked about trivial things such as boys and gossip, and deeper things, like what they each thought happens when people die, until the sun started to come up. Nora said she believed in heaven, and Erica believed in reincarnation. She wondered now if Erica's beliefs had changed the way hers had.

Nora put her hand out for the flask, and Erica passed it to her, eyes widening with surprise and delight. Nora wanted to have fun, but more than anything, she wanted to forget.

By the time they left the church, Nora was already wobbly in her heels. She felt warm and dizzy and weightless on Eli's arm as they headed toward the reception hall, partially due to the vodka, and partially because Eli had squeezed her hand as Charlotte and Robert recited their vows to each other.

The reception space glittered with gold and pink shimmer, and Nora smiled at how much it looked like Charlotte. Maybe she had been too rash. Maybe they could get close again. Or maybe she was just drunk.

She searched for her escort card on the table outside the reception hall, smiling to herself at the calligraphy that noted Eli as her date. She plopped down at table 12, tossing the card on the white linen that covered the table. Erica took the seat to her right, and Eli her left. She didn't recognize anyone else sitting with them, barely gave any of them a glance - until a statuesque young woman in an emerald dress that matched her eyes gracefully stuck her hand out across the table and introduced herself as Angel.

Any other day, Nora would have simply exchanged pleasantries and forgotten all about her the second after they met so she could get back to flirting with Eli, but this girl brought a sickening sense of familiarity, the kind that brought instant panic. She wasn't a dead ringer for her, but she resembled Caroline.

Nora instinctively grabbed the champagne the waiter had placed in front of her ahead of the toast, and downed it despite the bride and groom not yet being announced. She didn't care that it was bad luck. She didn't believe in luck, anyway.

She imagined Angel as Caroline's cousin, someone who had lost their family member and was desperately searching for answers, while Nora sat across from her, inside a moment of happiness, sandwiched between her best friend and her love interest. Though the scene played out only in her head, guilt engulfed her. Here she was enjoying herself just weeks after a woman had been killed, and there was Caroline's doppelgänger to look her in the face while she did it. She excused herself and made her way to the bar for something stronger than champagne.

Nora didn't know if it was the whiskey or the fact that she was at a wedding, or maybe the events of the past two weeks had been catching up to her. As she danced with Eli through the night, she suddenly felt as intensely for him as she had the day she kissed him in his doorway. She felt closer to him today than she had in months. The way he looked at her directly in her eyes, his strong hands gripping onto her, pulling her close as the dance floor surrounding them seemed to disappear. Every touch of his hands on her hips was electric, and every so often they'd slip lower until they were resting on the top of her backside. Their bodies kissed each time they swayed in the low violet lights, until she leaned her head on his shoulder and he bent his head so his nose was in her hair, breathing her in. She couldn't help but smile to herself as she realized she could feel that this was happening again.

On the way out of the reception, Eli slung his coat over her shoulders, and she clung to it as she strode beside him to his car.

She could see out of the corner of her eye that he was stealing little glances at her. It was past midnight, and she was in the haze that only accompanies a drunken romantic encounter. The quiet darkness surrounding the two of them inside his car made it feel like a dream sequence. She stretched her body over to the driver's seat, chest pressed into his right shoulder, her breath just barely grazing his ear as she whispered, "Let's go to your place," and he grinned, immediately shifting into gear.

She wanted to be with Eli, but more than that, she truly did not want to go home, to return to reality. She wanted to stay in the bubble a while longer, inside a moment of normalcy.

Erica watched from the Uber she'd requested as Nora stepped into Eli's car, smiling drunkenly at him as he shut the door for her. Saw her lean over and whisper into his ear, saw the back of Eli's ears turn up as he grinned. She watched them pull away, turning right instead of left onto the main road, so she knew they were heading to his place instead of Nora's. She shook her head in exasperation and closed her eyes as she felt the car roll off to take her home.

TWENTY-FIVE

Casey's eyes shot open. She'd dozed off after the man came to visit, the way she always did after he left and the drugs coursed its way through her veins. But she woke up feeling something she hadn't in a long time. Anger. She was done accepting this. This wasn't going to be her life anymore. Today, it was time to fight.

It was the first time since she'd been abducted that she'd remembered - really remembered - who she was. She was no coward. She was Casey. The girl who got so angry over a school bully taking her friend's lunch money that she'd punched her in the back of the head. The girl who petitioned to start a lacrosse team at her school and led them to victory in a violent final game. The girl who no one at school messed with, because they knew better.

Her name was not Virginia. She did not want to read children's books to soothe a man who held her captive. She did not want to feel his disgusting embrace or wear his disgusting clothes or look at his disgusting face ever again. Escape meant risking he'd kill her. But if she stayed, she was already dead.

She sat up, willing the nausea down, gently smacking her cheeks as she geared herself up to think. She didn't know how, but when the time was right, she was going to escape. She was getting out. She could feel it in her bones.

TWENTY-SIX

As Nora pushed her key into the lock, she waved to her new neighbors across the street as the family bustled from their minivan to their house, arms full of paper bagged groceries as children yelled to each other indecipherably. She felt a weight lift as they smiled at her and waved back. It was important to her that they felt like they made the right decision moving in, so she made an effort to make them feel welcome any time she saw them. The homes on her block had remained more or less the same since she was born, save for a fresh coat of paint on a few shutters or a new set of windows, but the families living in them had mostly moved on. The kids she'd grown up with were long gone, most of them moving into the city, and their parents had downsized from their grand Victorian homes that required a great deal of upkeep to something more manageable as they aged. Each time she saw a 'For Sale' sign go up, a small piece of Nora felt less connected to the neighborhood. She yearned for the nostalgia of racing her bike up and down the block, naming the families aloud as she passed each home - ten houses down, the Kline house, was where she had to turn around, diligently using their driveway as a u-turn without ever thinking twice about breaching the verbal contract her parents had enacted in exchange for her going alone. The Klines had long moved on.

She watched as a German Shepherd greeted the family at the door, and they tousled his fur as they crossed through the entryway. She'd always wanted a dog, but the thought of caring for an animal that relied solely on her seemed like a responsibility she wasn't quite ready to take on. The thought had crossed her mind again after the break-in, but instead, she'd opted for a camera system. If they came back - for whatever it was they were after - she'd at least catch them in the act. She almost wished they would come back, so at least she could see who it was that was disrupting her life. Maybe it would become clear what their end-game was. She wondered if her neighbors wanted to know what was going on over there in that old house with the lonely girl, who within the course of a week had come home with no car, had police stationed outside her door, and had installed a noticeable camera on the scaffolding covering her porch. She didn't want them to fear their new neighborhood, or to become too afraid to associate with her.

She sighed as she tossed her keys on the table and started to really think about the events of the night prior. Eli had always been clear that he was uninterested in being tied down to a relationship, and lately, she'd been acting as if the past had taught her nothing. She'd let the romance of the wedding cloud her vision and the liquor make her brave. But now, it seemed clearer that she'd made a mistake, because she'd been down this road with him before.

When they'd first started sleeping together two years ago, she'd convinced herself that she didn't care about his past, about his reputation as a womanizer. She secretly wore it like a badge of honor, that this gorgeous Casanova had come back for more. He'd chosen her to spend his nights with when he could have had anyone else, and they spent most of their time lazily in bed, laughing and sharing memories of their parents and dreams for the future. Eli looked almost sheepish as he shared that he wanted to open his own brokerage, and she hadn't truly known until she said it out loud, but she wanted to go back to school so she could finally become a journalist. Dreams, she was sure, they didn't share with anyone else. But he was always difficult to pin down, and she saw how easily he chatted up other women, well after their relationship had turned physical. She'd told herself he was busy working. He was just a flirt. He liked the attention. It was harmless. When the conversation with a beautiful stranger ended, he was coming back to *her*. She doubted he ever - no, she was certain he didn't - speak to other women the way he spoke to her. She could see it in his eyes one night, toward the end of an hours-long conversation in his bedroom that went into the wee hours of the morning - he'd hesitated before saying "never mind", but she knew in her heart that he had wanted to tell her he loved her.

She wanted to be near him whenever she could, to take in his scent of cloves and cinnamon as he wrapped her in a bear hug whenever she saw him, nestling her cheek into his soft, black hair. A huge grin plastered her face whenever they were together, even though she knew it was obvious to him and to everyone else that she was more interested in him than he was in her. He didn't prioritize their meetings over work or the gym or even nights out with his drinking buddies, but she assured herself it was part of the deal they'd made, and that eventually, he'd start to become more available as things got more serious. She had even had a brief pregnancy scare, and he'd been so supportive, holding her hand as she shook and silent tears fell down her face while they waited the longest two minutes she could imagine outside the closed bathroom door, as if the test may be nuclear and explode onto her.

He'd rubbed her shoulders and kissed her forehead as they waited, seated beside each other in the hallway. "It's going to be okay. No matter the outcome. We'll figure it out," he'd assured her, and his voice never wavered. She had always imagined she'd be a mother someday, but she wasn't ready. She could barely take care of herself, and that had suddenly become startlingly clear. She'd nearly gasped at the negative result, laughing through more tears, and he'd taken her into his arms and moved his hands gently through her hair, whispering in her ear that it was okay, she was okay. She remembered, vividly, how grateful she was to have gone through it with Eli. But in the following days he became more evasive, and she heard from Charlotte that she'd run into Eli at a bar downtown with a friend. When Nora pressed her on whether the friend was female, Charlotte's face had flushed, and Nora had her answer. She eventually got the hint that this thing they had - she refused to call it 'friends with benefits', because she knew it was more than that - was never going to progress the way she wanted it to, and she felt like she had no choice but to end the relationship.

She'd been too nervous to talk to him in person, so when he'd texted her at midnight one Thursday after a night out asking if she wanted to come over, she'd responded that she couldn't, and that she didn't think they should sleep together anymore. *I don't want to lose you as a friend*, she'd said. *You mean a lot to me, and I don't want either of us to get hurt.* She pressed send before she could second-guess herself.

It's cool. See you this weekend! His only response, and the last they'd spoken of it.

Even though it had been her decision to end it, his lack of reaction had stung like he'd slapped her. She'd even thought that maybe he'd change his mind about wanting to be single. Maybe he'd text her the next day saying he missed her, that maybe they should give it a real shot. But that conversation never came. She felt more stupid than she ever had. Ashamed that she thought they were something that they weren't, that he could have changed for her. She'd cried to Erica about it, how she felt like an idiot, that she didn't want things to be weird between all of their friends now that everyone knew it was over. Erica had assured her that this wasn't her fault, and she'd had nothing but nasty things to say about him - that he was arrogant, and selfish, and that he'd "always been a douchebag."

But Nora's feelings of disappointment eased when Eli kept

calling, kept wanting to be in her life even when the physical aspect of their relationship was over. They would go out for drinks in the city or go for walks around her neighborhood together, and they would leave separately, hugging goodbye like old friends, as if they had never been together in a physical way. She'd felt awkward at first, timidly approaching their table of mutual friends and avoiding eye contact with him until he came over and wrapped her up in the embrace she'd grown to cherish. They found their rhythm again easily, and she tried not to make it obvious that she looked forward to seeing him, putting a little extra effort into her appearance any time she knew they'd see each other.

Over time, she found that though she cared for him more than she could remember ever caring for another man, she had more control as friends. There was no more waiting around for him to call on her - at least, not that she'd let on. Now, she took just as long to answer him as he had for her, a silent punishment of sorts while she could pretend that she was too busy for him, even though it had taken practice and restraint and a scolding from Erica to get there. Maybe this was better, that he respected her and wanted her company even though they didn't have sex anymore. Or so she'd told herself. Now, she was back to square one.

She couldn't help thinking that this time felt different, though. He'd been more attentive than he'd ever been, showing her affection in intimate ways he hadn't since that day outside the bathroom, brushing her hair from her face when it covered her eyes, gently leaning her shoulder into his chest to steady her as she struggled to walk through a whiskey-induced fog. He'd shown real interest when she'd told him about what she was working on with David, allowing her to go on and on about it without interruption, urging her to keep working on it and to keep fostering her relationship with her uncle. That was more than she'd gotten from Erica. Maybe seeing her in the hospital had upset him. Maybe the accident had been a blessing in disguise, had made him realize he cared about her more than he realized. He'd turned 30 earlier in the year; maybe he'd had a moment of clarity, and he was finally ready to settle down.

He was gone when she woke up that morning, and her solitude in his apartment had brought back memories of so many times she'd been left there in the past. He was an early riser, so he'd be at the gym or at work by the time she woke up after spending the night. She'd gotten used to watching the cherry wood headboard as she lazed on her back before rising to look out at the towers of the city, her favorite view, a view even she, with her inheritance, couldn't afford. She yawned as she stretched and moved her gaze to the neatly stacked rows of old records above the player, seeing that Sinatra topped the collection, wondering if she had time to sort through them before he got back. She thought better of it and moved past a whiteboard in the living room covered with Eli's perfect, small handwriting displaying graphs and numbers and blocks of three letters that she never even tried to understand, and out into the kitchen, its stainless stove untouched since he'd moved in. She pulled a ballpoint pen and pad from a drawer to leave him a note that she'd gone home. Her hand hovered over the paper, wondering whether she should leave a little heart on it to show she was interested, but of course he knew she was interested. He bounded through the door before she could make her mind up, fresh coffee for them both in tow, and she'd crumpled the note and shoved it into the sagging sweatpants he'd lent her. He asked her to stay longer, and the twinkle in his eye and the hand he slipped slyly around her waist told her what that meant. She'd said she wanted to get some rest, watching his face as she sipped the coffee he'd ordered just right, iced lavender latte with an extra shot of espresso. He'd kissed her with vigor on her way out, saying he'd call her later as she thumbed the silver chain over his chest. She found herself thinking that maybe it was possible for leopards to change their spots.

A text from Eli popped in. *I miss you already.* Her heart fluttered as she responded that she'd see him tomorrow.

She smiled to herself before stretching out on her bed, kicking off her heels and wrapping herself up in her duvet, the warmth enveloping her body like velvet. *It feels so nice to think about something normal*, she thought wistfully, before drifting off into a deep sleep.

TWENTY-SEVEN

"**B**uenas días, Mami." Erica wrapped her long, slender arms around her mother's tiny waist from behind her, resting her head on her mother's shoulder as she squeezed.

"Buenas días, Mija. ¿Como estuvo la boda?" Gloria turned to face Erica, lifted her hands to cup Erica's cheeks and gently brushed her fingers under Erica's eyes.

"The wedding was good." Erica grabbed an apple from the counter and slid into the orange booth that wrapped around her kitchen table, taking a juicy bite and stretching her arms above her head as she yawned.

She drummed her fingers against the pictures of fruit that lined the cracks in the table and stared off, her brain foggy, but clear that something was off.

"What's wrong, Mija?" Gloria's face turned to concern and she slipped into the booth across from her daughter, sliding a coffee across the table to her. Gloria was seven inches shorter than Erica, standing at a mere 5'1", but when they sat at the kitchen table to have their big talks, the table was the great equalizer. Erica had gotten her height and her athleticism from her father, but the strong intuition, the feisty personality, the passion to stand up for what was right, no matter who she was telling they were wrong - that all came from Gloria, and she lit up every time she saw it reflected in her daughter. In the few moments that Erica looked lost like this, it tormented her.

Erica had always been a precocious child. With an IQ of 125 at just seven years old, Gloria knew that her daughter wasn't going to be an easy one to parent, and Erica had proved her right. She'd challenged authority at every turn, giving all of her teachers a run for their money. When she lovingly characterized Erica as 'bossy' to their family, she knew she was putting it lightly. Rather than watch cartoons as a child, Erica preferred to build intricate homes with her blocks or line up the vegetables in her play garden just so, in perfect, perpendicular lines. Gloria never questioned her or tried to guide her toward a different activity; she knew it would be a battle she'd lose. Instead, she would assist silently with a ruler when the eye became too unreliable for Erica's liking. She'd watch her daughter carefully, tiny fingers gently patting the clay soil as if a real carrot or turnip were to sprout at any moment.

She'd let her grow into the woman she was meant to become. She'd taken a job at the Parks & Recreation department because she loved the outdoors and the hours allowed her to attend law school in the evening. She'd completed her Juris Doctor in just two years, and she passed the bar exam on her first try. She always knew the answer, no matter the given situation, even when she pretended not to.

But here she was, mulling over Nora's behavior, without a clue what to do about it. It was clear to Erica that Nora was slipping back into self-destructive habits, but she didn't want to start a fight with her about it.

She'd wrestled with herself before deciding against calling 911 after she'd pumped the water from Nora's chest after finding her unconscious in the tub, but she was protecting her the only way she knew how. The same way she'd protected Nora when they both cheated on a math test in junior year and she took the blame for both of them, accepting a zero even though she knew she'd catch hell for it from her mom. The same way Nora had protected her when Erica got too drunk at a party at her own house, banishing everyone outside as she held her hair and rubbing her back while the night's events wretched from her body and into the toilet. An unspoken pact of sisterhood. Putting each other before themselves.

She'd mentioned Nora's struggle with depression to her only once since, in an attempt to gauge how she was feeling, but Nora had tensed up, barely able to stammer "I'm fine" before pivoting to the subject of reality TV, so she didn't ask about it again. It killed her, not knowing. But she'd watched her, carefully. After she tried to kill herself, she started seeing a therapist, but she went through a brief period where Erica could tell she was drinking too much. Any time Eli called her, she'd drop everyone else - Erica included - like a bad habit. She could deal with the lack of text exchanges while Nora was grieving, but to suddenly have plenty of time to talk to Eli was a slap in the face. Erica had snapped one day in her own house, after Nora spent a girls' night texting Eli instead of laughing along with her during their monthly 80s rom-com marathon. Nora had barely lifted her head as she revealed she'd be leaving early to go meet him. Erica had clamored to her feet, hovering over Nora in a wave of fury. She'd told her that she was sick of playing second fiddle to a guy who would never be Nora's boyfriend, that she'd better get her shit together before she didn't have any friends left. Nora just glared back at her, face beet red with tears in her eyes, and stormed out without saying a word.

She had been treating Nora with kid gloves since her parents had died, and all of her frustrations had come out at once. She felt guilty about her delivery, but the sentiment was true. Eli was a fair-weather playboy who she knew would leave her feeling depressed and inadequate, and that's not what Nora needed. Frankly, Erica was sick of hearing about a guy who would inevitably break Nora's heart.

Erica knew Nora would never be the first to mention their fight, so she'd made the first gesture and apologized the next day for overreacting. Nora had said it wasn't a big deal, but she felt that something shifted between them on that day. Nora never wanted to deal with confrontation, even when it was necessary. At times, Erica tried to get her to engage in an argument - sometimes, just to see how far she could push it - but Nora would rather sweep everything under the rug. But after this squabble she seemed standoffish, and things weren't quite the same between them until she had, shockingly, ended things with Eli. Erica had been right about him, of course, but she'd decided it was kinder if she refrained from pointing that out.

Now, Eli was back, in the midst of another Nora Crisis. It was no surprise - the one time Nora attempted to meet someone new, a fiasco ensued, and he'd been waiting in the wings to save her. She was sure it wasn't a coincidence. Whenever Nora was experiencing a moment of weakness, there he was. *This dude is a cockroach.*

Erica sighed.

"Just thinking about Nora, Mami. It's no big deal. Don't worry about it." She offered a meek smile and squeezed her mom's hand from across the table to prove she was okay so that she wouldn't agonize over it too much. She knew it was an insane ask; her mother constantly worried about her, whether it was warranted or not.

As she always did, she offered Erica a knowing smile, and simply stated, "It's my job to worry about you, Mija."

Erica never chastised her mami anymore. They had always been close, but Erica knew she hadn't exactly made her mom's life easier when she was a teenager, constantly coming home after curfew and exploding at even the implication that her mother suggested she was out drinking - which, of course she had been, but she'd never let her mom have the satisfaction of a proper scolding. After Nora's mother passed away, their bond had become inexplicably stronger. They had known Nora's family for years, and they both took the unexpected death hard, clutching each other's hands at the funeral as if at any moment it could be one of them in the casket.

She still felt a pang of guilt every time she complained about her mom to Nora, because Nora would never have the chance to fight with her own mother again. When she talked about going shopping or to dinner with her mami, she could swear she saw disappointment in Nora's face, which was understandable; she would never experience another memory with her own parents, even the most mundane everyday moments. It was the only subject she tiptoed around, because she truly did not want to upset her friend. She didn't know how to talk to her about it, so she thought it was best to avoid the subject as much as she possibly could.

"Is Nora okay? That poor girl has been through enough." Gloria shook her head.

Erica swept her hair into a loose bun and said, "Yeah, yeah, mami. Just girl stuff. Eli's back." She rolled her eyes and chuckled to put her mom at ease, though she didn't feel much like laughing. She felt anger, deep and intense, boiling under her skin. Nora was shutting her out, and she suspected Eli was the root cause.

He was slick, and she knew better than to ever give credibility to someone like that. Everything about him made Erica sick. His arrogance. His need to gain the affection of every female in the room, right in front of Nora while she pretended not to see. His carefree nature while upending Nora's life. The guy was untrustworthy, at best. Erica was constantly looking into his eyes whenever they were in the same place, trying to work out what his deal was. He was good-looking, she had to admit - though he was much too clean-cut to be her type. And from what she could tell, from his designer shoes to his constant need to pay the tab for the group, pretty well off. But any time she heard him talk, it was artificial. All bullshit. She barely knew anything about him, and it seemed like Nora didn't, either. Or if she did, she never shared it with Erica.

Though they rarely spoke beyond the mundane conversation

of acquaintances, she could feel his presence was back just watching Nora's demeanor. She wasn't fully there when they spoke to each other. Half-listening, bailing last minute every time she was supposed to come over. That was the problem with Eli - he wasn't just playing with Nora, who was all too happy to accommodate anything he asked of her. Was he the one encouraging Nora to play detective? Now this melodrama was trickling into hers.

"Oh no, not again. What is it this time?"

Erica shook her head, staring off as she cracked her knuckles. "I don't know. But I'm gonna find out."

Erica sat with her windows cracked, fingers floating in front of the vents, gently brushing her sea salt freshener as the air conditioning blasted her face. She needed better vision past her tinted windows without the possibility of being seen.

Eli stood with perfect posture in his tailored suit at the desk of O'Malley's Laundromat several yards in front of her before grabbing an armload of items covered in plastic from the clerk.

Erica watched as he exited the building, effortlessly weaving through the bustling hordes of people that trickled in and out of the colorful shops on Tressler street, and hung the items in the passenger side of his car. She readied herself to shift into Drive, but after he closed the car door he kept walking, crossing the street to a coffee shop at the corner. *Aha.*

Either he was meeting someone at the shop, or he'd leave with two drinks, giving him away.

At the wedding, it was clear that Nora and Eli were back to being - what could she call it? *Fuck buddies? Nora wouldn't like that,* she thought, giggling to herself devilishly. The two were inseparable, pawing at each other like high school kids. Nora had barely talked to Erica the entire night. Nora had called her this afternoon, pretending like she was calling for their usual gossip session after an event, and then not-so-casually dropping that she'd spent the night at Eli's. She'd braced as she waited for Erica's reaction, and Erica had replied, "No shit."

Nora told her she felt like things were different this time. Erica had heard it all before. She'd clearly rehearsed what she was going to say, getting herself worked up for no reason. No point in chastising her. All Erica ever wanted to do was protect her, and in any case, Nora needed a great deal of protecting.

Her eyes fell to the orange folder sitting beside her in the passenger seat, its contents hidden, though she'd read the documents so closely she could recite the lines from memory. An associate attorney offer from Stearns, Canning, & Brooks, one of the most prestigious law firms in New York City. A fat salary. Opportunities for domestic and international travel. Civil litigation, where she could stick it to the man. A job she knew she couldn't take until Nora was steadier on her feet.

She'd been noticing a lot of changes in Nora lately. She'd been more assertive in little ways - she'd first noticed when Nora, for the first time in her life, had sent back a drink that was made incorrectly. Erica beamed with pride; she was finally rubbing off on her. But she was clearly exhausted. She had bags under her eyes, and she was nearly skin and bones. Her mind seemed unclear, and she only half-listened when Erica spoke. And Eli was problemo numero uno. Once he was out of the picture, she was confident the rest of Nora's problems would follow suit. But Nora never liked to be told what to do, and *that* Erica understood. So she was going to get proof about the kind of man Eli was so they could kick him to the curb for good. She'd waited outside of his apartment complex as she surrounded herself in the aggressive energy of old-school hip-hop, the bass vibrating through her bones as it amplified her mood, and as if on cue, Eli pulled out from beyond the gates of his building. She felt a surge of adrenaline and pulled out of the lot, following a few car lengths behind him, and he hadn't gone far before pulling into the heart of downtown.

She had expected Nora to ask her to come over and thought she'd have to come up with an excuse about why she couldn't, but she'd said she had to work on the case. It was weird, how much time she'd been spending with David, working on something so morbid. It seemed like such a strange thing to be interested in. But she didn't knock her for it. Nora needed a hobby, and more than that, she needed real family. Especially now, with a brand new trauma rearing its ugly head. There was no doubt that Nora was working through some heavy PTSD, experiencing a painful accident the same way that her mother died. But she wasn't sure this was the greatest idea, to be helping with murder cases. She made a mental note to make sure Nora was still seeing her therapist.

She couldn't see Eli once he'd disappeared inside the coffee shop - only the pattern of dark bricks and the edge of its red awning hovering over two wrought iron tables outside. She turned her attention to the effects inside his car. She squinted to decipher the outline of the garment bag he'd retrieved. The O'Malley's logo blocked most of the contents, but she could see that whatever was hanging there was a blush color, and it looked like it was silk or satin. She grinned smugly. Eli wasn't exactly the type to wear blush.

She debated risking getting out of the car to peer through the window and see if he'd grabbed a table, and then she could take a closer look. She rubbed peach lip balm on her naturally full lips as she watched herself in the side mirror. She was pretty proud of her sneak-around clothes, with her hair, usually cascading down her back, tucked up inside a plain baseball cap. She never wore t-shirts when she wasn't at work, preferring a bolder, sexier look, but today she was wearing a black tee normally reserved for the hours she spent cleaning her car every month. *Let's see what you're so busy doing.* It was kind of exciting, watching someone who didn't know she was there. Especially such an asshole.

She mapped out the best route to take, ready to make the one solid second she'd have count. She'd pass the shop and cross the street down to the haughty boutiques on 4th Avenue before he could catch a glimpse of her. She'd duck into one of them if she had to, pull a *Pretty Woman* since she was practically in rags. Before opening her door to check out what was happening in the shop, she closed it again abruptly and covered her face with her hand as Eli walked out alone. One coffee.

Her heart pounded as he stopped, seemingly jogging toward her, but he doubled back and bent low, lending a strapping arm to an elderly woman hobbling across the street, who looked all too grateful to have a handsome young man like him to help her. She thanked him profusely, and dimpled cheeks turned up in a big smile as he waved good-bye to the stranger he'd escorted. Erica rolled her eyes and to no one but herself, said, *"please."* No one patted himself on the back quite like Eli.

She waited a beat before pulling behind his Supra, slipping her Audrey Hepburn sunglasses on and making sure once more not to get too close to his car. Was he going to a girl's house? Heading out for the night? She squinted in confusion as he turned back in the direction of his building. Nora always talked about Eli being a workaholic, but Erica had assumed that was an excuse to spend time with other women. Could it be possible that he said he was busy because he actually had work to do?

Eli lived in a posh structure with a doorman and the gate to his lot was guarded at all hours. She thought briefly about flirting with the gate operator to get inside the lot, then remembered how she was dressed and cursed herself for playing down her features for once. She wouldn't be able to slip in, but she could wait a bit to see if he left again. He was a night owl, and it was barely 8:00.

She allowed her car to get closer to see if she could get one last look at the garment bag, readying herself to cover her face as she passed by, but just before he turned right to get into his lot, she caught him looking at her. Quick as a flash, but the intensity of his golden eyes were unmistakable. She opened her mouth in shock and sucked in sharply, but quickly shut it and kept her face expressionless, remembering that he couldn't see her seeing him behind her sunglasses. She dared to look again as he turned, waiting to see if he would watch her pass, but his attention had turned completely to the young man at the gate, and Eli said something, and they both erupted in laughter before the electric fence swung open and Eli waved goodbye to the man, gone in a flash.

She could swear she'd been caught, but he'd moved right past, as if he hadn't seen her.

But he had to have seen her.

Now things were getting interesting.

TWENTY-EIGHT

Nora lay sprawled out in her bed as instrumental music flowed from her phone, thinking about the call she'd had with Erica that afternoon. She'd said so many things: she thought she and Eli were going to give it a real shot. Had she used the word 'exclusive'? He hadn't explicitly said that's what he wanted, but they'd texted all day, and they already had plans to go to the old cinema that week to catch a showing of *Casablanca*. He'd asked her to stay that morning, and she'd been the one who decided to leave. She didn't want to leave. Ever. She didn't want to dance at a wedding with anyone else, ever again. She'd said as much to Erica, who had gotten quiet. She'd barely squeaked out a "Hm." And then she'd changed the subject.

Oh, well. She couldn't bother to find meaning in the silences and inflections that Erica used anymore. It didn't seem as important, with everything that had happened. It wasn't long before the facts of Caroline's case drifted in her mind as the ebbs and flows of violas gave way to piano.

After she'd revealed the break-in to David, he suggested she do a better survey of her house than she had the day it happened, look through every room again, sort through drawers and take better note of minor changes that the intruder could have made. She didn't know what she could possibly find after so much time had passed, but she decided he was probably right, and she knew he'd ask about it when she went to his house that evening. She begrudgingly made her way downstairs to take a better look.

She started in the kitchen, sifting through old spices in the pantry and cookware in cupboard doors. A thin layer of dust settled on the rims of the pots and pans, and an insect of some kind scattered as light broke in through the door. Not a finger had swiped over them.

She sifted through her junk drawer next, stuffed full of takeout menus and receipts and odds and ends she could never find a good place for. Nothing she hadn't put there herself. If someone had taken anything, she wouldn't even know. Things only went into the drawer, and never got looked at again.

She spun around, hands on her hips, and bit her lip. *If I were a burglar, where would I look?*

She started from the beginning and moved to the front of the house. She imagined slipping through the front door - somehow, unlocked. She'd been so sure she'd locked it, but when the police had pressed her on it, they'd looked like they didn't believe her, and she started to second-guess herself. It wasn't like her to leave it open, but she'd been so exhausted, her mind so out of sorts from the accident, that she assumed she must have.

There wasn't much to look at in the foyer; she'd already replaced the flowers that sat on the table by the stairs. The family room to the right had only couches and a television. She lazily bent down to check underneath them. Nothing but dust bunnies.

She made her way to the den in the back of the house, checked the back door for a second time for signs of anything strange, and came up empty.

She stopped as she arrived at her dad's desk. She normally barely glanced in its direction, but now she took it in. The cherry wood had dulled from the sunlight and dust had settled on it the way it had on the cookware. It hadn't been touched since he'd died. *I guess now is as good a time as any.*

She picked up the papers that sat atop his legal pad that were now caked with grime. Bills from two years prior. They'd been marked past due, but she knew money wasn't the issue. He'd never recovered after her mom had died, and the mundane of everyday life had been too much for him to handle without her. No one had said it out loud, at least not in her presence, but she'd read about it in stories of older couples who died within days of each other. He'd been much younger than the couples in the articles she'd read, but she knew the connection her parents had with each other, and what it meant for him when her mother had died. He died of a broken heart.

She'd felt guilty that her father's death hadn't been as hard for her as her mother's. She loved him just as much, and she missed him every day. But she knew once her mother died, that the man who was her father had died with her. She'd never tell anyone, not even her therapist, but in some ways, she thought it had been a gift that he didn't have to go on without her. The heart attack had taken him quickly, and now, at least, he wasn't in pain anymore. She shook her head and ignored the tears that threatened to fall from the pain that pricked the back of her eyes.

She winced as she opened the drawers of his desk, mindlessly sifting through innocuous paperwork. She was thankful her parents had left their life insurance information in a separate folder for her so she didn't have to go through his desk until now. This would have been too painful, to comb through the complexities of her parents' everyday business, invoices from food wholesalers and order forms for cakes for celebrations of all kinds that her father had canceled, like he was just waiting to die. She realized how far she'd come since those first few days alone, when she never would have had the courage or the mental capacity to handle looking through the carnage.

She reached further into the depths of the drawer, until her hand hit something hard and smooth. She squinted, puzzled, and pushed the oblong object against the side of the drawer so she could see what it was, out from under the mountain of papers. When she saw a flash of color, she audibly gasped and ripped her hand from the drawer, as if bitten by a snake lurking inside.

"What the fuck. What the *fuck*?" She said aloud, the volume of her own voice jarring her further. Her heart beat ferociously, and she thought she might actually faint as the blood drained from her face, leaving her an unnatural shade of grey.

Aqua. A case. Surrounding a phone. *Her* phone.

TWENTY-NINE

Nora had run through a range of scattered thoughts before she mustered the courage to pull the phone from the drawer. She set it on the desk and stood staring at it, moving from ringing her hands together to rubbing her face as she paced across the room and back to squeezing them together again. She felt almost immobilized by fear, like she could not do or think of a single thing until she made sense of what was happening to her. What *was* this? *Is someone fucking with me? Is this the world's cruelest, longest, prank? Why would anyone do this to me? Am I crazy?* She was having an out-of-body experience, her mind becoming cloudy.

She could not let another minute pass without telling someone. In any other case, she would call Erica, shrieking, and she'd hurry over. Erica would poke holes in her theories, find an explanation to put her at ease, and that would be that. But she knew this called for someone with a little bit of a different outlook; someone who could provide some kind of explanation as to what was going on. She raced up the stairs to her replacement phone and dialed David, her hands shaking furiously as she forced tears down until they caught in her throat.

"What's up, Nora?" he answered.

"David, I need you to come to my house. *Now*." Her voice had gone shrill, and she didn't even try to attempt to hide her fear. This went beyond her constant need to come across as having her life handled. She understood now that she did not.

"What's going on? Are you okay?" he demanded, and Nora realized his panic mimicked hers.

"No, David. I'm not. My phone is here. The one I lost in the accident. Come now."

"Don't touch it. I'm on my way."

David arrived in uniform straight from work, standing on the porch of a home where he hadn't been welcome for years. He'd lied to the Sheriff and said Briana had needed him, and no one in the station batted an eye since they knew she was ready to give birth any day now.

He exhaled deeply as he allowed himself to gain familiarity again with the stately brick home he'd approached, apprehensively, so many times. Years had passed, and so much had changed, but the house remained, stoic and untouched, and inside its walls, it held feelings of angst. His hands shook as he thought of all the times he'd fought with Irene in this very house. He could hardly remember a time he'd been here that hadn't ended in heartbreak, for him or for his sister. That was how Nora must remember him. When her mother died, she'd thought he was still a junkie. He hadn't mustered up the courage to tell his sister he'd gotten clean, because he wasn't so sure himself that it was going to stick. He didn't want to let her down as he had in the past, and he wasn't ready to tell her all the things he knew he had to say. How yes, he did steal from her and Brian, and he was ready to admit it. That when Brian had grabbed him by the shirt collar and dragged him through the house until he forced him onto the porch and warned him not to come back, he knew he'd deserved it. He'd felt betrayed, because they were the ones he'd leaned on when he needed help the most. That it had been necessary, and he knew that now. How he knew she had still loved him, still wanted to help him when no one else on the planet did, and he'd ruined that too. That he was ready to repair their relationship, if she'd allow it. And then just like that, she was gone, and in her soul, he'd be forever a junkie.

It was painful in a way he hadn't experienced since he'd first heard about Irene, to stand at her doorway and know for certain she wouldn't be the one answering, now, or ever again. She'd always been his protector, from elementary school bullies all the way through his addiction. He'd crumpled into the fetal position in her living room, sweating, gasping for air, when he'd been unable to find money for heroin and came to her, desperate. She never judged him, at least not to his face. She'd wrapped her arms around him and held him there, motioning for Brian to bring her the phone, where he heard her bark orders at a rehabilitation facility that had been full but somehow made room for him. He hadn't been inside the house since he'd been clean, and certainly not since Irene had been gone. But he had to put it all aside, for Nora.

Every time she arrived at his house, he couldn't help but admire the scene unfolding when she and Briana embraced. It had been a thing of his dreams, to connect them. The last time he'd seen Nora, she was just a kid, timid and shy - but when he was goofy with her he could get her to smile, and the innocence of it brought such light to his day. He hadn't seen that smile since. The bony, awkward teenager he was familiar with had transformed into a striking young woman, poised and measured, carrying so much weight on her shoulders.

It was so strange, and so wonderful, how these turn of events were starting to bring them all together. He'd been so uncertain about reaching out to Nora when he noticed her name on the accident report, but he knew it was his only shot at seeing her again.

He'd been secretly thankful it was her that had been in that accident. It had to have been fate.

He took a deep breath and rapped on the door. Nora nearly jumped out of her skin at the heavy knock, though she knew he was coming. It was only a few seconds before she was ushering him inside, wild-eyed and frazzled, looking past him out the front door suspiciously before slamming it shut.

"I know you told me not to touch it, but I had to. I had to look and make sure it was mine. I took the case off and there's a small scratch in the top corner on the back. That's it, it's mine." She spoke hurriedly and excitedly, the words tumbling out faster than she could manage them. She had attempted to turn the phone on, but it was long dead.

David sighed in exasperation, but he empathized with her plight. "It's okay. Grab a baggie, and we'll put it in there. Don't touch it again with your fingers." Nora handed him a Ziploc as he slapped on latex gloves before gently dropping the phone into the bag.

He examined the phone through the plastic.

"Did you notice anything weird? Any blood, hair, markings, anything like that, before you touched it?"

Nora suddenly felt stupid, like a child who had gotten caught with her hand in the cookie jar.

"No, I didn't. I should have tried to look harder. I'm sorry."

"Well, what's done is done. I don't see anything here but I'll have forensics take a look at it."

Nora looked at him desperately as worry shrouded her. She closed her shoulders and made herself small, like no one would be able to see her if she held herself hard enough. "You're going to bring this into the station? Am I going to get in trouble?"

"No. I'm going to send this to the state lab myself, and if anyone asks, I'll say the phone was recovered from the road. But I doubt anyone is going to notice. Did you ever describe your phone or the case to any of the officers?"

"I don't think so. But, I mean, I don't really know *what* I'm doing anymore." She took a seat on the sofa and dropped her head into her hands.

David sat next to her and after a moment of deciding whether he should, he gently rested a hand on her back.

She flinched under his hand but quickly felt the tension ease. He was clearly uncomfortable, but he wanted her to feel safe. She had to admit to herself that she'd unclenched a bit as soon as he'd walked in the door. He'd become a more familiar face than she'd anticipated, and having him here, he felt like the uncle she remembered from when she was just a child, before he'd had a problem that had taken over his life. Until now, she'd forgotten her impression of him before his addiction - that he had been kind, and smart, and sometimes he'd even been fun. It was nice to not be alone in this.

David waited for a moment before removing his hand and taking out his notepad.

"I'll admit, when you told me about the break-in, I wasn't sure it was related," he began. "I didn't see how it would be. But you're sure - and I mean, absolutely *positive* - that you didn't...you didn't have your phone when you came home?" Nora looked at him with surprise and venom in her eyes, but he continued. "You had a concussion, right? Is it possible you just forgot where you put your phone?"

Nora stood up and moved to the couch opposite him. The moment of closeness was over.

She answered him as she shook her head in disgust, practically spitting the words out. "Yes, David. I'm pretty fucking sure. It was a huge ordeal. I didn't have my phone in the *hospital*. I didn't have my phone at the *police station*. I had to get a new one when I got *back*." She ticked off the moments on her fingers as he took notes. "What are you taking notes for? *I didn't have it!*" She screamed angrily. "I know my phone was gone. I was there. If you're going to question everything I say, then you can just get the fuck out of here." She'd lost control of herself completely, disbelieving of the words that escaped her mouth. She was sorry the moment they left her lips.

David flipped his notepad shut and looked at her in surprise, and she could see the hurt in his face, though he tried to keep his expression even. "I'm sorry, I'm sorry. I just...I'm just trying to make sense of all this."

They sat silently, the air thick with intensity.

After a moment of staring anywhere but at each other, he cleared his throat and began carefully.

"Do you have any idea as to how this happened? Or *why* this happened?"

Nora silently shook her head. She was suddenly exhausted. As drained as she'd been when she first arrived home from Woodbridge.

"I'm guessing not, but I have to ask. Do you have anyone you'd consider...you'd consider an enemy? Someone who wants to hurt you? Someone trying to make you...make you question yourself, for some reason?"

"You think someone is trying to gaslight me?" she asked doubtfully, giving him a questioning look. "I really don't think that's what's happening. I don't know anyone who would want to do that. And I don't think anyone I've ever met would consider me an enemy. That seems pretty harsh. And anyway, how would they have gotten my phone? They would have had to have access..." She trailed off, realizing there could only be two options. Only someone with access to her car could have taken her phone. It was either the police, or it was the person who killed Caroline. *Or are those one and the same?* No one else would have had the opportunity. She shuddered, thinking of some creep reaching over her, brushing against her skin, plucking her phone from her car. But why? And why would they then bother to bring it back? *Does Caroline's killer know where I live?* She straightened her back as chills ran down her spine, her distrust for David suddenly renewing.

She stared at him and he stared right back, looking as though he was reading her mind and not knowing how to respond.

"Did the police ever say anything to you about my phone?" she began carefully.

"No. I didn't work the case."

"What about my car? Did you ever see it while they were searching it? Did anyone look like they were...overly interested?" She danced around it, but she wasn't as good at this as David was. He could read between the lines from the way she asked.

"Nora," he began, scooting closer to the edge of the couch so he almost stood, his piercing eyes boring into hers. "I did not do this. I want you to know that. I would never...I would never, ever do that to you. I need you to trust me on this." He seemed desperate for her to believe him, and he spoke very deliberately and sincerely, his hands shaking so slightly it was almost indecipherable.

"I do. I believe you." She didn't. Especially now that he sat across from her, the first time she'd seen him in uniform since she'd noticed his presence walking by her at the station. It almost felt like he was a different person entirely than the one she'd been working with all this time. She didn't know if she would ever trust him. She'd felt herself becoming lax, becoming comfortable, the way she'd promised herself she wouldn't. This was a stark reminder of why she hadn't wanted him around. "I just want to know who would have been able to get a hold of it and then somehow bring it back to me. I thought you might have an idea of who would do something like that. Maybe you work with someone who seems...off."

He shook his head, pondering what she'd asked, before answering. "I don't think any of those guys would have the motivation, or the wherewithal, to do something like that. Except..." He trailed off.

Nora looked at him eagerly, waiting on pins and needles for his answer. But he said nothing.

"Except who?" she demanded.

David cleared his throat.

"I'm just grasping at straws, trying to get this to make sense."

"You said it yourself - you think all these 'suicides' are murders. And there's at least some semblance of a cover-up."

"I wouldn't...I wouldn't call it a cover-up. Just...turning a blind eye."

She stood up, balling her hands into fists like a toddler throwing a tantrum, and said, "David, you better tell me right now, or this - all of this - is done."

He looked at her, appraising her condition, which he would categorize as unhinged, or at the very least, unbalanced. She'd been through so much. *They'd* been through so much. So he gave her a name.

"Detective Percy. He's the only one who's worked all of the cases."

Nora squinted at the name and then recalled the man smoking the cigarette outside the woods, the one whose hand rested so easily on his gun. The gold plaque on his jacket had read PERCY. She shuddered at the thought of being so close to him.

"Well, he and Sheriff. And there's Bill, the Medical Examiner. Those three are the only ones who have their hands in every case. And they all...they all hush up about it as soon as I ask any questions. Tell me it's none of my business. But, I...I don't want you thinking any of them did this." He gestured to the phone. "I'm really just spitballing, here."

"You came to me about this whole thing because you think something's up in the department, right? Maybe they're trying to make me question what I saw."

David's face turned white, and then he nodded. To Nora's surprise, he stared right at her and said, "Maybe you're right."

THIRTY

"I have to tell you something."

Erica fidgeted with the gold rings that adorned each of her fingers, the way she did any time she knew she was about to cause upset. She sunk herself down in Nora's desk chair, putting herself at eye-level with her.

Nora's mind raced at the possibilities. She was already on edge from finding her old phone. She hadn't even gotten the chance to tell Erica about it yet. She cleared her throat.

"Okay...so tell me."

"This is going to sound weird, but *hear me out*." Erica flashed a smile as she put her hands up in defense. It had gotten her out of plenty of predicaments before.

"I saw Eli downtown last night." No reason to tell her she'd gone looking for him.

Nora's face fell.

"Okay..." she said softly.

"You said he was busy, right? But he wasn't busy. He picked up some dry cleaning and a coffee and went home."

Nora waited for more, a look of perplexity crossing her face.

"And?"

"The clothes he picked up...I think they were for a woman."

Nora's eyes flashed, but she said nothing, so Erica continued.

"And...he saw me driving, but he pretended *not* to see me!" She put her hands up toward wide eyes, as if it were a major revelation.

Nora shook her head.

"I don't get it."

"I...okay, I saw him get into his car, and I thought I'd just see what the douchebag was up to, since he's trying to start things up again..."

Nora stood up. Erica expected her to start crying, but instead, her face twisted in rage.

"Let me get this straight. You followed Eli all around town." Her voice had raised several decibels, her face growing dark.

"I wouldn't say that. It was like, a mile drive." Erica casually fussed with her nails, chipping away at dark polish.

"And he didn't wave to you, and this means...what?"

"I don't know. That he's shady, at the very least."

The situation was so absurd that Nora had to laugh, though what she wanted to do felt much more violent.

"I tell you that we're getting serious and the first thing you do is follow him? Are you trying to make me look stupid?" Nora spewed.

"Of course not! I'm just making sure he's not lying, like before..."

"You have so little respect for me, that you assume I can't handle my own relationship? I have news for you, Erica. Eli doesn't *like* you!" She screamed, her reaction startling Erica as she retreated backward in her seat. "Of course he pretended not to see you," she went on, knowing that she should stop, but finding it impossible. "He thinks you're a stuck-up, know-it-all bitch. Why *would* he want to talk to you? The only one who looks *stupid* here is *you*."

Erica rose slowly from the chair, her face sullen, squaring herself up with Nora, gold chains catching the glow of Nora's screensaver, overpowering her in more than stature.

"Is that what Eli thinks of me, or what *you* think of me?" she pressed, her eyes boring holes into Nora's.

Nora fell back on the edge of her bed and drew silent. When she didn't answer quickly, she knew what it would mean, but she didn't bother to protest. Erica huffed, rolling her eyes as she hustled out the door, muttering in Spanish to herself words that Nora was sure were of the vicious variety.

She winced as she heard the front door slam, distress settling around her like a cloud of smoke.

That night, Nora found herself fighting off racing thoughts, once again unable to find sleep's elusive embrace as she lay staring blankly at her ceiling.

Nora knew something had to really be bothering Erica for her to take her own time, which she always said was her most precious asset, to follow Eli around, and then to put her tail between her legs and admit to Nora what she'd done. She must have been pretty sure she'd find him with another woman. But she hadn't.

The clothes were a bit of a problem. They could be his assistant's. But then, wouldn't that be her job to pick up his clothes? Was she being blinded by his charms, yet again? Or was Erica just *that* jealous?

It had truly felt different with Eli this time, but she had to admit, it had been hard to see things clearly lately. Something wasn't sitting right, her stomach turning in knotted anxiety, but she didn't know where it was surfacing from. Above all else, it nagged at her: just as she knew in her bones that Nora needed her that night in the bathtub, Erica's intuition was never wrong.

THIRTY-ONE

After yet another fitful, restless night in bed, Nora awoke early to a pit in her stomach. She hated being on uncertain terms with Erica. She knew she had a right to be angry. But when the two of them weren't in a good place, the world never sat quite right. She didn't want to fight, but knew she couldn't let this one go. She cursed Erica for putting her in this position at all. *Time for a distraction.*

She stretched as she yawned in bed, pulling her arms to the right and then the left, noticing her shrinking stomach as she pulled on a sweatshirt. She groaned at herself, realizing she still hadn't made it to the grocery store but knowing she had to eat. The enchiladas at David's had made her belly full and her heart sing. Though the tightness in her stomach lied to her about the need to eat, she noticed the difference in how clearly her mind operated after she'd eaten a proper meal. But she suspected she wasn't going to be invited to any more family dinners any time soon. Not after the display she'd made when he was just trying to help. She hadn't heard from him since.

She looked at the clock on her nightstand, which read 7:13,

and mulled over whether she should wait to eat. She wasn't in the mood for breakfast food, deciding not to read through her case notes until lunchtime. She reached for her phone and saw a good morning text from Eli, a first. A rush of warmth through her chest, and she grinned, remembering what happiness felt like, and cursed Erica once again.

She clicked through channel after channel as she sat with her back against the headboard, unable to focus on the meaningless exchanges between lovers on the television. She sighed when she realized she couldn't help but work on the case until she got closer to an answer.

She retrieved her moleskine from her purse and settled back on her bed, shaking her head as she flipped through the pages. Such a tiny book that carried such weight. She perused the pages of meetings with grieving families, squinting at her own handwriting that became sloppier as she raced to write during interviews. Past the notes she'd copied from the whiteboard about the killer's probable profile. And then she arrived at a page she'd starred during her visit to copy the land records.

V.E.M.?? It stared at her from the page, her own handwriting seemingly sticking out from the rest.

She grabbed her laptop and brought it to her bed, cozying herself under her covers as she searched for the business name. No results.

She located a business entity search page for the state of Pennsylvania, and punched in the keys. Seven pages of businesses appeared, blue links leading to each individual business. But only one specifically titled V.E.M.

She sat up straight, her body going rigid.

She hovered her mouse over the link, but before she clicked, she saw an address to its right, linked to the business. A P.O. box in Philadelphia.

Waves of adrenaline rolled through her now. A business in

Philly with property in Woodbridge? It didn't make sense. She closed her eyes and clicked the link, waiting for a name.

She gripped the sides of her laptop as she opened her eyes and scanned. There was a grid where officers for each business were listed, and her eyes rested on the name.

Virginia D. McKay.

It sounded familiar, but she couldn't place where, or when, she'd heard it.

She scrambled to her notebook and flipped frantically through its pages, through dozens of notes of jumbled blue and black ink, but never saw the first or last name among its contents. She sat, puzzled, her mind going slightly hazy, and she found herself getting dizzy. She shook her head at herself. *Time to start taking care of yourself.* She grabbed her keys and headed out to grab food.

She took her place in the drive-thru at Lori's Bagels, sighing at the sight of the line wrapped around the building. She rolled up her windows and turned her radio on, letting slow melodies of lost love and kindred spirits envelop her mind and wander back toward Eli, and the wedding, and what it felt like to let herself get wrapped up in the normalcy of it all.

She pulled forward to take her spot at the intercom, and suddenly it dawned on her.

The envelope.

She sat up straight, her hands growing slick with sweat, as she let herself recall where she'd seen the name Virginia McKay. Her eyes darted as if the envelope, one that looked like a bill, had presented itself in front of her.

Nora sat, quaking, immobilized by fear.

A deep voice came over the speaker, making her jump.

"Welcome to Lori's, can I help you?"

Nora didn't answer and instead whipped her car out of line, pulling into the first available spot before slamming on the breaks, her body heaving forward with the sudden jolt. She could hear her own breaths growing quicker and more panicked as she replayed the scene in her mind. *Inhale, one, two, three, exhale, one, two, three.*

She ripped her phone from her pocket and fired off a text, never thinking twice before sending.

Something is wrong. I need you.

The text had barely left her fingertips before Erica responded.

On my way.

THIRTY-TWO

Erica was making things difficult, but that was nothing new. As Eli helped an old woman get safely to the sidewalk before he slid into his car, he'd caught a glimpse of an old Impala facing the sidewalk he'd traversed. He didn't make any sudden movements and continued fiddling with his radio as he started the engine, but he used his peripherals to confirm what he'd suspected: Erica in the driver seat. Attempting to look nondescript, but for a woman that tall and that striking, that was impossible. He considered that it could be a coincidence - she came into the city pretty regularly to meet friends. He was too far from her to see what she was doing, but she was alone and sat very still, facing him. He watched her pull out behind him when he left, darting his eyes to the rearview mirror once he realized she was following him.

Well, that changes things, he sighed. Virginia will have to wait until tomorrow. He went back the way he came, searching his mind for reasons she could possibly be interested in his whereabouts. *Always knew she had a thing for me.*

Eli prided himself on his discipline. He found that he rather enjoyed the rigor of keeping a regimented schedule. He was up at 5 a.m., usually laying with eyes peeled, motionless in bed, before his phone alarm went off, whether he'd slept the night before or not. Clothes freshly pressed, apartment pristine, cold, and angular. When he was in what he called 'Replacement Mode', he'd take a seat at his couch and sip an espresso, the first of many for the day, as he perused the selection online under one of his aliases, looking for someone quiet and reserved, but not boring. No, she had to be interesting, or else it wouldn't be a suitable replacement. She had to live within driving distance to the cabin, but nothing too close to where she would eventually be found.

He looked forward to the days he had time to make the trek out to their cabin. Once he made it there, he would carefully select an outfit from his mother's wardrobe that he had relocated from his apartment once he'd found the perfect spot. He'd slip out of his apartment before 6 a.m. so he could help her get up for the day before eight. *Early risers are my kind of people*, his mother had told him in Kindergarten, rubbing his cheeks with her soft hands as she'd gotten him ready for school.

He'd eventually moved all of his mother's possessions to the cabin, because it was the place where he felt the most connected to her. Her books, where she'd made notes and highlighted passages she found intriguing; her photo albums, full of pictures of her before she'd had Eli and a few of the two of them together; her vanity, where she'd applied her makeup with perfect precision every morning, and lovingly brushed Eli's hair. She'd see Eli watching from behind her over soft waves of brunette hair, and toss him a wink in the mirror. He'd smile a goofy, wide grin, a smile so pure that only a child could create something so wonderful, and she couldn't help but stop what she was doing to smile back at him. He'd hadn't seen a smile like it since - bright and full of unconditional love. And of course, he had her clothes, stylish and expensive, full of fabrics like silk and cashmere, organized in the makeshift closet. He could swear they still smelled like her.

He'd smooth each item of clothing as he removed it from its satin pink hanger, smiling to himself as he came up with the perfect outfit for the day. *She'll love this.*

Virginia had left behind just one photograph of his father. The person who took her away for good. Eli had held the photo so many times that the edges had worn where his thumbs met the paper, wondering what life would have been like if his father had just stopped hitting his mother, if the last time he did he'd taken it a little easier and she'd stayed, and they were happy as they had once been. Deep down he knew there was a kinship with him, a likeness in their mannerisms, but he couldn't fathom committing such heinous acts as his father did to the angel who was his mother. He remembered huddling with his knees to his chest, crying silently so his father wouldn't hear him, feeling helpless and cowardly as fists thumped on flesh and his mother cried out for his father to stop. When she vanished in the middle of the night, she left Eli a note under his pillow that he never showed to anyone, explaining that she had to leave even though she didn't want to, that once she was settled and had the power to come back for Eli, she would. But she didn't. She'd taken the clothes on her back and nothing else, and Eli at just the age of five had put everything he could find that belonged to her into boxes that he stored hidden in his closet, the remnants of his most treasured relationship shoved into corners that he dragged out only on the nights that his father had passed out for the evening, sifting through her things looking for clues as to where she went, and over time, to help him remember her. He'd been shipped off to his father's sister a year after his mother left, once it became clear to his father that caring for Eli alone was a nuisance. He never saw his father again. He didn't know, to this day, whether he was alive or dead. But he didn't ache for him the way he ached for her. He'd spent nights staying up late just in case she came back, listening intently for footsteps on the porch, for the screen door to creak open. She wouldn't make it through the tiny living room, past TV dinner trays and scattered beer bottles, to his bedroom in the back. He'd be ready and meet her at the door. He had his dinosaur backpack ready next to her things in his closet, filled with snacks and clothes and his favorite books, so he'd be ready at a moment's notice to run away with her. He cried one final time when his aunt came to pick him up and take him to Pennsylvania with her, when he realized his mother wasn't coming back. Never since.

The man in the photo his mother had left behind stood alone, clear blue sky at his back, a faded trucker hat, tanned skin, thin smile. Long and lanky, leaning against a boulder in what Eli figured was probably Colorado, where he lived until he got shuffled to his aunt's family. The photo was generic, and there was no record of where it had come from; besides his complexion, Eli's looks favored his mother - so he decided he'd borrow it for his dating profile. It had yellowed with age, but online it simply looked like he'd used a vintage filter over a recent photo.

He was angry with his mother for leaving, but he still loved her, still remembered so many tiny moments that any normal five-year-old would have long forgotten, and he wanted to tell her that. He wanted to tell her how lonely it had been, how he'd never felt like he had a home since she'd been gone. The older he got, the more he thought about trying to find her. Eli made a lot of money as a stockbroker downtown - more than he ever needed - and stopped spending it on cars and frivolous expenditures, deciding to put the money to good use. A post-coital conversation with Nora had inspired him to finally do it, and last year, he hired a private investigator to place her whereabouts.

He'd waited anxiously for a call, and was surprised when just two days later the PI left him a voicemail stating that he had information for him. His heart pounded as he thought about everything he would say to her, how they would reminisce about the times they shared. *Maybe we can sing the song about the weather she made up! Will she remember it? Of course she will. I can finally talk to her about art, now that I understand it. What has she been doing all these years? Has she been happy? Did she miss me as terribly as I missed her? It seems impossible, but I know she did.*

He thought of her voice, how she would look older now but she would probably sound the same, and God, how he had longed to hear it every night since she'd gone.

He thought the anticipation might kill him as he hurried home from work, opened his laptop to take notes from whatever the PI had found, and dialed his number through shaking fingers.

What came next bore into Eli's brain like a parasitic worm. With two words, the investigator wiped away years of hope. They pummeled over him like a train. *She's dead.*

She's dead. She's dead. She's dead. He hadn't even considered it. She was only nineteen when she had Eli. She was only in her forties now. She was too young to be dead.

Once the initial shock had worn off, Eli pressed him for details. The investigator paused, asked him if he wanted to know how she died, even if it wasn't pleasant. Of course he had to know. He couldn't go on, not knowing.

She'd been dead for years. Twenty-four years, to be exact. She was found by hikers in Grand Mesa Forest. She'd been shot in the head, and it had been declared a suicide. Eli calmly told the investigator to hold as he walked into the bathroom and violently vomited. He'd barely eaten that day - he'd been too excited to get the details about what his mom had been up to all these years. But still, out it came, bile from his intestines until his throat burned. He'd spent nearly every night of his life willing her to come back to him. Thinking about where she was, teetering between anger, depression, and curiosity. He remembered when she first left, how he imagined her finding some faraway land, where beautiful trees and flowers bloomed and she could have a horse like she'd always wanted. As angry as he'd been, his love never faded, and he'd hoped wherever she was, she was happy. She was safe. He flushed his anger and disgust down the toilet before returning to the phone.

"What is the date, exactly?" he remembered asking, only for confirmation of what he already knew to be true.

"The date she died?"

Eli spewed vitriol. "Yes, the fucking day she died."

"She was found on September 25th. They put her time of death at 24-48 hours prior to that."

September 23rd. The night she'd left.

He knew why the police never came to tell him. His parents weren't married - there was no record of them being together. They moved constantly, her license never matching the current house in which they lived. They'd given a sophomoric effort to find her family and thought to themselves, *oh well, she wanted to die, so let's let her be dead*. But he knew the truth.

The morning after she'd left, Eli had woken to his father charging in the door in the wee hours, the sun barely rising. It was not unusual for him to be out all night, so Eli hadn't thought anything of that. But he'd heard the water sloshing in the washing machine, which Eli had noticed because his dad never, ever did laundry. But he forgot all about it, because he found the note from his mother, and nothing after that ever mattered again.

He'd followed her. His father had heard her leaving in the middle of the night, and he knew what she was doing. And he wouldn't let her live without him.

He was so stupid. He should have known she was dead. He should have put the pieces together on his own. She never would have left him all these years. Even after he moved to Pennsylvania, she would have found him. She would have clawed her way into the house and ripped him from their arms, holding him as she rocked him back and forth, telling him over and over that she was never letting go again - the way he imagined she would every night until he eventually became a cynical teenager, allowing his anger to overtake him.

Something changed in him that day. He knew it. It had been brewing since he was a tiny, lost boy whose mother had abandoned him. He'd been burying it, and this had flicked a switch inside him. And now, he was ready to unleash it. He couldn't help himself. He needed her. He *needed* her. And he couldn't have her, so he had to be creative.

THIRTY-THREE

To find a large chunk of land for sale in a town so remote had been a sign, really, that it was time for Eli to give himself what he'd so desired. He'd purchased three acres from the township at an insignificant price several years ago, and the surrounding woodlands had been abandoned for years, evolving into an untamed wilderness. He'd built the cabin himself; no permits, no electricity, no running water, though he'd put in a sink, because he planned to eventually spend more time there. For now, he only needed a few rooms with extra insulation to protect sound from escaping in case somebody decided to get ornery. He'd gone to the cabin every sunrise to work on it, wheeling out planks, hammering them piece by piece, racking his memory for the things his father had taught him as he worked on their old bungalow through gulps of whisky and jumbled words. He'd work until his hands bled, until the sun had completely disappeared, knowing in his heart that it was all worth the sacrifice.

The woods surrounding his property sat outside the confines of Tuscarora State Forest, so there was no reason for a ranger to pass through. The forest attracted tourists, but there were several points of entry throughout its 90,000 acres, and Woodbridge was far enough from the interstate that no one ever came through that way to get to it. And if one ever decided to take the route less traveled, the state-of-the-art cameras he'd installed surrounding the property would send an alert to his phone before they had time to poke around. Thank God he'd found a satellite service kit to install the security system - he was certain he was the only one for miles with any kind of service. It had taken him several days and three smashed cameras to hook everything up, but he'd meticulously moved each camera millimeter by millimeter until he got every inch of the outside of the cabin and the perimeter of the vast property covered. No one could get in or out without him knowing about it.

Caroline - who was known to him only as Virginia, as were all of the girls he selected and brought home - had made a fatal error by underestimating him. She didn't know there were cameras, but of course there were cameras. Did she think he'd leave anything up to chance? He shook his head and smiled smugly at the idea that anyone could possibly think they could escape him. Why would anyone want to? He'd give them quite the life, if they would just act appropriately.

Eli knew he was good at his job, not by the quarterly bonus check that reliably ranked five digits, but by the way he could effortlessly weave in and out of personality types to suit the buyer. Since he'd been a boy and bounced from school to school, changing friend groups as he pleased, he'd been a salesman through and through. His riches had allowed him enough money to throw at all the things that people pretended made them happy - cars, women, travel, a room with a view. Still, the void. A heavy hole. A darkness money couldn't, and wouldn't, cast out. He was chasing what didn't exist, until he *made* it exist.

He'd convinced Harry on a late night at the office over an expensive meal and plenty of brandy to work from his loft most days so he could care for his ailing mother. All his red-faced, coked-up boss cared about was money, and Eli made him plenty of it.

Through smacking lips and a butter-stained jacket three times the size of Eli, Harry had grunted and said, "Don't fuck up my bottom line." And Eli sat back with his arms crossed above him, staring over Harry's sad hairpiece to the city skyline, lights twinkling brighter now, knowing that it was the beginning of a new era.

He knew from the start that this would have to take top priority. He took such careful care of them, feeding them just enough heroin to feel euphoric and docile, giving them the proper attention. He could feel them shudder as he brushed their hair and sang them their new name, which he found so curious in the summertime with the hot, stale air enveloping them. He'd pull a sweater over their heads, covering their bony shoulders, but it didn't seem to help them warm up. A minor side effect from the drugs, he'd determined.

The first girl he'd chosen was a random pull from two towns over, and she proved to be too much of a burden. He'd wrestled with her as he handcuffed her to the cot he'd set up, but that made it too difficult to dress her and groom her, so he'd made the mistake of telling her not to scream and took them off. She'd sat for only a moment before making a mad dash for the door. He grabbed her by the waist as she kicked and flailed, screaming for help. He couldn't understand why she was acting so rash when he'd been treating her so kindly. His expression was blank, but his mind raged: *I'm not letting you leave me again.* Alas, it was too much of an undertaking and she made it too much work for him - this didn't resemble Virginia's personality one bit. After only a week of her trying to dodge him, screaming every time he entered the room, he'd had enough and smacked a hammer into her skull. One swift *thud* to her crown, and then it was quiet once more as her body fell. He slipped off the red garnet ring she'd been wearing on her middle finger as a souvenir of their time together. Though their relationship had been tumultuous, he'd always think of her as the one who'd helped him formulate the more sophisticated and meticulous plan of action he had now.

Her dead weight proved hard to move, which validated his decision to obtain such an obscure property where he wouldn't be seen no matter how much time he needed, so he buried her behind the cabin. He'd never dug a hole quite so deep before, and it proved to be much more laborious than he expected, the hardened dirt refusing to give way the first few breaks against the shovel, splinters forcing their way into hands already marred by scratch marks as he finally broke ground. Even through his fitness and muscled triceps, he could barely muster the strength to roll her body, heavy with death and covered in tarp, into the hole, and had to take a break for lunch before he covered the hole with the dry, crumbled ruin.

The whole thing had been a mess, literally and metaphorically. He resigned to the fact that he'd chosen the wrong girl and decided he needed a more methodical approach. He'd pondered how he could choose more wisely. After a few days of mulling it over and taking diligent notes, he'd settled on utilizing an online dating service that didn't require much vetting from its users. Cupid's Arrow, full of lost and lonely women looking for something more. He could hand-pick who he wanted - a meek girl who could be trained for her new role, and he could introduce them to a better life than they were living now. Real companionship. He thought that would make the experience much easier and more enjoyable for him, and, quite frankly, for the girl.

But as each of them grew thinner and duller and just as non-responsive as the day he brought them home, he'd begin to lose interest, and before he knew it, it was time for a replacement. They were doing him a real disservice, not acting like his mother used to at all. Didn't he deserve a mother worthy of the title?

The second girl had been an accidental overdose. There was a learning curve with these things; he couldn't exactly practice in advance before he went for the real deal. He learned from Virginia #1 that he'd need something to sedate them with for at least part of the time, to keep them subdued so they could spend some real quality time together, learning from each other. He'd simply given her too much for her body to handle, but it did make the cleanup much easier for him, which sparked his plan - ingenious, if he did say so himself - to overdose them once their time together had come to an end. Heroin had solved both of his problems, and it was cheap and in ample supply in Woodbridge; he spent a great deal of time in bars watching carefully to see who had what he was looking for, and the slender, tracked, red-eyed customers always led him where he could find the goods.

When he was done with his girls, he would dump them elsewhere in the woods without having to dig a hole - an especially helpful desertion in the frigid winter months when the ground became too difficult to break. When it was time to move on, he'd simply overdose them and wheelbarrow them out as far as he could from his property. Everyone would assume they were junkies, and when junkies died, the authorities thought of it as one less blight on their township: a win/win situation. And he knew quite well that the sheriff's department, which was all but inept in both skill and servitude, was not equipped to handle someone of his own intelligence and fortitude. He'd instructed them to bury the cases without them ever knowing, and they'd happily obliged.

He wasn't certain at first what he would end up doing with the new woman in his life - he'd imagined having just one girl to fill the role, but after he replaced her once, he found it much more satisfying to do it again. And again.

He didn't have a timeframe for how long they'd share their life together - it was up to the girls, really, how long they stuck around before they began to disappoint him. It really didn't matter. All he wanted was to find someone who could provide him the kind of relationship he'd been searching for since he was a scared five-year-old, using all of his might to manifest her.

Until that need was fulfilled, there would have to be sacrifices.

THIRTY-FOUR

Nora's car stuck out like a sore thumb when Eli arrived at Jimmy's last month. He usually took a quick appraisal of the cars in the lot and could match each car to its owner; the old pick-ups rusted around the edges with age just as their owners had. The silver SUV was the only new car in the lot, and when he went to get a closer look, he recognized the Philadelphia Parks and Recreation sticker in the back window that she'd gotten from Erica. He guffawed in utter shock when he realized it had to have been Nora he'd been chatting with under his Ryan Williams pseudonym.

He stopped dead in his tracks and stormed back to his mud-caked Ford pickup, his Woodbridge ride. It infuriated him that, just as he hadn't put the pieces together about his mother, he'd once again been fooled. She'd said her parents were dead, but didn't give specifics. She'd used a pseudonym and a faraway photo that looked vaguely like her, but wasn't. He was better than this; he was getting distracted. It was too much to take on a second girl while managing the first one. He'd thought it was a great idea; a natural progression. He'd fantasized about expanding his cabin with more rooms so he could keep an entire house full of girls, all that he'd treat so well that they'd never even consider leaving him. She'd tossed a stick of dynamite into his dream without a second thought. He lingered at the driver's side of his pickup, hands grazing the metal handle as he fumed, and with balled fists and pure rage, jogged back to her car and kicked the side of it in frustration. *How dare she do this to me.* He couldn't do this with Nora. He couldn't use someone who was already tied to him. Plus she was stronger than she thought she was, and he didn't want that much of a fight again.

He leaned against her car with his head down for a moment to gather himself as he decided what he should do. He didn't want to give up so easily. He wanted more girls, and that was that.

I guess I'll do it the old-fashioned way. He had all of his tools in his car and he'd cleared his schedule for the night, and he figured he shouldn't waste it. He'd been in the mindset of this plan all day and without being able to execute, it left an insatiable need in his body. There was a bar in the next town over, so he headed there and hoped for a junkie looking to score or a floozy who was drunk, thinking they were going back to his place for a one night stand. *Easy pickings.*

He'd been sitting alone in the back booth facing the door, watching the patrons as they walked in, then out to smoke a cigarette, shivering as a cool breeze followed them back in again. He watched carefully out of the corner of his eye as he saw a woman stumble. He took a better look and saw immediately that she was too old. A forty-something wouldn't do for this. He sighed, exasperated. Then his phone began to beep, loudly and hurriedly.

He hadn't heard the sound since a deer had walked up to the back of the cabin in the spring. He casually grabbed his phone and loaded up the camera system connected to the cabin, then stood up with a start at what he was witnessing.

The tiny window in the kitchen had been smashed. He

rewound sixty seconds and saw Caroline standing, disoriented, cowering, outside of his cabin. And then she took off.

He threw down a twenty on the table and bolted out the door, seething in anger.

He threw his truck in gear and took off, his body bouncing with the mounds on the dirt pathways, jutting in and out of back roads only the locals were privy to, knowing he could cut her off at the pass if he played his cards right. She was weak. She couldn't get far. And he would find her. And she'd be sorry she disobeyed him, especially on a night like this.

Like a lion stalking an antelope, he slinked through the woods. He'd spent so much time trekking through them that he could navigate without making much of a sound, even at night without much help from the moon. Caroline was not nearly as quiet. He could hear her in the distance, breathing heavily, sometimes gasping for air, snapping branches of trees as she ran, leaving an invisible trail to her whereabouts. He honed in on her sound, concentrating on her and only her as he took long strides, clutching his hands into fists, letting them go only to carefully move a branch out of his way or to ensure his tool belt was still secure, and then balling them back together. He could tell she was getting close to the main road, and then he heard a car. Panic began to prick at him, and he picked up his pace to a dash, caring less now about being heard and more about getting to her before she got herself to the street. And then he heard the car. *Fuck.*

He'd been careful to ensure that there was no road leading to his cabin, so he usually parked his car just inside the woods in a clearing before hiking the rest of the way, but Nora had made that impossible when she'd almost hit the Old Virginia. He'd watched silently as the whole scene played out: Caroline launching herself in front of the SUV, Nora swerving into a tree, Caroline unsuccessfully attempting to wake her. Nestled safely in a blanket of dark trees, he calmly followed her as she descended back into the forest. It had been her calamitous choice, going back into the forest and not keeping to the road. He snapped a twig off a tree in an attempt to get her away from the car. The last thing he needed was Nora seeing him out here. He watched her, her head on a swivel, as she decided what she should do. He grew impatient, snapping another branch off a tree and breaking it in anger over his knee. That one got her moving, and he smiled to himself when she made the strange decision to go back where she'd come from.

He knew she'd tire eventually. This was exactly why he kept them docile and hungry while he kept himself fit and strong, and he made a mental note to properly thank himself later for his fortitude. When she'd shown her weakness, running so slowly it was barely a jog, he'd made his move, calmly and soundlessly approaching as she fumbled with something in her hands. He wrapped his left arm around her torso as his right angrily swept a knife cleanly and deeply across her throat. He made it quick so she didn't have the chance to make a sound. Her hands had tried to pry his knife off, but the attempt was feeble, and they dropped lifelessly before he released her and her body crumpled to the ground. He stood over her for a moment, seething with anger and breathing heavily as euphoria wrapped his body, before deciding to leave her there. She'd never had a chance.

A phone lay next to Caroline, inches from blood that had pooled around her head. Eli plucked the phone from the earth, its plastic case foreign against the natural, eyeing it and suddenly realizing it was Nora's. She hadn't been waking Nora up; she was taking her phone.

He couldn't risk going back to return it. There was no telling when Nora would wake up. He couldn't toss it in the woods; if it were found, and he was sure it would be if Nora were on the case - they'd have reason to believe it wasn't suicide, and he wasn't looking to get Nora into trouble with the police. They were desperate to close a case as soon as it opened, and they'd be looking for any excuse to pin it on the easiest person to blame. He couldn't keep it on his person - it was too risky in case they decided to bring in the big dogs and suddenly use real tech. He tsk-tsked as he thought, knowing time was of the essence.

He used a fallen leaf to brush off a drop of blood before slipping it into the pocket of his gym shorts until he decided what he wanted to do with it. Nora had given him a key to her place once so he could meet her there for a late night tryst, and he'd made himself a copy before giving hers back to her, just in case. He thanked himself again. Always ten steps ahead.

He'd considered moving Caroline's body for a moment, but thought better of it; he knew the police would eventually be coming to assist Nora, and he couldn't be nearby when they arrived. He slowly approached her car from the passenger side and peeked in to make sure she was breathing - not that he'd be able to help if she wasn't. This was really her fault, anyway. He watched carefully for movement before he heard a long, primal sound as she came to. As silently as he'd come, he descended back into a cloak of darkness.

Nora had, once again, thrown a wrench in his plans when she called him to meet her at the hospital. He'd rinsed himself clean in the rushing river that cut through the trees, the deer that shared the woods with him not thinking much of his presence as they dipped their heads to drink from the water he was sullying. Shortly after he'd finished, she'd called, and he did the math in his head - he had about 45 minutes to jog back to his car and get a fresh set of clothes on before he had to drive to the hospital. He smiled to himself as he changed, patting himself on the back to have the wherewithal to always have a fresh set in his vehicle. He stuffed his bloody clothes into his gym bag, making a mental note to toss the set in a dumpster outside of town when he came back for it, but not close enough to the city where there'd be cameras of him doing it.

He shook his head at the lack of battery on Nora's phone on his jog back toward his car, smiling. She was so predictable. Once it was dead it would be much easier to move it. He watched her as she slept in her hospital bed, thinking of the best place to put it back. He knew Nora never went into the den. He remembered her confiding in him that she never went through her dad's desk after he died, that she had no plans to. Perfect. She was out of it, it would take weeks before she even realized it was there, and by that time, it wouldn't matter. She'd second and third guess herself, and eventually land on it being her who had misplaced it.

When Nora had shakily whispered "that girl is dead" as she sat in his car the day after her accident, his blood ran cold. He felt his blood pressure rise, his temples throbbing. It normally took days, sometimes weeks for them to find one of his girls, and that was by design. The longer the decomposition, the more any possible evidence degraded - not that they were even looking for any. Nora was smart - it was what he liked about her, but it surely didn't help him here.

He'd watched unsteadily as Nora marched up to the officer, and had tried to remain as cool as possible while he waited as she spoke to the sheriff. And it had worked. She could play detective with her wannabe brother uncle as long as she wanted. She'd give him the inside scoop.

The drive home with her had been quiet, and he could tell she was exhausted. He waited patiently until the middle of the night, when she'd be fast asleep, to let himself into her house. Once he slipped the phone deep into the crevasse of the drawer in the den, he looked for a copy of the police report. He wanted to know what she saw, what she heard that night. Gloved fingers rustled over papers on her dining table. It was a mess; he wouldn't be able to find anything in a hurry. Then he heard her stirring upstairs, and he booked it. He had no choice but to leave the papers strewn about. She hadn't even noticed anything different about them.

Caroline had been in Eli's clutches the longest - she always seemed so interested in everything he said, listened so intently when he read to her, and put great emphasis on her words when she read to him. She'd even talk to him at times, saying she liked his outfit and, on a good day, that he looked handsome. But still, the nagging hole remained, and he began to draw up plans for adding a second girl into the mix. And then the fiasco with Nora happened, and Caroline blew it. "What a shame," he'd murmured to himself as her body slumped to the ground. *We could have really had something.*

THIRTY-FIVE

Eli had just finished packing up the last of his bloody clothes that he'd left by the stream he'd used to wash off after Caroline, heading toward Jimmy's for a burger before returning to the city, when he saw a flash of blonde against tanned skin. A young woman walking from her car, the lone vehicle in the lot, to the only gas station for miles, that sat kitty corner from Jimmy's. Casey strode into the metal doorframe covered in weathered bumper stickers to pay, face focused on her phone, unaware of her surroundings. He slowed the car and watched as she walked. She was young and looked distracted, and didn't notice him watching her. Perfect. He'd been spooked by his near run-in with Nora followed by the catastrophe with Caroline, but he felt a familiar thrill pulse through his body and knew this was too good an opportunity to pass up. The cabin had been empty a few days already, and loneliness stirred within him. From her designer summer clothes and her perfectly practiced makeup, it was clear she was an out-of-towner passing through, unknowingly crossing into his hunting ground. He thought about this most interesting proposition for only a moment before he knew that it was her. She was next - it was fate, that he'd crossed her path. He'd never done it like this before, but he was much more practiced now than he'd been when he first started. He figured he'd give it a whirl.

He pulled to the right shoulder abruptly and hopped out hastily, grabbing a nail from his toolbox, pricking it against his finger to make sure it was sharp enough to do the job. The only thing his dad had ever taught him was to have a fully equipped toolbox, and it always came in handy in the least expected places. He jogged across the street to the station, glancing over his shoulder as he crossed the road. The silence in the street amplified the crunch of gravel beneath his feet, and he watched the door intently for signs of movement as he glided toward her car. His heart beat a little faster, breath quickening, as he knelt down and began to pierce her tires, one, two, three, four holes, for good measure.

He pulled into Jimmy's Bar, as he had many times before, and backed into a space, watching in silence as she filled her gas tank. He doused an old rag with the chloroform he kept in his toolbox, mopping up the beads that trickled down the labelless bottle, careful not to let any go to waste. As she pulled out of the station, she didn't seem to notice the slow leak in the tire. He waited a beat before pulling out and heading back west, following at a distance, careful not to get close enough to register on her radar, relieved that she was going the direction he needed so it would be easier for him to get her where she was ultimately heading. He saw the tire beginning to flatten, slowed his pace and then pulled over again, waiting patiently around the bend so she would be nice and panicked, grateful to see a car even though it was a stranger, to not just accept but to *ask* for a ride. He only needed her in the car for a few seconds.

His looks were always advantageous at times like these. She'd smiled at him flirtatiously, didn't think twice before entering his vehicle. She seemed to tense up quicker than he anticipated, and he knew it was now or never. He watched her fumble for the car handle and wrapped her in a bear hug. He pressed the cloth hard against her mouth, slowing whispering *"shhhh"* into her ear as he felt her protests soften, before her body gave way to his.

She'd had such a fiery spirit, that first week. Then she'd gone docile and much more agreeable. Now, she was barely there. It was like all she cared about were the drugs.

He mulled it over in the hollow silence of his loft, allowing discontentment to surface as he sat atop his pristine, five-thousand dollar, incredibly uncomfortable couch. The espresso at his fingertips had grown cold, the sunshine behind him disappearing so it cast a shadow of himself on the bare wall he faced. The charts on his laptop sitting atop his African Blackwood coffee table jumped, intersecting lines of green and red and yellow, bearing numbers and letters that most people didn't understand but made perfect sense to him. He didn't notice. The familiar desire for a fresh girl was settling in. Yes, it was going to be time to upgrade soon.

THIRTY-SIX

Nora hadn't stopped shaking from the time she messaged Erica through the ride into town. Just seeing the Woodbridge sign gave her heart palpitations.

Eli had never, ever mentioned having any business in Woodbridge, let alone owning property there - whether it was his, or his mother's. He was much too vain to be seen in a place like that. She remembered his haughty response when she'd told him which hospital she was in. *But he was here. The night of my accident.*

It had been nearly two in the morning, and he'd been awake. She assumed he'd been with a girl. Maybe the girl was Caroline.

She tried not to get ahead of herself. *This doesn't mean anything, this could be nothing,* she repeated, the words bouncing frantically through her brain as she gripped and released her seatbelt over and over, knowing she was lying to herself.

She'd noticed an envelope on Eli's counter over a year ago after spending the night, the quartz of the countertop sparkling at its edges. Jealousy pulsed through her; she assumed it was a secret live-in girlfriend. She'd picked it up and held it to the light to see if she could read it, but then she heard the jangle of keys, and she dropped it back on the counter.

Eli had just gotten back from the gym, his shirt damp with sweat.

"Who's Virginia?" she'd asked casually once he came to greet her with a kiss, though she could feel her face burning.

"Who?"

She lifted the envelope and shook it in the air, watching for a reaction. He had none.

"Oh, I think she used to live here before me. That reminds me, I have to stick that in the mail." He grabbed a pen from the drawer and wrote 'Return to Sender' in perfect penmanship, sticking it in his laptop bag.

She'd laughed at her own foolishness. How could he live with another woman without her knowing about it? She hadn't thought of it since that day.

The first place Erica had taken her was the P.O. Box, located just a mile from Eli's building. She surveyed the inside from the nearly empty lot to be sure he wasn't there. Only an elderly man was inside, struggling to use the copy machine. Erica had volunteered to go in - Nora was still a mess, and would have given away that something was wrong.

Erica pushed her bust out and put an extra sway in her step as she strode in, locking eyes with the middle-aged man at the counter and smiling flirtatiously at him. He returned her smile, his pale face turning red, and she knew she was in.

"Hi, hun. How are you?" She leaned her forearms on the counter, sticking her backside out.

"I'm good, ma'am. Thank you for asking. How can I help you?"

"I'll pretend you didn't call me ma'am," she said, and winked.

He shifted uncomfortably and cleared his throat.

"I was wondering if I could drop something off for someone. I can't remember their box number." She pressed her hand to her cheek and faked a pout.

"Oh, sure. Who is it for?"

"Eli Moreno."

He clicked the keys searching for the name, then frowned.

"I don't see a box listed under that name."

"Hm, that's weird," she said, putting her hands on her hips in feigned confusion. "How about Virginia McKay? Maybe it's under her name."

More clicking, his slender fingers moving with ease.

"Oh, here we go. It's Box 187," he said, beaming proudly. "Down the hall to your left. Let me know if you need assistance." His pale eyes sparkled.

Erica nodded.

"Well, I want to make sure I have the *right* Virginia McKay, you know? These photos...I mean, this *document* I'm dropping off, is kind of personal, you know what I'm saying?" she said, and she winked again, looking down at her chest and then back at him. "Can you check her home address to make sure it's her?"

He pulled at the collar of his uniform and chuckled, shaking his head and smiling as he pulled up her file.

"I don't think I can give that out, ma'am. But let me see...oh yes, it's the one you're looking for. Her son is listed as an authorized user. Eli McKay. Oh..." he said, and his face burned red, realizing he'd given out information for a name that didn't quite match.

"Her...son." Erica blinked, then peeled herself from the counter. "Okay, thank you." She turned on a dime and hustled out the door, barely registering the calls from the man telling her she was going the wrong way.

Nora had opened the door to the car and vomited right there in the parking lot when Erica shared the news. But after she got it all out, she wiped her face with the back of her hand and directed Erica towards Woodbridge, knowing she had a long day ahead of her.

She'd laid everything out to Erica in the car, the words tumbling out hysterically as she detailed the points of the case.

How she had been just miles from his property line when she'd shown him the location of her accident, and he hadn't breathed a word of he or his mother - who he'd told her was dead - owning any property there. He'd lied about the envelope, pretending he'd never heard the name. He was an avid hiker, he could make it out there easily. But he didn't hunt. Why choose this place? She expected Erica to tell her she was being crazy. She'd drive her there to show her there was nothing to worry about and then she'd roll her eyes and tell her to call her therapist again. But instead, she'd gone completely silent, and Nora could feel tension coming in waves off of her. Erica subconsciously drummed her fingers on her steering wheel and pursed her lips together again and again, her posture completely erect in her seat. Once Nora had finished explaining, she took a deep breath and waited for Erica's response.

It didn't come. Minutes of silence as Erica cracked her knuckles, her fingers barely grazing the bottom of the wheel as she stared out into the trenches of beyond, knowing this day was taking the turn she feared it would. Finding it impossible to wait any longer, Nora demanded, "Tell me what you're thinking!!" Her voice had gone shrill from panic, causing her throat to go dry.

Erica looked at Nora in the passenger seat, so frail and frazzled, fear emanating from every part of her body, then turned her eyes back to the road and quietly said, "I'm thinking...that we need to call the police."

Nora whipped herself to face Erica, the belt startling her as it jolted her back into her seat.

"What in the hell are you talking about? We don't know what we're going to find. We don't even know what we're looking for. What are we going to tell the police? 'Hi, my boyfriend might be a murderer, just gonna check out this weird piece of land his family owns, can you come with?' What are you even *saying*?" Nora was hissing now, finding it hard to catch her breath. "And what is Eli going to think when I bring the cops to his property? I already broke his trust by looking this up."

Erica shook her head, then muttered under her breath, *"He's not your boyfriend."*

"What?" Nora's eyes went wild. "Did you just say he's not my boyfriend? That's what you're taking away from this? Wow. I knew you were jealous, I just didn't know it was this bad." She threw herself back against the seat and crossed her arms, shaking her head in disbelief.

Erica let out a cruel laugh.

"This dude could be a murderer and you think I'm jealous. That's rich. I've told you from the beginning to stay away from him, but you didn't want to see what was right in front of you. Eli is a piece of shit; he's always been a piece of shit. And I think now we both *finally* know that." She didn't bother to hide her condescension.

Tears stung Nora's eyes as she watched the road ahead, trees whipping past them and back into oblivion, fearing what Erica said to be true. The details rolled through her brain and into each other; how she'd never been able to get comfortable in his apartment, and she could never pinpoint why; he was gone for hours, sometimes days on end, and he never offered any details where he was going. She'd pretended not to notice that he was ultra private about his laptop and his phone. He'd snapped at her when she'd handed him his phone as an alarm sounded, telling her he could hear it and he could get it himself. She told herself it must have been something about work - his job was high-stress and he didn't like to talk about it. But the back of her mind had set off silent alarms that she chose to ignore. She thought it might be because he was talking to another woman. But this new connection got her mind racing back to every little thing that had ever pricked at her senses, screaming answers at her, if she would just dare to look. If there was nothing to hide, why was he hiding it?

Erica glanced from the road over to Nora, who sat silently trembling, and immediately softened her stance.

"Nora, I'm sorry. I don't want to fight with you. Especially now. I didn't mean to be a bitch," she said, gently rubbing her hand on Nora's knee.

Nora didn't respond and cracked her window to let some air in.

"Look, you can be mad at me. That's fine. But we need to be smart about this. We need to tell someone what we're doing."

Nora let her anger fade and slowly nodded.

"You're right."

"Why don't we just call David? He's police, and you guys have been working on this, right?"

Nora shook her head as her eyes welled again, her emotions coming in uncontrollable waves now.

"The last time I saw him I all but accused him of being the one responsible for this. All he's wanted to do is help and I basically slapped him in the face. He's not going to want to help me anymore." Her voice shook as she let the tears fall silently, not bothering to wipe them. She had a feeling there would be more before the day was over.

Erica abruptly pulled to the side of the road and stopped her car.

"What are you doing?" Nora sat up straight in her seat, clinging to her seatbelt, her guilt turning to panic.

"Let me see your phone."

Nora watched her, eyes narrowed as her breath quickened, and didn't move.

Erica smiled wickedly. "Don't you trust me?"

Nora didn't know how to respond. Everything she thought had been true, she'd been wrong about. Maybe she was wrong about Erica, too.

Erica scoffed and before Nora knew what was happening, she'd slipped the phone out of Nora's pocket.

Nora flailed and clawed at her, trying to rip it away. But Erica was much stronger than she was and tossed her a pathetic look, as if a bunny were trying to scare off a lion.

"Are you calling Eli?"

Erica threw her head back in manic laughter.

"You're funny."

She pressed the phone to her ear and smiled at Nora, shaking her head.

"Hi, is this David?" she asked sweetly, winking at Nora.

Nora covered her face with her hands.

"Hi, David. This is Erica, I'm a friend of Nora's. She found a very important piece of information about your case. This guy she's been....*dating*, he might be the guy you're looking for. We're going to check out some property he's connected to and thought you might like to come along."

Nora's face turned crimson as she listened in shock. David was never going to trust her again.

She heard a muffled voice but couldn't make out what he was saying. Erica gazed at her nails as she listened, and Nora took the opportunity to snatch her phone back and put the speaker on.

Erica jumped in surprise, but didn't fight her. Nora could swear she detected a hint of admiration, but there was no time to relish the moment.

"David? It's Nora." Her voice shook.

"Nora, thank God. Whatever you're about to do, you need to stop right now," he said, as forcefully as he could, though he was shaking too. "Tell me...tell me where you are."

"We're going to check out that V.E.M. property - it looks like it's tied to Eli Moreno - or maybe, Eli McKay. It's in his mother's name - Virginia McKay. I've known him for years and he's never mentioned it, but it's three acres of land that are close to where I got into the accident. There's no address or anything, just coordinates. We're not far. I've got my map and we're gonna follow it and see what's there."

David lowered his voice until it sounded almost menacing.

"Nora, DO NOT...do NOT go into those woods without me.

Stay where you are and wait for me, do you hear me? Tell me where you are."

Erica mouthed *Okay, Dad* and shook her head with a grin.

"We'll call you when we get there," Nora said brusquely before clicking off the phone and shoving it into the pocket of her shorts.

"*Damn*, girl. You don't want him to go with us?"

"I do, actually. I'm scared shitless. But I don't want him to get there and then tell us we can't go. I need to see for myself, with my own eyes, what's there," Nora said. "I wasn't lying, I'll call when we're there. He can meet us."

They sat in silence the rest of the drive, following the pavement as it circled its way around the town, past the unkempt houses and their hapless residents, past the hand-painted sign pointing toward Jimmy's, until they found their way to the tree where Nora had lost consciousness. She felt her gut clench with guilt. "Here's where it happened," she murmured, more to herself than to Erica.

"Do you want me to stop?"

"No. Keep going."

They made it a few miles further as Nora used her finger to trace the map as they drove. Finally, she took a deep breath, and said firmly, "Here."

"Uhhh...where?" Erica leaned toward the wheel in her seat as if a different angle would produce something new to find. "There's nothing here."

"Pull over."

Erica obliged, though there was no shoulder and her car rocked over the grass, leaving a meager trail behind them. She looked to Nora for further instruction with eyebrows raised as she cracked her knuckles again, one by one.

"Hope you brought your hiking boots," Nora said.

"You know I always have them in the trunk for work."

"Good. Put them on. Do you have supplies?" Nora had been so disheveled that she hadn't thought about needing basic essentials for the journey in.

"What, are we camping out here? I always have tools in my backpack. I didn't pack extra water, I didn't have time. I can bring my canteen if we find water."

She popped her trunk as she slinked out of the car, slipping her weathered boots on seamlessly with her legs as she fished through her bag. "Flashlight, compass, duct tape, binoculars..." she called, bending low behind the trunk so she was out of Nora's vision, and pulled up her leggings to wrap the black plastic sheath shielding a thick-bladed knife around her calf, and then stretched the elastic and cotton back over it. She frowned at the bulk, but figured Nora would be too distracted to notice. If anything went down, she'd have to be quick. She slid her hands over the black cloth, memorizing where the knife lay and the quickest way to access it.

"Looks like there's a stream on the way," Nora called, moving her hand over the waterline on the map. She fumbled with her seatbelt, barely able to get it off of her shoulders before climbing out from the vehicle and into the silence of the forest. "I think it's only a few miles in." Nora stared into an abyss of thick brush looming before them, the smell of fresh pine trees flooding her nostrils, imagining what could possibly be awaiting their arrival beyond the trees. She moved to the trunk beside Erica to gather their makeshift bag and handed her the map.

"There's no vehicle access?" Erica asked hastily.

"Doesn't look like it."

Erica shivered as she shot her a warning look, rubbing her bare arms, though the heat stuck to them like molasses. "That's fucking creepy, Nora."

"I know. I'm gonna call David." In the stark quiet, Nora was suddenly desperate for David's calming presence. Erica's cool demeanor was starting to wear off, and Nora was uneasy leading the charge.

She pulled her phone from her pocket and redialed David. His number sat as her phone attempted, and failed, to connect. Her heart sank at the tiny X where bars should be.

"I'm not getting service. Try your phone."

Erica pulled her phone out, the lotus flower on the case failing to bring calm.

"No bars. These hillbillies just don't have phones out here, or what?"

"Does your car have OnStar?"

Erica chuckled, shaking her head.

"No, my twenty-year old car does not have OnStar, Princesa."

"Fuck." Nora ran her hands over her forehead through the thick of her curls that had already begun to grow in the humidity, and started pacing, kicking up tiny chunks of gravel into wild, tall grass.

"Let's just go back. No big deal." Erica swung her keys in her hand, watching as Nora began to shake her head.

"I don't know where we're gonna get service. It could take us twenty minutes to get back."

"You have somewhere else to be?"

"It's getting dark soon. I don't want to be out there at night." She shuddered, remembering how much darker it had gotten the minute she stepped into the trees beyond the caution tape, where Caroline had spent her final moments.

"Let me see the map again."

Nora handed over the pages, crinkled from the many times she'd folded and unfolded it while she worked over the body locations. Erica noticed the circles on the map but said nothing, moving her finger across the page, tracing the invisible line they'd have to take. She shrugged.

"That's more than three miles, babe. But I'm up for it." She looked into the clear sky, shielding her face with her hand as she appraised the sun's location, calculating to herself how much sunlight they had before it disappeared behind the trees. "It's gonna take us a bit to get out there. I'm sure this terrain isn't the easiest to climb. You're right. I don't want to try and find my way out of these woods in the dark." She bit her lip and looked over

Nora. She was visibly shaken, but she seemed determined, and Erica found herself wondering the last time Nora seemed this interested in doing anything.

"Nora," she began softly. "Whatever you want to do, I'm with you. But we can go back. We don't have to do this. We don't know what we're going to find. You sure you want to go?"

But Nora did have to do this. The closer they'd come to this space, the more she'd felt, deep within her body, that something was very wrong. Her gut told her to press on. And for once, she decided to listen.

She slammed the trunk shut with a forceful heave, brushing her hands off as she looked Erica square in the eye.

"Let's go."

THIRTY-SEVEN

David looked at his phone in disbelief as the call ended abruptly. He bolted for the den, frantically whipping open the bottom drawer of his desk and jumped as it reached its breaking point and clanged. He knew where the map was but somehow it seemed to take an eternity to find it, then he exhaled in short-lived relief as he found its ragged edges and where he'd noted *V.E.M.* the day Nora had texted him about it. He stared at their whiteboard, now filled with names and details and theories, as he unlocked the top drawer and pulled out his Smith & Wesson, checking the ammunition for full rounds before smacking it shut and sliding it into the back of his belt. He kissed Briana on the way out, barely stuttering that there was an emergency at work. She scrunched her nose and he assured her everything was fine, that he'd be back before dark, avoiding her eye line.

His pickup rattled over dirt road after dirt road, a short-cut as long as he was willing to handle the rocking, his hand shaking as he pulled up a number he'd saved to his phone when he first started noticing that something wasn't right in Woodbridge. This was past Sheriff Townsend and office politics. It was time to involve the

FBI. He'd deal with the consequences later. He had to save Nora, no matter the cost.

Eli had just settled in to order a burger at Jimmy's when he felt a sudden buzzing from his secondary phone in his pocket. He pulled it from his jeans, wondering if it was a deer or a raccoon today that was crossing the threshold to his property. The camera loaded as he took a swig of his beer, never daring to drink the local water. Two familiar bodies appeared, moving hastily through the grass as they breached his perimeter, causing him to jump up from his stool, and the haggard men at the opposite end of the bar turned to watch him. "Jimmy, I gotta go," he called just a tinge too loudly, slapping down a $20 at the bartop, his glass, still full, nearly toppling at the vibration.

"Take care out there, ya old hound," Jimmy said, stuffing the bill into his pocket, watching as the door whipped closed behind Eli's harried exit, and turned back to drying streaked glasses behind the bar.

Panicky thoughts raced through his mind as he threw his Supra into gear and peeled out of the lot towards the woods, his feet floating over the clutch and the gas before pounding them to the floor, cursing to himself that he didn't have time to switch back to his pickup truck. What could he tell her? How was he going to fix this? It was only a matter of time before they found his cabin. Overwhelm consumed him as he thought about losing his mother once again. He couldn't protect her before; he was just a small boy. But now, he was a man, and it was his job to protect her at all costs. Nothing would stop him this time.

A deer and her fawn darted in front of him and he braked hard and shifted the knob down, using the time for the two to cross his path to check underneath the passenger seat for his tool bag, though he knew it would be there, and he thanked himself for always being prepared. He yanked it from its hiding place and tossed it on the seat beside him. He'd never wanted to use his kit for Nora, though in the back of his mind, he knew this day might come. Once the deer had finished crossing safely, he roared past them, and the pair scuttled hurriedly to the opposite end of the woods.

He shuffled through the black, heavy bag, using his hands to feel for his knife, and unclenched as his hand found where the plastic met cool metal, and he thought about how the next part of this would go. Maybe he and Nora could work something out. Erica, on the other hand, would be a pleasure.

THIRTY-EIGHT

The sun's shape had gone absent in the shadow of the elms just as it had as Nora approached the spot Caroline died, rays finding their way through surface openings as if descending directly from the heavens.

"At least at work we have trails to follow. Watch out for poison ivy." Erica's voice echoed through the valley of trees, and an unseen bird in the distance answered her, squawking and cawing as it rustled through branches.

Broken twigs rolled under their feet, occasionally snapping beneath them, and Nora was exceptionally aware of every sound they were making against the stillness of the forest. Lanky weeds brushed against her bare legs as they moved deeper, lower into the valley, where the air was much cooler, and Nora wondered if the bumps that covered her body were because she was ill dressed or because she was so terrified of what she would find at the end of the path.

Not fifty feet from their makeshift trail, in a perfect ray of sunshine cutting through the branches, Nora saw a shadow that stopped her cold. She grabbed the back of Erica's tank, stretching its cotton so roughly that Erica's body recoiled against her hand.

Nora put a finger to her lips, her insides lurching, as they waited silently for movement. After the shadow came crunching of browned leaves that had already fallen in anticipation of winter, and then a doe, gingerly stepping forward as she watched them, her baby trailing behind her. They stared in wonderment as the doe crossed their path, never flinching, never allowing them to stray from her eyesight, as she led her spotted fawn away safely.

Nora began again before Erica stopped her. "Nora, wait. I'm getting a really bad vibe." She grimaced as she wiped a bead of sweat from her brow, her other hand on her hip. She breathed deeply as she looked to the trek ahead, trailless forestry and, from what she could hear, a stream of some kind nearby.

"That's the point." Nora knew she was close to being talked out of this entirely, so she turned her back to her and marched on, ignoring the pooling sweat as it began to act as glue between her back and her t-shirt. The terrain became tougher still the further they traversed into the woods, where climbing over long-dead trees and their uprooted stumps was the easiest path to avoid the thorns and the prickles of the bushes and branches that clung to them as if to claim them for their own. They grunted and groaned and their muscles burned as they traveled uphill, but neither of them uttered the slightest complaint, for they both knew that this had to be done.

Finally, the terrain seemed to level off, and through interlocking branches, Nora could see an opening. She grabbed Erica's arm and pointed, and they wordlessly, breathlessly ascended toward the clearing, slower now, cautious not to create a sound. As they pushed back the branches, a shoddy, handmade cabin revealed itself. The workmanship of an old shack, but large enough for it to look like a tiny home, whose only neighbors were the looming trees.

"Nora." Erica said softly, then cleared her throat. "You need to prepare yourself for what we might see here. There could be...let's just say whatever we find, you can't unsee it..." She found it difficult to find the words for once, but Nora flicked her flashlight on as she eyed the setting sun, bounding forward as Erica trailed behind her.

Nora's blood pressure rose, the sound of her thundering heart clear and heavy in her ears now, telling her to run as fast as she could, miles and miles back where she'd come from. Back to a safe and boring life, where she could forget about Caroline and maybe even Eli, and she'd never stick her nose where it didn't belong again. But her body disobeyed her fear, and it drifted toward the cabin as if it were being carried by a cloud.

"Is this the witch's house from Hansel and Gretel?" Erica's attempt to lift the mood fell flat when she found she was unable to keep her voice from rattling as they moved, slower and more deliberately now, almost tiptoeing, toward the cabin. Finally, they found what appeared to be the front door, a small pathway having formed from someone moving in and out, and beside it, worn grass that circled toward the back of the cabin. Nora moved to follow where it led, still leaving a careful distance between herself and the cabin, and found that the path stopped beneath an old, heavy wheelbarrow. It had once been bright red but the paint was chipped and faded, and atop the rust, what looked like dirt and hair and sludge.

She stared at the wheelbarrow, trying to piece together what he'd been using it for. Her mind wouldn't stop racing long enough to piece it out, but its looming presence made her uneasy. She broke her gaze from its stoic form, lonely against the backdrop of an empty forest, to move back toward the front of the cabin before she talked herself out of it, and finally made her way toward the door.

The first thing Nora noticed was the smell. The stench of urine and something rotten, though she couldn't quite place the scent. The foulness was a strange departure from the fresh, clean air flooding her lungs on the way in. The mixture of putrid and fresh pine churned her stomach.

"What's up with that?" Nora pointed to a piece of thick board hammered into the side of the cabin, what looked like a late addition.

"Look at the ground."

Shards of tiny glass sparkled in the light, and she winced as her shoes, caked with mud, crunched over the pieces. She listened for a second before moving again, though she wasn't sure what she was listening for. When she was met only with an oddly discomforting breeze, she moved closer to the structure, putting her hands up to the pale grain that formed a rectangle above much darker, longer pieces of wood that made up the bulk of the cabin. She moved her fingertips above her head underneath the plywood, using her hands to tell her what she couldn't see, until a sudden sting caused her to reflexively withdraw her hand. Droplets of blood and dirt covered it, and it itched as if she'd just drug it through fiberglass.

"It's a broken window. Watch your feet."

"Not that. *That*." Erica motioned to a mound of disturbed earth about sixty feet east of the front door, an oval of darkness just beyond the wheelbarrow.

"What's he doing out here?" Nora murmured to herself.

"Are you sure you don't want to go back and get David? This feels like something," Erica said as she drew closer to the mound but stopped a few feet before she reached it, leaning the top half of her body nearer as if she were prevented from approaching any closer by an invisible fence.

"He'll figure out where we are."

The padlock that encircled the door handle began to make Nora feel nauseous, and she seemed to be growing more lightheaded with each passing second. What didn't he want anyone to see?

"Good thing I brought these babies," Erica said as she reached deep within her bag and revealed bolt cutters. Before Nora could protest, she snapped the link in two.

Nora stared, bewildered, as the lock clanged to the dirt, breathing hard in the stillness.

Erica thought about what she'd just done. They were breaking and entering; she could be ruining her career before it started. But she knew that wasn't what was really bothering her. It wasn't just the shell of a makeshift cabin in the vastness of remote woods, the weight of the quiet that surrounded them putting pressure on her temples. It was what waited for them beyond the door, because she knew in her heart of hearts that there was something wrong here. She bit her lip and stared at the ground, then back at Nora.

"We had to get in," she said quietly, reassuring herself as much as Nora.

They looked at each other for a moment, then both nodded in silence as Erica slowly pushed the door open. It creaked softly and they both froze with the door ajar, waiting for someone to come bounding to the door. But no one came, and through heavy, hushed breaths, they pushed it open together.

Nora didn't know what she expected, but she knew it wasn't this. A tattered recliner sat directly in front of them, staring at the door as if it was waiting for them to enter. The floor was made of hardwood but the planks were unfinished, and the slats didn't line up quite right. The recliner was oddly the only thing in the room; no television, no knick knacks or signage about a man cave or *Gone Fishing* on the walls. Erica slid her hand over the wall next to the door to look for a switch, finding nothing. "I don't think there's electricity," she whispered, frowning at the thought of someone sitting in this chair in the darkness.

Nora stepped, deliberately and gently, into a kitchenette to the left of the front room. A rusted refrigerator that wasn't plugged in to anything, a sink, and the wooden planks they'd seen covering the window above it. She moved closer and saw that the planks she was seeing were not the ones she'd seen outside; there was wood covering both sides of the window. She shivered. *No one is getting out of here.* When she saw how small the window was and thought of the glass outside, it seemed that someone had broken it from the inside. Tiny triangles of glass dotted the sill, and atop them, specks of brown residue. The only window within the structure, the only source of light.

Nothing about this cabin reminded her of Eli. He wasn't interested in solitude; he was a partier, a lover of night life and all that the city had to offer. His loft was filled with giant windows that sprawled nearly floor to ceiling, and his home had been designed by an interior decorator. This place, this dark shack that smelled like hot garbage, certainly didn't reflect his taste. He had new everything - cars, furniture, even appliances, though he never used them. He could afford a second home, something beautiful on the beach. Maybe this was all a mistake.

But as she looked past the kitchen down a narrow hall, she saw, in the darkness, a gleam of metal. Another padlock. Erica gripped Nora's arm suddenly, and they both froze and stared at a thick and uneven wooden door that looked handmade, not by a carpenter, but by someone frenzied and unpolished. She went to shush Erica, for her breathing had become audible, and then realized that the noise was coming from her own body. Nora felt herself go weak, her legs turning to jelly, her eyes watering. There was no light from the uneven crack under the door, no scuttle of movement. But if they were going to find anything - anyone - that's where they would be. There was nowhere else to look.

Nora called out, so frail and meek she could barely hear herself, her voice catching in her throat.

"Hello?"

THIRTY-NINE

Casey huddled at the edge of her bed against the back wall, hugging her knees. She didn't know if this was a trick. She'd never heard a woman's voice in this place. Then she heard the links clinking against each other the way they did when the man came. They had a key.

But then she heard fumbling, hushed voices that seemed like they were trying not to be heard. The links dropped to the ground, and an angry jangle echoed as it hit the wood. The man never dropped the lock. Then she saw the handle moving and failing to open, and then Casey could hear frustration between the voices. Yes, there were two of them, at least.

She could hear some banging, and the door flexed. She began to shake, the sounds reverberating so harshly she covered her ears. Suddenly, the brass handle she'd been staring at, her only chance at a life, was ripped from the door, flecks of wood flying with it, and suddenly, she was staring at a hole, with two anonymous bodies behind it, and she held her breath and braced for what awaited her.

Erica took a second to find her footing. Her knee burned and spikes of sharp pain shot through the foot in her boot. But she'd had to kick the handle off. They weren't leaving without finding what was behind the door.

Erica's bag fell to the ground with a thud as her shoulders dropped.

"What the fuck..." Erica breathed heavily, looking from Nora, her hands over her mouth and frozen in panic, to the tiny person in vintage clothing, as if she had been there for decades. She stared silently at them through wide, exhausted eyes, and then Nora saw the chain. Her ankle was bound to the floor, and in that moment, it was clear. This was where Caroline had been, all that time she was missing. Nora had barely processed what she was witnessing before Erica bounded across the room. Casey recoiled and put her hands in front of her face.

But instead, Erica rushed to the rocking chair, lifting it from its rails, groaning at the weight of the cherry wood, and heaved it over her shoulder, bolting toward the front door that had been shielded with a padlock. She shoved the chair underneath the handle, shaking her head as she raced back, knowing this would not keep him out. It would only alert them when he arrived, and if he could keep this up, this secret, psychotic life, without anyone knowing, then he already knew they were there. She looked at her phone once more for service, knowing the X was waiting, taunting her.

Casey dropped her hands when Erica exited hastily from the room, realizing that the two new faces had not anticipated her existence within the walls. Hope flurried within her, and tears began to form. Somehow she found her voice, and though small and weak, barely a whisper, she pleaded, "Please help."

Nora dropped to her knees in an instant, her hands trembling, nearly breaking the zipper on Erica's duffel bag, and searched desperately for the bolt cutters. She breathed a sigh of relief when she found them, as if they may have disappeared in the minutes since Erica had used them. She rushed toward the girl so quickly that she almost toppled into her on the stained mattress, her knees weak and her legs uncontrollable. She fumbled with the bolt cutters as she attempted to keep her hands steady, the rust on the steel of the tether making it difficult to break. Sweat rolled down her back as her t-shirt clung to every bit of her torso, the warmth and panic of their bodies elevating the temperature.

"Nora, hurry up. We gotta get the fuck out of here," Erica warned over her shoulder as she watched the front door, shifting her weight from one foot to the next with each passing second, the knife that she'd hidden on her calf already gripped tightly in her hand.

"I'm trying!" Nora cried, but she'd been careful not to hurt the girl, whose skeletal ankle looked like it would snap if she touched it the wrong way. *Fuck it*, she thought, pushing the bolt cutters against the bone and under the chain. Casey cried out in pain, and Nora tensed at the sound of a snap, but then the chain fell, and she was free.

Casey looked at her ankle in disbelief, then back up at the black-haired stranger yelling at her to get up, that it was time to go, hurried but somehow in slow motion, as if she were in a dream. She looked at the room around her, the tiny, musty place she'd somehow grown accustomed to living in, her mind clouded and unsure, and then the red-haired stranger lightly touched her arm and looked at her sincerely and told her she was safe now, and then she was somehow back to herself, and rising up, slowly but steadily.

They all jumped at the harsh ringing of wood against wood at the front of the cabin, and Erica quickly shushed them and ran out of the back room, closing the door behind her. She went to duck and remembered there were no windows in this place, so she rushed to the rocking chair in the living room. She threw her back against it as she worked to keep her breaths, near hyperventilation, from becoming audible, waiting for a shadow to appear in the doorway, clinging the knife against her heart with both hands. Once he realized something was blocking his entry, Eli threw his body weight against the door, his anger and desperation making short work of the heavy chair.

Eli's eyes flashed in the darkness as he gripped a hunting knife, and he instinctively went straight down the hallway to the room where he kept his Virginia, his most prized possession. No one was going to take her from him again.

Nora trembled as she heard the heavy steps come down the hall and swing the door open. She wished it wasn't Eli, and in a way, it wasn't. She barely recognized the large, menacing figure that towered before them, anger and venom and panic showing on his face. She wanted to call out to him, to say, "It's me, can't you see it's me? I love you," anything to stop him, but the words caught in her throat. She did not know this man, this projection of evil, this was not her Eli, they were two separate people, she did not know this man, she did not know this man.

Instead she kept her arms around the girl who had said her name was Casey, suddenly implored to protect this stranger, as if her arms could save her from what was to come. She whispered to her again and again, "It's okay, you're okay."

Erica took one last breath, squeezing her eyes shut and willing her mami telepathically to hear her tell her she loved her, and before she could overthink it, she crept behind him, shakily and quietly, while he was fixated on the girls in the room. Nora kept her eyes fixed on Eli so as not to alert him of her presence. But he'd seen them both enter the cabin, and Erica hadn't anticipated that he'd trained himself to hear even the slightest of sounds in his range. When she hesitated just a second before lifting her knife to plunge into his back, he whipped around and knocked her to her feet with a hefty shove, pinning her down with his knee as he struggled to pry the knife from her hands, shoving his own weapon into the back of his pants as he wrestled to get to hers.

Casey mustered the anger she'd been yearning for. This was her one and only chance, and she was going to take it. She sprinted suddenly toward him and tackled him from behind, attaching herself to his back in a whirlwind of chaos, punching the back of his head with infinitesimal fists as she wailed, her flailing bare feet kicking his ribcage. He cried out, more from surprise than pain, losing his balance for just a moment before thrusting her off of him with ease. Her tiny body hit the wall with a sickening thud, sliding down the wall before crumpling into itself. He felt for the knife in his pants but it was gone, and his anger swelled inside his chest like it hadn't since the day he found out his mother was dead.

He breathed maniacally as his eyes, bugged and strange, searched the floor. Erica instinctively moved closer, clutching her knife with both hands now, but froze as he stood up to face her, his height towering over her as he puffed his chest, which rose and fell with such volition that Nora could see his breaths from his back. Erica knew her knife wasn't going to do much more than slice his hand, and that would have to be enough.

Her eyes darted back and forth between Nora and Eli, her body paralyzed with fear. Nora mouthed *"run"*, but she knew Erica wouldn't leave without her. As Eli cautiously moved closer to her, Erica began to tremble, and whispered, desperately, "Eli, no. Please," her voice catching in her throat as she slowly backed away, the knife pointed at his chest shaking so violently she could barely control it.

Breathe in, one, two, three. This is it. Make your move. Nora sprinted to the edge of the closet, behind an antique vanity that faced them, using pure adrenaline to topple it to its side. Its substantial weight created a lilt in the air as it bounded over, the mirror shattering into shiny, glistening shards.

Seven years bad luck. *No such thing.*

Nora scanned the broken pieces and in one smooth motion gripped the largest shard as she strode, sure and quickly, her shoes cracking tiny pieces that flitted into her shin bones, and menaced toward Eli, who stood between her and Erica, rocking his head between them like a cornered animal. She didn't think, she didn't feel - she moved wordlessly toward him. Erica watched as Eli turned his attention to Nora and sprang at the opportunity, gripping onto his arms, crying in pain as he attempted to wretch her off of him, averting him for just a moment but it was enough, and as he wrestled with Erica he knew Nora approached him from behind, and he cried out "Nori!" - and only then did Nora hesitate, but her body moved her forward still, below the hand that was struggling with Erica, and swiftly, firmly, angrily swept the glass across his jugular vein, the same vein he'd sliced on Caroline.

She took a step backward and exhaled in a tiny cry as blood spurted from where she'd maimed him across Erica and all over the floor he'd built himself. Nora clutched the glass against her hand so hard it carved into her flesh, her blood mixing with his. She watched as he fell to his knees, clawing at his throat, gasping, life trickling through his hands and down his chest, soaking his clothing so quickly that she knew there'd be no coming back from this. Betrayal and sadness veiled his face as he watched her looking on in horror, and then he was looking past Nora, his eyes unfocused, and through gurgles, she thought he might vomit, but then he fell onto his back, reaching toward her with his free hand for help, until eventually both of his hands fell lifelessly to his sides with a heavy thump.

The weight of what she'd done came crashing down on her, the pressure suddenly unbearable as she fell once more to her knees, breathing heavily through her mouth, her breaths the only sound they could hear now. Erica's hands covered her mouth in a prayer position as she stood motionless, the first time Nora had ever seen her speechless. Tears fell silently down Casey's face, her bony shoulders hugging her knees, softly rocking herself, her mouth agape in agony. Nora's breathing quickened, causing her to go lightheaded as she gripped onto the doorway over him, and then he spoke.

"Mommy," he murmured, and something resembling a smile overtook his face, until his color drained completely and turned a shade of ash.

FORTY

He hadn't expected Nora to hurt him, and he could see she hadn't expected it either, her face twisting in horror as she watched him fall. What a pity, that she hadn't given him time to explain. He could fix this. He could show her what he was doing was kind and just. The world was cruel; she understood that more than anyone. He was providing unbridled affection to these women, the kind that could only be shared between mother and child. It was a gift. She'd understand. Instead, she sliced him open, fear and pain marring her eyes as her bloodied hand covered her mouth, bewildered at what she'd done.

He grasped at his throat, bitter liquid filling his mouth, his balance becoming more off-kilter as blood rushed out of him. His vision blurred before turning brighter and brighter, until he could only see whiteness, the absence of color surrounding her - yes, it was her. She was waiting for him. All this time, she'd been waiting.

He choked out, extending his arm toward her, and Virginia wrapped him up in her arms, the embrace he'd been looking for since his lonely nights as a five-year-old, waiting in his bedroom, ears alert, for the sound of creaking footsteps. His backpack packed, his cherubic face stoic and naive, knowing she'd come back for him. He'd waited so long to feel her again. She was here. He was home.

FORTY-ONE

Nora held a bouquet of wildflowers in her hand so tightly that her hand turned white, rounding the corner toward a private room at the county hospital, while press of all kinds waited on the outskirts of the property. She'd shielded her face and ignored their intrusive questions as she hurried inside, but knew she couldn't balk at them; they were doing their job, and before long, she'd be one of them.

After she was finally able to leave Woodbridge, after hours of questions from the FBI, where they'd shown Nora the photos from the cabin that included the picture she thought had belonged to someone called Ryan Williams, she'd nearly passed out. She had no choice but to hand over her moleskine, and likened it to handing over her firstborn.

Erica had been persistent that she felt okay to drive, knowing she was still shaky but wanting more than anything to see her mom as soon as possible. They sat in silence for a while and then listened to the radio, knowing that they would soon be having an hours-long conversation about what happened, but not today.

Nora had opened the door to her house and stood in the entryway, cradling the handle, staring at the dying peonies on the table that faced her. Their edges had dried and crumpled, their color faded. Then she looked at the stairs, the ones she'd rushed up as a child in front of her mother before she could catch her, giggling all the way. The banister she'd leaned against the first time Eli came over, pressing his body into hers in a way that told her he was spending the night. She felt sick. She stepped backward out the entryway and onto the porch, shutting the door as if she were slamming it in her own face, and dropped to her knees, sobbing violently into the ether, for her, and for her parents, and for Eli. She texted Erica to turn around and take her away.

She put the house up for sale the next day, not bothering to clean or stage it, sending Erica in to collect her things for her while she sprawled out in silence on Erica's bed, rubbing the stitches on her hand that had already begun to itch. She could tell that once the swelling went down, the gash would still be there, where their blood had become one. He'd be with her for life, that much was certain.

When Erica returned, Nora had said blankly, "I want a fresh start."

Erica had asked, "How fresh?" with a Cheshire grin on her face, tossing her offer letter on Nora's lap, and asked, "You coming, or what?"

When a family of four sent an offer 48 hours after she'd listed it, Nora barely glanced at the contract before telling her agent to accept their offer. It had become abundantly clear that the house was no longer the home she'd shared many nights of cards and holidays and laughter with her parents. She'd been so afraid to erase the memories there. But that's all they were now. Now, it was just a house, waiting for a new family's memories. It was time to finally let go.

The story had gone viral immediately, beginning on reddit and eventually leading to soundbites on CNN. National reporters interviewed David and he'd kept his composure better than Nora expected, and she'd followed suit, wanting to shape her own narrative before someone did it for her. She pushed her shoulders back and thought of her mom, how she'd beam with pride if she could see her now, and in those interviews outside the old Huntingdon County Police building, she felt a buzzing energy surround her, and she let herself be honest and vulnerable.

The nation was gripped by Nora's heroic save, and she'd had her pick of colleges and internships before settling on a transfer to NYU's journalism program, agreeing to move in with Erica as long as she got to choose the apartment, a deal which Erica, begrudgingly, accepted. Nora's guilt hadn't waned, but she knew there was no other option. And as much as her brain lied to her about it, she knew that moving on did not pay her parents a disservice. This is what they would want for her.

Nora found Room 313 and took a step in and then back out to recheck to make sure she was in the right room, but it was her. She barely recognized Casey, who had color in her cheeks, an IV of fluids and clonidine, and her mother by her side.

"Mom, this is Nora." Casey smiled as she introduced them, and Nora swore she even sounded different, more spirited, more alive, though it looked like it was still painful for her to move as she winced to sit up in her bed. Now that she was out of Eli's mother's clothing and had some food in her stomach, Nora could see that what she'd read in the papers was true. She was barely out of high school.

Casey's mother nodded silently, then let tears fall as she wrapped Nora into an embrace so heartfelt that Nora felt it in her bones. She released her and then gripped her shoulders in her hands, her face puffy from days of crying, and though she couldn't muster the words, Nora knew she was trying to thank her.

She wiped the tears from her eyes and chuckled.

"I'll leave you two for a moment." And in an instant she breezed out the door, calling to a nurse that her daughter needed more pain medicine, and could they bring her *green* jello this time, please?

"Things are different between us now. Better," Casey said. She recalled in her mind the primal cry that escaped from deep in her mother's gut when she arrived at the hospital and saw with her own eyes that her baby was alive, and the release of anger and despair and desperation between them when they finally embraced and let love and hope wash over them.

"But she's still driving me crazy." Casey shook her head as she grinned, and Nora laughed, because she knew what she meant.

Nora squeezed Casey's hand as tears pricked at the backs of both of their eyes, though neither of them let a tear fall. They both knew that this was the last time they'd see each other. They were both ready to start a new life, one that didn't include the other. When David had arrived at the cabin, Nora was still gripping the mirror, but she'd had to sit down to put her weight against the wall - she had no energy left to stand, and running was out of the question, but then, there he was to catch her. He'd rushed to Nora's side, but she'd pushed him toward Casey, knowing just by looking at her that she was malnourished and in need of a doctor's care, for both her body and her mind.

They didn't discuss what happened to them, but they didn't try to exchange false pleasantries, either. They were past small talk but beyond the possibility of friendship, somehow. A purgatory of shared traumatic experience. Nora pulled her into a hug, expecting resistance but feeling none.

"I'll be seeing you," she lied.

"O'Shea. Get in here." Sheriff Townsend removed his hat as David entered his office, red-faced and slightly sweating. He stood at the doorway until Townsend nodded at him to take a seat, and he watched him silently as he fumbled with the chair until he was directly across from his superior. The reporters hadn't left the outside of the precinct since the kidnapping victim had been found on Eli Moreno's property, and David had bitten his nails down in anxiety for the wrath that awaited him at work. The FBI was in the process of excavating the perimeter and had already found two bodies in the vicinity of the cabin where he'd found Nora and Erica and the girl who had since been identified as Casey Hansen, all of them nearly comatose from shock. He'd been careful not to move anything in the ramshackle structure though it was clear he'd just missed complete chaos, and he immediately radioed the sheriff's department while he checked for a pulse on Eli, knowing from his coloring and the enormity of blood beneath him that he would find none.

Townsend sat with his hands together so they formed an arch, and waited a beat before he began, watching David squirm in his seat.

Finally, he said, "I put in for that transfer you asked for."

David's face lifted.

"In...in Pittsburgh?"

"Yes, in Pittsburgh. Looks like because of the Moreno case, they're going to find you a spot. Possibly in Homicide." He leaned back in his chair and ran his hand over his stubble. "There's nothing more for you here. On to bigger things." He smiled grimly. He'd be out of his hair before the new year. David's face beamed.

"Sir?"

"What?"

"It's...it's been an honor, sir."

Townsend looked at him and blinked, then returned his peaked hat to his head, which signaled that it was time for David to leave him be. Once David was out of sight, he picked up the phone to call Jimmy and see what was going on down in the woods.

"Looks like they found another body," Jimmy said, then sighed, and Townsend could hear glasses clink as he dried them. "Word is, they think there are more victims somewhere. Too bad. I liked Eli."

Towsend closed his eyes, knowing it was only a matter of time before they tore apart the department he'd been so careful to protect. The suits had shaken his hand and explained where they'd be doing their business, but they hadn't asked many questions yet. They'd said they were going to be looking at his case files, and he knew they'd make good on that. This town really had gone to shit.

That night he thought, well, the Barone case is over. I'll finally get some sleep. He turned over on his squeaky mattress, facing opposite Darla, and tossed her a "g'night", but she was already asleep. And there they were to greet him. The girls, within the walls of his decaying old house that he never could get around to renovating, still grey, still covered in dirt, still dead. Still coming for him.

FORTY-TWO

Just a day after she'd left Casey, here Nora was once again, at a hospital. No reporters this time.

She'd barely had a moment to herself the past week. Maybe it was better that way. It kept her mind busy. She'd been furiously working to set up a foundation that she could seed with a substantial gift. Erica had helped her talk to lawyers and non-profit directors to put something in place. She'd been on the phone nonstop. In between reporters asking for interviews and comments about what happened to her and her relationship with Eli, she traded minor quotes for information about noteworthy donors to assemble a Board of Directors, and she found herself saying no when she wanted to say no and yes when she wanted to say yes. She'd asked Gloria to be a part of it, because she knew she could trust that it would be run properly and effectively, and she wanted no part in running the thing herself. Gloria's eyes had watered as she embraced Nora and thanked her for entrusting her, promising that she'd treat each application with the respect it deserved, and Nora smiled, because she knew she meant it.

Nora was adamant about establishing the foundation in memory of Eli's victims, attaching their names and nothing more.

Eli and his sickness would not plague this money. She would not let what happened to these women become their legacy. She hadn't forgotten the long list of missing women in Pennsylvania. Part of the money would go toward private investigators for families searching for loved ones who had been shut out by police. More would go toward mental health services for the women who were found.

She'd considered donating some money to childcare services. Maybe if things were different for Eli when he was young, this never would have happened. She'd ultimately decided to hold off, to get a better grasp on where the money would be going before giving anything, and though she wouldn't be donating in his name, she knew deep down, it was for Eli. She hated him for what he'd done. To these women. To her. And it made her sick, but she felt sorry for him. Maybe she could make sense of all this somehow. One day. Not today.

Today, she arrived at a hospital room that was filled with pink and yellow balloons, and her breath caught at the sight of her. A beautiful, brand new baby, sleeping soundly, a head of strawberry blonde hair and tiny pink mittens on impossibly small hands. Nora felt her eyes well as she stood in the doorway, awestruck in her presence. Innocence and goodness and all the promise in the world, right in front of her in a hospital bassinet.

And then she saw Briana and David, eyes underlined with purple bags, surrounded by the glow that only new parents achieve, smiling proudly, at their baby and at her, and they beckoned her to come in. She felt warm and strong and sure, and without a second thought, Nora went to them.

ACKNOWLEDGMENTS

I would like to acknowledge a few people who have had a profound impact on helping me reach my dream of publishing a novel.

Thank you first and foremost to my son, Ronan, the center of my universe. At its core, this story is about the relationships between mothers and their children. Even though at the time of publication you are too young to read it, this novel would not exist without you.

To my husband Joey, who has always supported my dream and tells me that I can when I think I can't. You have always been the biggest champion for this book and made me believe it is worthy of reading.

To my most in-depth beta reader, Tommy, who spent time giving me copious notes over the course of many months that drastically helped me improve the manuscript. Your input is invaluable to me.

To Steve and Rachelle, my best friends, who not only gave me notes on my manuscript but have been there for me through every step of the extremely long, emotionally difficult process of writing and publishing a novel. Your friendship is one of my life's greatest treasures.

To Laura, who mailed me handwritten notes and pushed me to keep going. You are the first person who ever called me creative and I will never forget it.

To my parents, who fostered a love of reading in me from a young age, effectively turning me into a writer. I know you have been dying to read the book and now you finally can.

Thank you to Lindsay Newton of Newton Literary Services for your editing expertise, encouragement, and for helping me develop the manuscript in ways I would not have achieved on my own.

To John & Olivia from Check the Locks podcast, thank you for being so supportive of my writing and allowing me to join you for our tradition of a Halloween episode every year.

For my dog Chandler, whose death required a pause in my writing but allowed me to return with an understanding of the stages of grief in a new way.

I would also like to thank myself for not giving up on my dream, even when it felt impossible.

Thank you, Mrs. Jeziorski, for telling me on that last day of 5th grade to keep writing.

ABOUT THE AUTHOR

Jessica Gomez is a horror film columnist and writer of editorials and introspectives on parenting. She graduated from the University of Michigan with a Bachelor's Degree in Public Relations and currently lives in Michigan with her husband and son. This is her first novel.

Sign up for her newsletter at WriterJessicaGomez.com.
Instagram: @WriterJessicaGomez

Printed in the USA
CPSIA information can be obtained
at www.ICGtesting.com
CBHW012031140924
14418CB00002B/2